TOM TUCKER

THE DISAPPEARANCE OF JOSEPH TWEDDLE

1843-1875

An American Novel

By: T. E. Carlsen

Based on true events

Tom Tucker: *The Disappearance of Joseph Tweddle*

2nd Edition August, 2016
ISBN-13: 978-0989172417

For book purchases and comments,
tedwincarlsen@gmail.com
facebook.com/tomtuckertweddle

Cover design by Joe Mancino
www.jmangraphics.tumblr.com

Charlie Tweddle / www.charlietweddle.com
Printed in the United States of America

DEDICATION

This book is dedicated to *Charles Irvin, "Charlie" Tweddle*: musician; artist; author and cowboy hat maker to the Super Stars. For without his steadfast support and dedication to his great-grandfather's story, as well as to his beloved Kentucky, this book could have *never* been written. You can read about Charlie's incredible life and work at: www.charlietweddle.com

SPECIAL THANKS TO:

The Livingston County Historical and Genealogical Society and especially to *Mary Lou Smith* for her tireless service to help make these words as historically accurate as possible; *Tom Burness* for his knowledge of antique firearms and weaponry; *Donald Brubaker* for his wealth of information concerning the history of the American Railroads; Canadian folk legends *Stan Rogers* and *Gordon Lightfoot* for their inspirational music and stalwart research of nautical sailing terms and expressions; *Carl Johnson* for writing the "John Tweddle blog" that aided with the Tweddle family timeline; to my good friend and surrogate father, *Roy C. Schlotthauer III*, as well as to *my Sons* & family for their undying emotional support throughout this long and arduous process; and last but certainly not least, the people of New York, and the wonderful folks of Livingston and Crittenden Counties, Kentucky – Thank you all.

- CHAPTERS –

CHAPTER one
THE VOYAGE OVER

JOSEPH'S TORSO slammed against the mid-ship's bulkhead hard enough to render another man unconscious. Fortunately being twenty-five and strapping, the slight bruise he received above his eye was just enough to aim him back toward his hammock. Taking a well-needed piss off the main deck under the darkness of a new moon, coupled with an impending Atlantic squall will have to wait he thought. So he leaned against an all familiar timber truss where he added to yet another splashing bucket of yellow.

The scuttlebutt that commenced a week ago that land would soon be spotted not only kept Joseph in a heightened state of expectation, it kept him clothed in the best he'd brought with him. Thanks-be to God he thought of the thirty-four year sea veteran who gallantly informed him the ship's lookouts should spot 'the Americas' by late tomorrow. Yes, thanks-be to God the captain said just two hours before most of the ship's passengers and some of her crew began throwing-up their supper of potatoes and fish; hopefully for the last time. The salted cod, strong like wharf pilings, contrasted the sweetness of the gentle potatoes day to night; even if most of the potatoes were rotten by this stage of the voyage and the remaining apples in the barrels were too.

Later that night in the same mid ship's store room, Joseph swung in the interim birth he'd stretched between two creaking timbers under which a dozen whisky casks were tightly secured. The potatoes and the cod he felt were the only food sources that occasionally had the ironic ability to settle his stomach and equalize the nausea set forth by the rolling and pitching of the vessel: nausea which seldom ceased.

POTATOES, the main stay of the human existence, or so it seemed in many parts of the civilized world; not that Joseph, for the last ten years you see, had been anywhere outside of his native England. For Ireland he'd read was *the land of green and mist*; where those beautiful little bulbs were so plentiful, and an entire nation and its lovely people were doomed to perish unless the ruthlessness of his own industrialized power lords could see beyond their greed.

To be certain, this was not a vision to manifest in the near future of that country. Because for its people not to starve, the English men-of-industry would have to refrain from taking every last bulb, even the puny and rotten ones, from the soils and shores where they grew, away for a grander profit. This, in and of itself, if dwelled upon, was enough to cause Joseph to throw the potatoes and fish from his own belly to the sea. But in respect of his hunger, and the tranquility his stomach now felt, he turned his thoughts elsewhere.

HELENA, as she was lovingly christened in 1841, was one of the first American three masted clippers built. She was on a run from China to London with a hold of Oriental teas, silks and oils; and then on to *The Americas* with a light load of passengers and a commensurate haul of assorted whiskeys. Steam power was becoming more practical and this improved method for transporting vast amounts of cargo would eventually take over, but for the next thirty years, these sailing wonders would remain the sleekest and fastest vessels to slash a course anywhere in the world.

Twas the spring of 1843 and despite Joseph's roving eye and penchant for women and foolery, John Tweddle wanted his eldest son; an engineering graduate from Oxford, to be with him for his greatest venture yet; the construction and implementation of the largest carriage building factory in America.

For John Tweddle; being a wheelwright and in love with the world of engineering, this was his most daring dream, but it was not Joseph's. Joseph was amiably content to remain in Victoria's Court where he could spend unearned income on as many maidens as he could possibly devour; tumbling them again and again, only to be disappointed on every occasion that money and power were all they sought. And it wasn't until John Tweddle himself; after years of tireless legwork, along with the force of money 'n men, made the voyage back to England to track the boy down, did Joseph finally succumb to his father's wishes. John Tweddle you see used what his son liked most and best: the promise of new wealth, and fresh women.

TODAY was a day like many before aboard *Helena*; all except one distinct difference: this new day smelled different. The air and the breeze had a sweetness added to it. And like most of the other passengers that hadn't noticed this sublime addition to their passage, Joseph too hung his head over the side and retched out his guts to the sharks and crabs.

By this point in the voyage; and despite high seas and three storms, vertical stripes of bile, old and new, had bleached its way down the hull to the water line. Seagulls now hovered for their breakfast; winging and wheeling and plunging into the foam before the morsels sank beyond their reach. Listening to tired and worn-out words about how the Americas were getting closer bore no merit until these airborne scavengers turned up to actually provide the proof needed: that the land of hopes and dreams would soon be walked upon and kissed.

Twelve days ago, the pitching n' rolling of the ship was so severe it took the life of Clive Wilde when he disgorged so hard, a piece of his stomach lining came up and lodged in his windpipe, ultimately suffocating him as he sadly lay in his birth. He was buried at sea the next morning with his widow and his widow's son beside Joseph. The boy held Joseph's hand; looking up at him in hopes the young engineer might take on the role as his new dad, yet this was not to be. The widow and the boy soon brought up pieces of their own insides; the widow bleeding to death and the boy to succumb like his father. After a short-worded ceremony by the captain; the last of Wilde family slid overboard at sunrise; all souls fleeing their earthly bonds only days before making port.

FROM the CROW'S NEST a sailor shouted, "LAND HO!" and in an instant the ship took on a frenzied excitement. Passengers and crew alike scurried in all directions. Telescoping-oculars, purchased specifically for the occasion, were retrieved from every cubby-hole and compartment one might imagine them to be stowed. All persons on board wanted to see America. Even the sick and dying raised their heads for as long as their weary neck muscles would allow. This was what they came to see and what they paid their passage for: a new land with new possibilities. Thoughts akin to this had mounted in these traveler's heads for weeks. America was fertile, and perhaps the last place on earth where one might be liberated long enough to actually experience what the word freedom meant.

Out of nowhere a young cabin boy, all of eleven maybe, grabbed the back of Joseph's trousers and with every bit of his seaworthy size, jerked the man from his head-hung position back to standing. And in the sweetest Irish voice, a brogue that hadn't quite cracked from childhood, yet strong enough to know his place on deck shouted, "Joseph! Joseph! We've spotted'er; the Americas."

Joseph Daniel Tweddle, with the aid of the boy, brought himself erect. Wobbly, he wiped the bile from his chin. Rising up to his full five-foot-eleven inches; skyward for an Englishman, Joseph was lean, strong and the epitome of a British cocksman; everything but the vomit on his coat. With a grosgrain ribbon tied to the dark brown tail of his eight-week old Thom Jefferson cut; a cut he procured shortly before *Helena* set sail, he caught his breath and nodded to the boy, grateful for his assistance. Along with his matching trousers, knee-high socks and cuffed jacket; all a dead give-a-way for a young aristocrat of moderate means and a weak stomach for sea life, Joseph stood as tall as the cutter would allow him considering her list and speed. He accepted the spyglass stuffed into his hand by the young mate who ordered, "Right there!" where he pointed again, this time with the hand that was absent his ring and pinky fingers; lost during those first important moments as the ship's sails were being unfurled.

As soon as her lines were cast and her bow turned accordingly, the wind picked up and the commands were shouted, "Run out the jib!" "Rig the boom!" In seconds sailors moved about faster than fast and the boy's hand, being in a place it should not have been, became encumbered in a line going aloft where it was beginning to take him up as well.

The first mate; middle-aged and stalwart of experience had no choice. So upon the boy's permissive nod and curse of, "Grip hard and slice be done ya!" the man severed his fingers: flesh through bone.

In truth, the main line was more important than the digits and the lad knew it. Grateful he was that it hadn't been his thumb, for this would have rendered the hand useless. Moreover, returning to port to administer medical attention to a worthless hand would have cost the voyage more in time than the kid was worth in appendages; regardless of their size or placement on his body. So in this way, the boy earned the respect of his shipmates well before making open water.

THE WOUNDS caused by the first mate's blade were almost healed now. And good for the boy the man had severed body parts before, because knowing to leave an ample flap of skin to cover the wound with was something only experience taught.

Directly after the amputation, he carried the traumatized youth below deck where he turned him over to the ship's cook; who if he wasn't at work feeding the passengers and crew, could easily be found with his head stuffed into one of the ship's many scuppers agonizing from a bout of staggers 'n jags. But at this particular moment the boy found himself with luck because the ship had just set her sails and the cook was neither drunk, nor at work, so he doused the bleeding wound with rum to impede any tissue from rotting. He then held the screaming boy's mouth open and gave him a hearty tang and one for himself before he commenced the crude process of trimming the skin and suturing the flap over the wound with a sharpened cod bone; more durable than anything currently manufactured, least wise in the mind of the cook.

A thick, lavender color scar now covered the sensitive area. The patch was also itchy and oozed some from the antibodies doing what God employed them to do: mend completely and infection free. But at this moment it appeared more of an annoyance to the mate. Still though in secret, he confessed to God the ordeal was worth counting his blessings over; because an infection, while at sea, was almost a sure sentence of death.

"Look man, look!" the boy shouted again, but Joseph's head was unsteady. However it did rise and he eventually steered the eyepiece close enough for a look.

"See 'er?" posed the boy hurriedly, "You do see 'er, don't you?"

All Joseph could see through the tiny hole was low lying clouds.

"Not there!" snapped the lad, "there, at the fore!" where he pointed even harder toward the bow of the ship with the hand that contained four digits and a prized thumb.

Through the long device, Joseph finally saw an opening in the cloud cover. Then in an accent that couldn't have been any more formal he said, "I see her! O my, I do! I see her! There she is!"

"It's aboot time," snarled the youth nonchalantly, while at the same time attempting to retrieve the glass, "Give it up now! Others want to see." But Joseph's big hand was still attached, and though the boy was almost twelve, he was still eleven, and Joseph wanted to look some more.

Now with the whine of the youngster he still

was, the boy meekly asked, "Give up the glass, Joseph?…" Joseph looked at the mate. They both waited. Seconds elapsed - their hands on the instrument. "Joseph … ?" whimpered the boy, who finally submitted with, "Please…?"

Kindly and without fuss, Joseph turned the device loose and looked with his own eyes toward the land that everyone had acknowledged to be America, and he stared in awe.

The boy, glass in hand, ran up to Carl Malloy, an Irish widower who traded away his family's two-hundred acres and the majority of his personal possessions to a shrewd Englishman in exchange for a dream and two tickets to the new world; one for himself and one for his four-year-old son who was tragically taken overboard while being held by his father so he could relieve himself. All this happened in a matter of moments as the ship's bow pitched downward in a full spray. The boy, torn from Malloy's grip, was thrust along the side-deck where he slipped through an opening and was out of sight in five beats of the average man's heart.

If it weren't for an impenetrable escutcheon inside Malloy's soul, along with the two sailors that stopped him, the man would have surely hurled his body into the chilly sea to tread water alongside his boy. But even if Malloy had chosen to jump, *Helena's* headway was far too swift to have come about and lowered a boat in an attempt to save the two before the temperature or the sharks had taken them over Malloy's arrogant stupidity. The captain you see, explicitly instructed Malloy time and again to never, under any circumstances, allow his son on deck without a line tied around him, and to use the buckets below whenever possible.

Now the young cabin boy held out his palm to an empty casing of a man from whence grew a dream. And the widower Malloy, who would take his own life before the ship docked, was all too happy to heedfully place a tuppance into the young mate's hand for his kindness; gently closing the mate's two fingers over the coin and kissing him on the forehead as if it were that of his own lost son's and saying, "Thank you, Martin." Martin however, was his son's name, and the mate knew this, yet said nothing because he too was on deck to witness the tragedy when the spray from the same wave that stung his cheeks, ripped the child from his father's grasp. This single incident; of a grown man howling through wind and seas, matured the boy's wits by at least ten years in experience.

ANYTIME Joseph felt the need for privacy he'd retire below to his mid-ship store room. Ironically the whisky casks stowed below his hammock were lashed stiffer and stronger than his own berthing arrangement. The futtocks and timbers constantly moaned and the ceiling above him percolated so bad it often times offered up inches or more of water sloshing below him. And when the ship was dark, the squealing rats were a regular source of non-tactile, yet organic stimuli. Yet for as good as the conditions were for some, this was Joseph's only place of solitude, if one could call it that.

The inherent dangers contained in this deportment of travel were more than obvious to those who accepted it; but for the mute, deaf, daft and dim-witted, it was further expressed in a lawfully written document that required their mark of acceptance.

For this reason among others, Joseph questioned his choice to return to America. Because for some inexplicable reason; as alluring as his father had made the adventure sound, Joseph knew his father's promise of women and wealth came unwarranted, and attaining this new and fragrant treasure would not be as easy as the old man made it sound. John Tweddle you see, being the richest man aboard ship next to Fraser Dunlop, was quartered rather nicely in his own stateroom. Yet, in the same split second Carl Malloy surrendered his choice to join his son; Joseph made his decision to book passage. Unfortunately a hasty accommodation was what one could expect in exchange for booking passage shortly before setting sail.

FOR almost FIFTY DAYS, Joseph restlessly waited. He waited as the captain and the crew talked of all the exciting harbors and townships along the eastern seaboard; with the first mate and his fingerless friend of course, offering up their faceless-fables before all. But Joseph knew better, yet it didn't stop him from fantasizing how the captain would find a port, chilly at best, where a passenger or two might board, or perchance some lonely cargo. Certainly not enough to come about for if lost at sea, making the vessel lighter and swifter, yet never to make it aboard without passage paid. Regardless Joseph thought, just steer the bloody thing into a calm port; any port and bring something aboard - or nothing at all. It didn't matter.

Just as long as the ship could lie at rest so his stomach could have a respite and his body could take a break from the anxiety of needing to always be on guard. But this could not be. There were no scheduled stops between England and America. No tiny islands in the North Atlantic with palm trees and warm winds; only an occasional ice berg and the hoarfrost that covered it.

IN SPITE of the payments offered up for turning *Helena* around to find missing chattel that had fallen overboard, this was the only kind of loss the captain smiled over. Because when Carl Malloy finally jumped, *Helena* was paralyzed with less than a knot of wind to her sails. Her speed and displacement, just enough to make the distance too great between the widower, who was now calling to be saved, and the men trying to save him. Nonetheless, as Malloy called for help, the ship and her crew could not have mustered any more speed and efficiency in repairing the longboat damaged in the storm the night before, than if the ship had a will of her own and a desire to manifest the intention.

With lost lines, a day's time and nearly the lives of two able-bodied men in the attempt, the captain and her crew, once the wind picked up, brought *Helena* about and made a daring and intrepid effort to save the doomed dreamer. Yet upon their return to the charted point from which Malloy had jumped, he was nowhere to be spotted.

The dreamer's face that beamed with joy as he and his young son boarded the cutter for their life saving voyage, dipped below the frigid waters less than four minutes after he'd made his fateful choice to join the boy. And to this day, no one knows why the saving-crew in the lifeboat continued to hear voices of inexplicable distress far longer than any mortal man could have stayed afloat in the subfreezing waters, but they did…

In THE END, the veteran mariner and provisional commander of *Helena* quietly went below deck and wept over the horrific loss of life his last voyage had cost. In so doing, he also recalled his overwhelming gratitude that he was never, in all his years at sea, been commissioned to command a coffin ship; vessels so filled with typhus and dysentery they merely served as burial platforms to extinguish hundreds upon thousands. Yet aboard *Helena*, he still ordered nearly one corpse every third morning over the side where it sank below sight.

Within a few years he withdrew to Nova Scotia with a fund, a new bride and a career to be proud of; only to depart for New Orleans shortly thereafter due to religious reasons and the bone chilling climate the northeastern territories possessed. A short time thereafter he signed on and trained as a boat pilot, but ironically due to his inexperience on the narrow and busy water ways, he was promptly terminated after he landed a rather large vessel on a sand bar. The error cost the company a considerable sum to have it moved to deeper water, but he only expressed amusement at his dismissal; feeling after all his years at sea, weathering the most dangerous waters the North Atlantic could throw at him, along with the perils that many of the other oceans had to offer, he of all persons should be given grace for such a trifle incident. For he was only making an effort to get ahead of a slower moving vessel in order to earn the company that employed him more revenue.

Yet this was not to be, and ultimately for good cause. This incident, among hundreds of others, finally led to the formation of an association disallowing sea captains, no matter their experience, retention of their vessels whilst entering the mouth of, or navigating the Mississippi River and many of her connecting tributaries.

In 1858; after sailing together nonstop through some of the coldest waters on earth; the cabin boy, soon to be twenty-six along with his finger-severing, first mate of a companion, wanted to make a voyage to a warmer part of the world. In spite of numerous offers paying substantially more to handle ships headed to the Northwest Passage, they wanted to see and experience something new and temperate.

The fifty-year old former first mate had decided

this was to be his final voyage, so together they teamed up and signed on with a two-masted schooner named *Clotilda* sailing out of Alabama at Mobile. They were informed the ship was a lawfully commissioned privateer vessel headed for Africa to patrol the waters in order to help stave off the illegal slave trade. But when *Clotilda* arrived and her crew started to hastily load enslaved Africans into her hold; both the boy and the older mate were desperate not to become ensnarled in something that had clearly been against English and American law for over fifty years; with harsh penalties to bear if captured. They also knew that if they were to make a fuss, they'd be dumped at sea, keelhauled or left in Ghana with the Africans. None of these choices were especially appealing. So the only smart thing to do they felt was to keep quiet and serve their sea-time.

During the final days of their return-leg back to America, a Yankee steamer hoved in sight, and due to the weather, the captain identified her as an American naval vessel. Either way, he and her crew were prepared incase such a thing were to happen. So rather be trapped and jailed, or worse for an obvious crime in waters this close to American soil, the captain gave the order...

While Clotilda aligned her port side away from the steamer's lookout, the crew, including the boy and the older mate, changed the slave's shackles from wrist 'n ankle irons to a single cuff around the waist. From the holds below the slaves were led up the stairs and onto the decking. Two sailors removed a section of port side railing and two others pushed a net load of ballast-rock over the side. As the counterbalance sank, it pulled behind it thirty feet of free line and the first chained and screaming African into the sea with many more to follow. The ballast continued to plunge and it took with it fifty men, women and children before the captain realized it wasn't a naval vessel at all and halted the valuable evidence from completely disappearing. This deadly calamity however, did not lessen the captain's paranoia over the more squeamish members of his crew: the boy and the older mate being at the top of his list. You see, to witness a natural death at sea was something any experienced seaman would hardly become delicate over, but to partake in the dragging of fifty souls to the bottom by way of a mistake certainly was, and the captain could see it in their faces.

That night while the warm gulf breeze pushed *Clotilda* north, the captain ordered seven of his most trusted to bludgeon the boy and the mate in their bunks and dump the bodies overboard. Sadly, for as much of a fight as the two mounted; clubs to the head and knives to the abdomen were no match for three fists and a partially useful hand.

JOSEPH ARRANGED his belongings as neatly as his droopy hammock would allow him to, taking time, along with care in his packing procedure. He examined his quills, ink, lead, parchment sheets, a volume on exploration, his two sketch books and his polished flintlock pistol; a formula he'd executed many-a-time during the voyage; packing and repacking; each time, spiritedly performed as he counted down the days to landfall.

Always one to travel in an uncomplicated manner, Joseph brought one large valise on the voyage: a lesson he'd learned while tending the female flock of Victoria's Court; in and out, quick and easy; all the while he and the ladies were achieving mutual satisfaction. That was until he discovered their principal intentions - which always soured his efforts to find heart-felt love. But what other methods were there; moreover, since this was the only manner Joseph knew of for pursuing love, what other conduct was there to exercise his efforts by than through his cock.

Joseph looked up when he heard a familiar voice say, "It's alleged that one cannot change an old person, and any attempt to do so, is surely a sign of madness," came the gentle articulation of John Tweddle, the forty-five year old family patriarch, veteran ale brewer, Freemason and investor. "I too pay a tuppance to see her every time I'm near," he added.

Reaching into Joseph's belongings, he pushed aside his son's pistol and retrieved a small oval locket containing the portrait of a young boy. With his arm wrapped around the same vertical timber the whisky casks were secured to, John Tweddle squared his feet and held the small painting to the light; where a sparkle pooled in his eye; a tear really. Morbid was the day too sad to recall, but here it was again. "He'd have been twenty-seven in June," said the man softly. His words not outwardly intended for the ears of the younger brother by two years, but John Tweddle hoped Joseph had heard them, yet Joseph simply continued to pack. These words had stirred the air before, so John Tweddle clutched the painting and stepped to a side scuttle where he looked out onto the cresting swells. He then looked back at Joseph's possessions where his eyes came to rest on the shiny pistol - and he implored, "This is a different land, son. Please, o please be mindful."

Joseph glanced at the pistol, yet chose not to engage over its inference and instead he replied, "Father, Robaré will never replace him, and Clara Pulling will never replace mother. She's only a year older than I am for God's sake."

"I'll hear no more of those words!" barked John Tweddle, and he turned his attention back to the white caps, "Leave a man to grieve in his own way! Besides,

Robaré's my son too now; and a fine builder!"

"He's a conceited, French pig!" countered Joseph, "and a furtive 'n whiney operate whose self-unity can always be purchased."

"And where have you been all this time, son, while Robaré's been working; tell me this?!"

"Endeavoring not to think of the way you abandoned mother - when she needed you most!" blurted Joseph; his outburst causing him to put even more of his mind on his packing.

The sudden pitch of the ship's downward movement caused John Tweddle the need to rebalance himself. "As I recall, you set forth for something new as well; and upon a purchase I'll add."

Joseph couldn't say a word to this. He knew the truth in his father's words.

"Too much had been set into motion by the time your mother's health took a turn. I informed you of this," said the man as he held the timber tight. "We would have lost much if I didn't depart for England to bring you back. I left her in good hands in America. Why bring this up now?" he asked, and his eyes returned to the sea.

"Still," rebutted Joseph, "You left her."

A deeper part of Joseph recognized how ill his mother currently was, and that God could very well seize her before he arrived, but what he didn't consciously know was that she would have never made the round trip journey. In fact she would have barely survived a few days on the first leg to England; even berthed in her husband's comfortable state room. And her crude sunrise burial would have made Joseph's outburst against his father even worse. He would have blamed him for bringing an unwell woman on a voyage she could have never made. Ultimately all Joseph had to rely on was what his father had told him of her debilitating infirmity; and his memory of her when he departed for England to attend school ten years ago; healthy and looking as beautiful as ever.

Both men gave the impression of being regretful. John Tweddle stepped over to the hammock where Joseph was mindlessly handling his things and looked at his eldest son with a yearning to embrace him, but men, especially Englishmen did not do this. Therefore when he handed the portrait back, he gently placed his hand on his son's shoulder and calmly said, "Dunlop and I are expecting you for dinner. Will you join us?" After a moment, Joseph nodded.

Then as respectfully as *Helena* would allow, John Tweddle departed. He carefully weaved his way back through the shadows where he found the need to duck under a cross beam just as the ship once again pitched down; causing the beam to almost break his head. He then continued into the darkness.

Joseph made his way to the same side scuttle where he too set his gaze upon the waters that had brought him to where he now stood. For it was not that long ago when two boys: Joseph Tweddle, ten and Robaré Pulling, ten years his senior played as best friends.

But as time elapsed, Joseph's mother, Sarah Dent Tweddle became increasingly weak from a degenerative illness; a disorder of sorts that set in shortly after Joseph's departure for England. Soon thereafter, Clara Pulling's fiancé, a much younger man in which John Tweddle was conducting some business, died from a minor infection that eventually turned septic. This was when John Tweddle began spending more time at the Pulling Estate than his own. This was also when the boy's behavior towards each other changed. During the overtly long courtship between John Tweddle and Clara Pulling, a courtship which continues to this day based on Sarah Tweddle's lengthy illness, the affection Joseph and Robaré had for each other eventually turned and disintegrated.

At first by wit and then by brawn, Robaré began to exercise every opportunity possible to publicly humiliate and belittle the younger Joseph; mostly over his lesser education and his desire to draw and be artistic, but also because the girls liked the kindhearted boy better. This was also when Robaré started to take advantage in private situations, tormenting Joseph physically. Robaré always used the excuse that since John Tweddle had made it clear on numerous occasions that no matter how wonderful the heart was that Joseph possessed, it was not as important as the academic achievements sought by Robaré. Because a generous heart, no matter how noble, would never take a man far in life, and thus a license of sorts, for Robaré to break it. This, in and of itself, drove the boys into many physical altercations with Joseph receiving far more than his share of embarrassing losses to the bigger and wittier French bully.

Matters only became worse by the impending union of their parents, known by many to take place after Sarah Tweddle's death, but Sarah's death, unfortunately or otherwise, had not taken place. She simply kept on living and withering away. Her condition becoming so dreadful it was necessary to place her into a facility shortly before John Tweddle boarded ship for England over five months ago. All of this, an undignified set of circumstances that had not set well with either boy, but Joseph more so.

Joseph absolutely loved his mother with all his heart. The mother Joseph sailed away from at the age of ten was a strong, yet compassionate and caring

woman; more so than most who marry for money;
which they all in some way made an effort to do. Why
this was, Joseph was outwardly aware of, except he did
not want to be. Going against one's own heart felt
unnatural, but he loved his mother more than her
reasons for marrying his father, and the union between
his father and Clara Pulling; for as magnificent as the
event was intended to be, and for as lovely-a-woman
as she was, continued to hang over Joseph and
Robaré's head like an executioner's ax.

The WHITE-CAPS had settled and the sea was calm
with a light breeze. So light in fact the sails could be
heard topside hard-flapping as they tried to catch more
wind than the sea would allow them to. With barely a
filament of light to see by, Joseph lay in his hammock;
and with his quills and lead, leaned over and drew the
engineering intricacies of a carriage wheel and its
suspension parts on the head of a whisky cask - upside
down. The drawing, so intricate, the bunghole of the

whisky barrel depicted the actual barring hub of the wheel, and the more natural lines of the oak wood revealed the quality lines of the wheel and its connecting points. Akin to a well used sketch book, there were several illustrations on each of the other barrelheads that depicted noteworthy drawings such as pistols; cannons; military hardware and a grizzly bear.

CHAPTER two
TILLINGHAST

HUNDREDS of TALL 'n short masts pointed to the clouds whereas the vessels that supported them crowded New York's busy harbor. And just as notable, a hundred times as many stevedores; black 'n white alike, lumped their cargo to and fro, offloading: boxes, trunks, furniture, textiles, sundries and seaweed; sophisticated possessions that had inserted themselves into the new world. All while sacks 'n barrels of corn, wheat, rice, cotton and tobacco were loaded onto ships that crept out of the harbor bound for countries in demand of America's new exports.

Bilge rats scurried, and if possible were hacked and tossed overboard. But for those that made it off ship, feral cats roamed the decks for a meal to feed their young by. Howling and hungry animals were hoisted from the bowels of the larger vessels and lowered into slatted crates; while just as many that failed to make the last day were wheeled to the end of the docks where their carcasses were raised high onto mammoth ox-drawn wagons bound for the factories.

Hundreds of people from all walks of life were greeted by loved ones, while just as many were alone and without. The passengers of steerage, mostly the starving Irish, were the last to depart. Their importance minimized even more by the fact the lifeless animals had preference over human existence; and only then were they allowed to leave ship.

In the streets, drivers of lavish carriages and coaches met their weary passengers who had already repainted themselves with a fresh tone of aristocracy and wealth. For at sea, if one were to complain over the stench of a rotten, yet still living animal bunking within nasal range, nothing could, or would be done. Unheard of equality in such closed quarters, but once off ship, their noses turned up and away from anything or any person that displeased them; and up and away they almost certainly turned.

On the other hand, an interesting point a commoner might titter over was the wagons loaded with rotting carrion and their accompanied smell. The biting reek they produced you see, held no prejudice over the sensitive nasal cavities of the gentry or their connected bloodlines. When the selected few that were privileged enough to ride in carriages were driven passed the fetid carts off-gassing their profusely sharp and offensive stench; which instantly made its way into the soft, plush interiors, it irrefutably caused many a coach door to open on the roll and vomit to splash in the street.

Closer to the docks, a winded constable chased after a young pickpocket only an arm's reach away. If caught, the youth would be dragged away, beaten and the lifted item filched again. Upon the thief's bludgeoning, his naked body would then be dropped into pig slop where the swine too had no prejudice of sex; color; country-of-origin or bone structure. Everything was eaten, shat out and the meat consumed by all who purchased it.

All of this raucous activity happened as sailors drank and celebrated over lost land time. And for as much as these men smelled of the sea, they loved lifting as many commoner's skirts as they might. Many a girl, of bleeding age and above, and some well under, were more than happy to take as much of a sailor's sea pay as possible in order to cover her own needs. These girls, overtly crafty, knew that a sailor's desire for rum over fresh water only made their job that much easier. This was due mostly to the fact that locating freshly boiled water, free of the parasites that caused malaria and yellow fever, amongst other diseases, was especially hard to find, making alcohol far easier and safer to ingest

DRESSED in HIS FINEST, Joseph stepped onto *Helena's* gangplank and bounced his way for the open dock. It had been a little over one-hundred 'n twenty months since he last set foot in New York and much had changed. Therefore his gait was lively and he carried himself and his bag as if he had a place to go and the knowledge to get there.

In the street, a five foot stump of a man was in the process of loading a flatbed wagon with six of the twenty-gallon whisky casks that Joseph berthed above during his voyage. As it turns out some of his drawings were clearly visible.

Watching the man work was Fraser Dunlop; a perfectly dressed, dashing Irish businessman in his early-sixties. He had a full head of greying hair covered by a fitted top-hat made of seal skin and was a standing member of the *Grand Lodge of Ireland;* which was no easy task, especially living in America. Beside him was his young, strong willed niece, Amanda Tillinghast. Her lime green gown, evenly marked by the muck below her feet, begged her spry and slightly pronounced breasts; coupled with her perfect posture, to jet beyond the expensive, tightly woven material and venture out into the brisk, naked air. Dunlop coveted his whisky as if there was no more on earth; and the parasol Amanda held in her brown gloved hand, gently rested on her shoulder as if to say, *ney* to the sun as it tried to make its way past her wide brimmed hat and onto her flawless, alabaster skin. With her arm locked into her Uncle Fraser's, they watched Innes manhandle the one-hundred-forty-five pound barrels into the wagon.

Innes, the forty-eight year old brawn of a man, stood atop the wagon bed; sweat dripping from every pore as he lashed down Ireland's finest. Only two of Joseph's drawings were visible, but Innes, a man that didn't know whom or what Joseph was about, could care less which direction the drawings faced or anything connected to the person that committed the art.

Dunlop on the other hand was a man of exquisite taste and loved the feeling of acquisition. He looked at his whisky and bolstered in a thick brogue, "Aye, Amanda darlin', there's nothin' like the taste of home." This was when a barrel slipped from the powerful man's grasp and banged hard on the wagon bed, "Shite," cursed Innes under his breath, looking to see if anyone had heard him.

"Careful, Innes!" shouted Dunlop, "Not a single drop, eh?" Innes, ever respectful, knew the importance of the barrel's contents and without another word, nodded in respect of his employer's requirements.

Joseph had finally made his way through the

crowd and stepped up to Dunlop and the Tillinghast heiress, "Aye me boy," said the man with esteem.

"Sir," replied Joseph, catching his breath. Instantly though, he was taken by Amanda and every part of her lovely stature pressing forward into the new world as if to say, *'I am here, and here I will remain'*. This time however, Joseph's cocksmanship was claimed by something altogether different; a woman who knew him not, and could care less about his money: for she had her own.

"Get your land legs back?" asked Dunlop.

"Never lost *those*, sir," answered Joseph, a bit embarrassed over his weak stomach; something a man of the day should not possess, much less admit he had, but it was difficult to disguise because of the vomit stains on his coat; discolorations he had a hard time removing with sea water alone.

Joseph clearly sensed he'd been looking at Amanda with too much initial interest, so he intentionally deferred to the whisky casks, "I can see you have many years of Irish pleasure ahead of you, sir."

"Years?..." scoffed Dunlop, "Weeks. I have eight more arriving in two months. I believe I must be a leprechaun," he said with a hearty belly laugh.

Amanda, who'd also been taken by Joseph, let her uncle know it by giving his arm a firm, yet unnoticeable squeeze. "Aye," whispered Dunlop where he secured Amanda's arm in his and turned squarely to face Joseph, but said nothing.

Aboard ship, formalities always took a rear seat behind the effort needed to stay alive, but Joseph remembered his station and asked Dunlop, "Sir, I do hope an introduction is in order?"

"Aye," bubbled Dunlop joyfully, "Aye, it is indeed. Joseph Tweddle, it gives me a great deal of pleasure to present my lovely and charming niece, Amanda Tillinghast. Joseph is quite the engineer; and here to help us get a rigid hold on our new venture. Dunlop's last few words caused Amanda's facial expressions to change from objectivity to aspiration.

Joseph respectfully bowed, but the finishing school Amanda recently completed did not pay off this time with a perfect curtsey. This was because her eyes hadn't allowed Joseph's to become disconnected from the gaze she cast.

"Miss. Tillinghast," announced Joseph in a stately manner, "It's an honor. Your Uncle speaks fondly of you, and often. It's as if I already know you."

Amanda's reply came as feisty, yet delightful and eloquently Scots Irish, "My Uncle's heart is open to that which he loves most, Mr. Tweddle: his family; his investments; his whisky, and now you – or so it appears."

A bit embarrassed by his niece's spirited nature; Dunlop genuinely liked Joseph. For what wasn't to like; jacket stains aside, the boy could accurately illustrate anything: animal, scene or machinery. He was honorable and forthcoming. He could socially indulge in drink without going beyond his limits; he could tell a joke, and he came from especially good stock. He also enjoyed the company of women, social and otherwise: an acquired taste so many of the eligible bachelors nowadays did not have or care to cultivate; enjoying their own company more; sodomites in the eyes of Fraser Dunlop.

Amanda's guileless nature left Joseph without words. Dunlop could see this, so he placed his arm around the girl in loving admiration and asked, "Where's your father?"

"He went on ahead, sir. Robaré hired a coach. Father's legs were troubling him, along with some family matters concerning my mother that required his attention."

"Aye, your mother… Understandable," replied the Irishman with compassion, along with a bit of letdown, "Well, not to lose sleep over. We shall all gather next month in Albany, as agreed, and turn the buggy world upside down. What say you that, boy?"

Joseph, who was filled with excitement through and through said, "I say that sounds like a plan, undeniably, sir."

Desirous to remain in Amanda's intoxicating company, and she in his, he was again lost for words and therefore felt the need to take his leave. Receiving her hand, "Miss. Tillinghast," he said, "It was a pleasure to be certain ... Sincerely ... Knowing about you... I mean hearing of you... No. I mean -- ..."

"Mr. Tweddle," Amanda replied, cutting off the foot Joseph had inserted into his mouth, "Hopefully it shall continue to be," - her sexual prowess, strong and alluring. With their hands touching, Amanda sensually pressed her thumb into the fleshy meat between Joseph's thumb and index finger and pinched the muscle. Joseph didn't know how to react to this. Usually he was the aggressor, but like his father said, he was in a new land now, and to take his sweet, cherubic time with this woman might not be suitable; especially after he'd heard aboard ship what a cocksman her Uncle Fraser was in his younger days.

Amanda not only exuded speed, she radiated the kind of heat Joseph had never felt before. He also knew, consciously or otherwise, he was being taken in at the romantic pace to which Amanda was accustomed. The only thing the boy could do now was to hold on - and hopefully follow.

JOHN TWEDDLE and his paunch of a thirty-five year old adopted stepson, Robaré Pulling, entered a warm library filled with books of regard, family paintings and beautifully crafted objects from both Europe and America.

Creating several suitable home environments for his family to reside in had not been easy. This is why John Tweddle wanted this crossing to be the very last one in which he shipped anything inanimate or otherwise to the new world. He was done with England and wanted to remain in America. It wasn't that he didn't care about his homeland, he did, very much so, but in every sense of the word, *artisan,* and its original meaning; he was a man at the top of his field; and he knew himself well enough to understand that what he wanted to accomplish could not be realized in all of Europe, much less England.

A large telescope pointed out to where mature, budding elm trees artistically lined the wide, dirt road. These full-size trees; five and more to a home lot, shaded and protected these large, well built, stately homes that beautified this colonized area.

Inside the library, trunks and crates lined the walls to make room for living, all while the sorting and arranging of the family's belongings could continue. In the adjacent room, women chitchatted as they cleared away the dinner dishes. They were happily doing what they liked to do best: gossip over their American environment and their rising socioeconomic class.

Joseph stepped across the library's threshold, did an about face and pulled the pocket doors closed. When he did, the women's voices along with the clatter immediately diminished. Turning for the fireplace, he rubbed his hands together and thought how wonderful this warm, dry heat felt.

His father and Robaré had already relaxed into matching bolstered chairs. Robaré's stocking feet rested on his own ottoman close to the popping embers and between the men's chairs stood a small round table on which a silver box rested.

After using his hands to lift each of his legs onto his own ottoman, John Tweddle sighed, "I do say boys; I'm as content as one man can be. All but these damn sea legs."

Robaré on the other hand; as if commanding a servant, said to Joseph in his Parisian, toffee-nosed accent, "Pour father and I a brandy, Joseph."

The Oxford engineer was grateful to be on land as well as someplace new, and therefore appeared completely naive to the way Robaré made the request. Knowing or not; and certainly too dignified to engage, Joseph simply reached for the decanter above the fireplace and poured two brandies into the nearby snifters. Then in a livened tone declared, "America's still everything you said it was father, and more! Thank you. I understand now what you meant by her perfume. She's so fresh and blue. The air I'm breathing… smells sweet."

Joseph handed the men their drinks; first his father and then Robaré. Lastly he poured himself one, dispensing less than a quarter of what he'd poured the other's, yet before he was finished, Robaré, with an impudent hand, beckoned more brandy into his glass and claimed, "A disgrace you've spent so much of your time thinking about useless things, Joseph. Wait until you see the new factory I have built."

Joseph refrained from looking at Robaré directly, yet no less humble, he grinned and chose instead to look around the giant room, "I cannot," he exclaimed as he examined the room, "I'm far too excited." He allowed his eyes to rest for a moment on several of the items he remembered as a boy growing up, conjuring up a few quick and colorful memories all while pouring the arrogant man more of his father's expensive liquor.

John Tweddle; the formal man he was, finally loosened his shirt collar and said, "Dunlop's an honest man with honorable intentions. This passage allowed me a completely new perspective of him, and his plans for all of our futures."

"And the contracts?" asked Robaré, always

40

suspicious.

Aware of his stepson's ongoing distrust of the Irish, he replied, "His word and his marks are high-quality. The contracts are in order and befitting all persons--

"He's still Irish," countered Robaré, snipping off the end of his stepfather's words. Then without warning the Frenchman changed chords and made a play towards Joseph, "Have you met sweet Amanda?" he asked, and he swirled his brandy, smelling the aromatic fragrance around the rim of his snifter like the nape of a woman's neck.

"I have," replied Joseph who became busy with the fire.

"Ravishing, is she not? I intend to--"

"I hadn't noticed," said Joseph, cutting off Robaré in turn.

John Tweddle smelled trouble, yet Robaré continued to press, "Are you blind little man? --

"No Robaré, I'm not blind. I've arrived back to help father build a new business, and that's what *I* intend to do," and he returned his attention to the fire.

"Well, so do I!" snarled the Frenchman, "among other things," and he sent a solid look to his stepfather and then finished his brandy.

Joseph looked into the flames and muttered, "Poor, starving bastards." He then turned and faced

Robaré, "What do you have against the Irish except what others have told you to have against them? If you hate these people so, why take an interest in their women? Still a hypocrite, and someone else's man, eh Robaré?"

John Tweddle clearly knew this would not end well if he didn't do something, so he interjected, "That's enough Joseph. You have only just arrived. There'll be plenty of time for that another day. I needn't remind you how much we have invested in Robaré's talents. You would be wise to learn from him."

Robaré savored the moment along with his brandy's bouquet while suckling the last drop that remained. On the same note, Joseph's anger quickly receded; an emotional skill he developed early in life over the need to protect himself from the constant torment that came by way of his older stepbrother.

John Tweddle opened the lid of the silver box beside him and retrieved three cigars. He handed one to each man and stated in a robust tone, "Right now, I want to celebrate with my new partners, and sons." This comment was almost too much for Joseph, so instead of creating a clash to cover his feelings, he inspected the leafy role, smelled it, and imitated his father's knowledge of them.

Robaré stretched forward over his own roll and

removed a flaming twig from the fire and respectfully lit his stepfather's cigar; but when Joseph moved in for the same light, Robaré cruelly held the flame just out of reach, forcing him to stretch, and stretch some more. But before Robaré had a time to react, Joseph took hold of the man's wrist and griped it like a vice. He then brought the flame easily within reach of his own cigar, but before lighting it said, "Ten years ago, your age and size over me was significant. Know this stepbrother, those days are well passed." For barely a moment, Robaré's eyes acknowledged a new respect. This was all Joseph needed in order to be satisfied, and because he willed it, released the pressure on Robaré's arm and resigned it back to him.

Puffing on his cigar, Joseph immediately hacked and choked. He caught his breath and laughed. This brought John Tweddle and Robaré into the fun with all three men breaking into paroxysms of laughter.

WHILST THE MEN drank and smoked, a soft knock sounded at the doors. Over his shoulder John Tweddle bellowed, "Come..." When the doors opened, a fifteen-year-old enjaneau with golden locks stood at the entry beside a black servant man holding a silver tray and tea set.

Ann Eliza Tweddle, or Annaleez to those who knew and loved her, was a naturally radiant girl with a cheerful countenance. Dressed in a light blue gown that was tightly drawn in at the waist and cut to the floor, she stepped across the threshold and was followed by the black man who set the tray down, bowed back and asked, "Will dat be all Masser Tweedle?" With a superior flip of his hand, Robaré dismissed the man and he left the room pulling the doors closed behind him.

Unlike Joseph who spoke in a formal British tone, Annaleez along with the rest of her siblings were American born and did not possess the same strong speech quality although they did speak with a tinge of English color due to the abundance of British descendents in the area. Nonetheless, like their oldest brother who was born abroad, they too were well bread, smart, and had a strong, underlying current of self-reliance. Annaleez in particular had proven herself to be playful at times, and at others, downright naughty. Conversely though she'd not always been like this. She'd only been different since nearly perishing on her return voyage to America not that long ago. Different in that her penchant was to disagree with all things asked of her; and to demand that *everything* be her way. This was, for the large part, becoming more than her family and those around her could bear. But since her dire bout with scurvy aboard ship which caused half of her twelve molars to loosen and fall out, she'd also gained a new lease on life, and a ishhealthy, 'live and let live' respect toward all things. It was a simple lesson and she learned it quickly. All the same, she still held concerns over her immediate family and wasn't the type who feared expressing of them.   She poured a cup of tea and announced in a scolding tone, "Father, you know what the doctor told you about the brandy, and smoking those things; here, drink tea instead."

"Nonsense, dear," the man cheerfully bolstered, and he shot a wink to Robaré, "The words of a physician are only meant for those who heed their advice." He still accepted the tea however, but pushed it aside.

Joseph could never understand how Robaré's self-importance seemed to win out over common sense, or decency. This made itself evident when his father allowed Robaré to convince him to forego the meeting on the docks after they'd arrived in New York;

the meeting Fraser Dunlop was very much looking forward to. The result being; family matters could have certainly waited an hour considering how long they'd been at sea, thus causing Joseph the need to fabricate a partial cover story. Therefore he allowed what he felt to pass because he loved his sister, and this was made evident by the way he stood beside her as she chastised their father.

Even before Annaleez turned twelve; and before she boarded ship for her return voyage to America, Joseph had a natural way of subduing her arrogance, and this was something Annaleez knew and grew to love. In fact, the simple gesture of Joseph moving to her side had already calmed the girl's nerves.

"A toast!" roared John Tweddle: "To Robaré, for all you have done; and to Joseph, for all you are about to do." The family elder raised his glass and waved, "To the wheel! …"

Cigars in hand, Joseph and Robaré raised their glasses as well. Joseph wanted to toss the smoldering roll in the fire and be done with it, but out of respect he refrained. "TO THE WHEEL!" they shouted, and they toasted and tipped their glasses. Annaleez; her eyes alight, watched her men with pride.

JOSEPH'S QUARTERS, similar to the warm library, were elegant, yet temporary. And akin to being aboard *Helena*, his belongings lay neatly on his bed next to his valise. A different African man had just completed the task of stoking the fire in the small hearth. He gestured to Joseph its readiness and asked, "Will dat be all, Masser Joseph?"

"Yes, thank you, Jeffrey," said Joseph in a tired, yet kindly tone. The man departed the room and gently pulled the door closed behind him.

Joseph stepped up to the door and made certain of its security. He then went to the window where he moved the curtains aside and looked down on the quiet avenue below. When he heard the distant echo of clattering hooves on cobblestone; he immediately recalled the time he'd spent in London and his affections for a woman he'd seriously considered spending the rest of his life with; a woman older than he by eight years. Unfortunately no matter how convincing he might have made his appeal sound to his father, Joseph knew he would have never approved of the union. Not because her means fell below his, which in and of itself was of reticent consequence to John Tweddle, and not necessarily that she was thirty-three and considered a spinster. And though she and Joseph were deeply in love, and she was enchanting and gorgeous through to her soul, as well as an English lady in every right; only four years widowed by an army Captain through an arranged marriage, she could not bear children. So to carry the Tweddle seed forward at Joseph's side was an impossibility, and more important to John Tweddle than love or money; and Joseph sadly knew this to be true.

So he wiped his tears with his jacket sleeve and drew the curtains closed. On his way back to his bed to commence his night time routine, a soft knock came to the door.

He opened it a crack and Annaleez excitedly whispered, "I overheard you and Robaré argue…"

Joseph looked down his nose at her.

"Alright, I was eavesdropping," she confessed. Joseph turned back inside and Annaleez squirted through. She closed the door tenderly, yet tight. "It always sounds so serious," she whispered, "Tis a wonder you two don't--

"It was nothing," said Joseph who was now warming himself by the fire.

Annaleez took a seat on his bed and started to bounce. Fiddling with his things she said, "Why must you leave so soon, brother? You've only just arrived and I've missed you. We barely saw each other when I was in England."

"I missed you too Ann, but we have three months until we relocate to Albany. Let us make the best of it, shall we?"

Annaleez picked up Joseph's book on exploring and remarked sadly, "While in England, I feared I might not see home again. Now I fear the same of you, brother."

"Don't say that. It's a fear you needn't conjure."

"I'm not built for another sea voyage, Joseph. I will surely perish. The first crossing tried to take me, but I fought back, still it took many of my lovely teeth - look."

Joseph sat down next to the golden haired girl and said, "I know, I heard." He gently placed his hands on her face. "Close your mouth. You look beautiful. Can you still eat an apple?"

Annaleez nodded...

"Good. Nothing to worry over," he said, trying to cheer her up, "All things for the best, eh? Albany's only a few days north; nothing like a sea voyage. As soon as we settle, father will send word and we'll all be together again."

"You promise?"

"You have my word," he said. This seemed to reassure the excitable teen.

"*Your* word I trust."

Annaleez always became tranquil when Joseph made her a promise that helped solve a concern she herself had no control over; for he has, to the best of her recollection, never broken a promise to any person. And this made perfect sense, because he never agreed to do anything unless he was certain of his ability, and most importantly, his willingness to accomplish the task.

Annaleez picked up Joseph's pistol and remarked casually, "You like her, don't you?"

"Give me that!" he snapped and he took away the weapon. On his way to the dresser by the window he asked, "You know her?" He placed the gun in the top drawer and then moved to the door to again make sure it was fastened.

"Of course, we're grand friends."

Of course thought Joseph walking back to the bed; why wouldn't Annaleez meet every fascinating person she could. Her new found zeal for life has turned her into a people magnet.

Annaleez flipped through a few leaves in one of his sketch books and said, "I know she's Irish, but *I* don't believe what people say about them; she's completely American."

"Yes, I noticed this too," said Joseph.

And like a preteen who's just heard the word *penis* for the first time, Annaleez dropped the book and bubbled, "She fancies you."

"No… ?" said Joseph in actual surprise.

"Mmm," remarked Annaleez nonchalantly.

"How do you know? --"

"She told me."

"She didn't? --"

"Mmm...

"But when did you see her?"

"After you'd met on the docks"

"Really... ? --"

"She's rightly straight forward; says what's on her mind."

"Yes, I noticed --"

"She wants you--" the teen pronounced.

"Annaleez.... Please, you're fifteen."

"Tis true, and she always gets what she wants."

"Sounds like her American ways have rubbed off on you."

"*Could* it be the other way around? Either way, I like it," and she popped up for the door. "We're to go shopping tomorrow and after, a picnic at the *Cleary Glen*." She stopped at the door, spun around and faced her brother who'd followed her. He was clearly a foot taller.

"You're invited too," she said palming her dress flat. She then leaned into him and whispered, "See you in the morning," whereby she gave her oldest brother, who was now agreeably corralled, a kiss on his cheek. "Good," she said, "Eleven A.M., and be prompt. No one wants to think of you otherwise."

"Alright, I will."

"O, and Joseph?"

"Mmm…"

"I know you had your reasons for wanting to remain in England, and I'm terribly sorry it didn't work between you and Margaret; really I am. I very much liked her. She was a delight to talk to, but… I'm so glad you've come home." And with a brightened smile, the baby girl who was delivered breech in 1828 and thought to be stillborn, slipped out the door the same way she entered.

FOLLOWING a LONG SEA VOYAGE, Joseph's exhausted body lay motionless in the soft feather bed. A gentle knock sounded at his door, but the worn out man failed to budge.

Out his window on this snappishly cool morn, the avenue below was now attentive with activity: people, horses, carriages and wagons; all with much to do. Another knock sounded, but this time a bit louder.

Down the street, Fraser Dunlop's man, Innes, now clad to chauffeur, was commanding a four passenger, covered chaise-carriage at a healthy clip towards the Tweddle home. The investor's coach was beautifully outfitted with twin brass lanterns, tuck 'n rolled interior and every shiny accoutrement available, including glass windows and room for a second driver. Elite chattel to be certain; topped off and drawn by a matching pair of gelded silver dapples. Their nostrils, like exhaust ports for steam powered machinery, snorted long, white plums into the cold air before them.

In front of the house, Annaleez and Robaré waited in the chilled air as Innes approached. They watched him skillfully negotiate the lightly weighted, empty carriage. No other driver required with Innes behind the reins, and no simple task on a slippery dirt and cobblestone runway, especially at the rate he was traveling. At the same time he crossed the road; he applied the brake and reined the animals back, bringing the large symbol of status to a controlled stop not two inches either way of where he intended; perfectly positioned so his passengers need not travel any more than one step-up and into the plush interior. No easy feat for the unqualified.

Innes Mac Lochlainn, *The Gaelic Viking*; a man

who in secret turned down a sanctioned assassination because he took personal pleasure stoving-in a politician's head like a melon for ritually sacrificing a twelve year old boy after he'd tortured and sodomized him. The money, offered up by the boy's heart wrenched parents to see justice served for their only son was all the funds they had, but Innes, a man of fierce loyalty toward the basics of humanity, saw a deed that needed doing and plainly did it.

Unfortunately for the lad who was only performing the rudimentary task of delivering a message from one man to another; all for the handsome pay of a half-dollar in coin, came too close to the politician's confines. The trap was set, snaring the boy and thus outlaying his life, but it also cost the life of the man who'd sent the message to the Satanist. Both men executed inside their coach as they engaged in lubricious acts while they waited for a third man, the man who ultimately discovered the broken bodies.

INNES climbed down from the rear driver's position and without a word, took on the footman's job and unlatched the door. An elegantly gloved hand extended past the door's threshold and Robaré reached for it, but inside, Amanda quickly rethought the act and withdrew it. She looked at Annaleez who in turn helplessly looked up at Joseph's window where there was no movement. Altogether embarrassed, Robaré sent his stepsister a rancorous glare.

The horses nervously pranced and nickered. One of them, the closest to Robaré, urinated loudly causing ammoniated steam to rise from the mud while at the same time splashing some his way.

Innes could hear and see everything as he held the door open, yet remained silent when Robaré incoherently mumbled while helping Annaleez into the carriage. Annaleez, in full knowledge that Robaré wanted to sit next to Amanda, plopped herself squarely beside the heiress. Having no other option, Robaré climbed in and sat across from the women. Looking at Amanda while she chatted with his stepsister would have to do. The three aristocrats then adjusted their dress and posture for the ride into town. Robaré shot another resentful look toward Annaleez, but a dignified squeeze from Amanda's hand calmed the girl. Innes closed the door and it clicked tight with the artisanship of nothing finer.

A DAPPLE'S WHINNY along with the sound of a barking dog finally made it beyond Joseph's window to pierce the sleeping man's deadened senses. Drowsily he reached for his pocket watch on the night table and muttered, "11:20... ... Damn!" He threw off the covers and jumped out of bed. Butt-naked with his breath fogging before him, he peeked past the curtains and could only watch as the Tillinghast carriage turned around in the avenue below and roll away. He sat back on his bed and rubbed his eyes. When he finally felt the temperature of the air, all that came from his mouth was, "Cold, bloody cold," and he quickly climbed back under the covers.

Twas a SPENDID DAY for a ride in the country. Spring was in the air and New York's promising skyline could be seen in the distance. Combine this with the shimmering beauty of the Hudson and Joseph felt right at home. Clothed in a pair of high black boots and English riding apparel, he slowed his sorrel steed from a canter to a trot. Up ahead three coaches were at rest. One of them was the Tillinghast carriage; all in a semicircle at Cleary Glen; a lovely, out of the way setting where the coming-of-age came to fraternize: the coming-of-age that had been given permission and held elite status.

With a large, park-like backdrop; Cleary Glen was bejeweled with sprawling oaks, elms and sycamores. It displayed a splendid, open green meadow with low-lying grasses and a brook; just a fleck bigger than babbling. Other coaches and buggies were also at rest throughout the area with their young occupants strolling about.

As Joseph rode closer, he saw seven young adults: three men and three women along with his sister Annaleez; the third wheel and self-proclaimed match maker, all milling about and socializing. The young men, though dapper in their attempt, tried to grow facile hair with seeming little success; revealing in some cases, vast patches where hair had yet to grow. The women, all dressed in elegant gowns, darted about and giggled anytime one or more of the gents made an attempt to get close; making the game of *hard-to-get* into a fun and open sport.

The coaches encircled two finely set tables abounding food and drink. Innes, one of three mature chaperons, stood guard. Positioned with a watchful eye over all; he was armed with two pistols under his cloak, a cudgel behind his waist band, a dagger in each boot and blunderbuss within easy reach. Plenty of armament in case a highwayman or two decided to originate a stupid idea.

Down by the BROOK, Robaré and Amanda stood on opposite sides. Amanda had been doing her best to prevent her dress from touching the ground while Robaré, who'd been drinking, paced the water's edge. Behind Amanda and over the edge of the bank, the picnic was underway.

"Yes, Amanda," replied Robaré," but it's been over a year since we were introduced and--"

"Please Robaré," the girl stated firmly while grasping her gown, "If I matter to you at all, then kindly bring an end to your assault against my feelings."

Robaré looked into the tree tops as if he were hearing voices and declared, "Your feelings? ... An assault? Well, pardon mademoiselle," and he tossed back another swallow from the one pint sterling flask his stepfather had given him on his thirty-third birthday.

"Aye, Robaré, I have pardoned your behavior more times than I care to concede."

When **ANNALEEZ** spotted her brother; she dropped her socializing and beamed like the sun. Joseph dismounted and upon tying his mount to the Tillinghast carriage, respectfully acknowledged Innes and then made his way towards his sister's group.

Annaleez rushed to him and said, "Joseph, I am so happy you could join us," then drew him in close, "You're late," she whispered, joyfully scolding him. She then spun around in delight and announced, "Is this not fabulous? Come, I want to introduce you," and she pulled him towards her friends.

FROM the BROOK, Amanda watched as Annaleez cheerily introduced Joseph to all her friends. Robaré however, appeared even more hapless. He was now allowing his shoes to get wet. "It's my family's money, or lack of it, is it not?" he demanded.

"It has nothing to do with money," she said, continuing to keep her gown and feet dry, "It never has."

"Then what could it *possibly* be?" he squalled tossing back another swallow.

"As bigheaded as you are," she retorted, "I have always taken you to be a sensible and intelligent man--"

"You would take any man for all you could!" the Frenchman sloppily bawled.

"Do you really want to know?" blasted Amanda. "Would you really like to hear it from my own lips why I don't love you?"

"Go ahead, say it!" shouted Robaré, "Cry it out to the whole goddamn world while you're at it!"

But Amanda's attention was suddenly drawn to the creek bank, "Joseph ..."

Joseph reached down and Amanda immediately gave him her hand and he pulled her up, all the while being careful not to dirty her gown.

Robaré took another swallow and announced, "Oh... Is this not fine! Little stepbrother, here to save my damsel."

"I am not yours, Robaré! I am no man's chattel," defined the girl, and she threw back her shoulders and turned for the picnic.

"I suppose you're HIS THEN …?!" he shouted, now standing in ankle deep water.

"I belong to no person!" came the volley, and she was gone.

Robaré looked in wonder at the scenery then begrudgingly proclaimed, "Little Joseph, your timing is perfect; your clothes are perfect; you are so GODDAMN PERFECT!" Off balance, Robaré slipped. In doing so, he put his hand on the pistol he'd tucked in his trousers. Joseph, overreacting, drew his pistol and pointed it. Pathetically though, Robaré fell into the water where he scraped his knee and sank his gun hand, "Go ahead, kill me!" he shouted with scornful pity, "Stand 'n deliver, stepbrother! SLAY ME!"

"You're drunk, man," said Joseph, and he returned his own weapon to his pants, "Sober up," and he too turned for the picnic.

Sadly, Robaré was clearly overwhelmed. He attempted to stand, but then elected to sit in the pebbly wet sand; caring not if the seat of his trousers became soaked.

AT A MODERATE three beat cantor, Innes drove the dapples parallel to The Hudson. Joseph's horse was in tow and could be seen through the back portal from inside the carriage. While Robaré snored against Joseph's shoulder, Annaleez and Amanda sat beside each other in console.

Joseph was genuinely concerned over his stepbrother's condition, as he well should be. His father dropped a substantial sum into his talents as an architect, builder and general business partner.

Robaré snorted some and then burped up. Joseph glanced at the mess on his coat and asked Annaleez, "How long? ..."

Annaleez was also concerned and there was humanity in her tone that superseded the fact that not only was Robaré far removed from her own bloodline, he was not in the Pulling blood line either; being adopted at the age of five from an abusive orphanage. On the other hand, her attitude toward the matter had also been tempered by Joseph's ten year absents - coupled with his much anticipated return.

"Since the return voyage," she replied. "He started with little nips of rum to combat the ship's motion. Then it turned into an everyday affair; at least it's the excuse he still uses. In your absence, father placed tremendous responsibilities upon him. He also doted on him and gave him much of his love; love you were entitled to.

"No Ann. There's plenty of love to go around and father's always given his freely. Robaré was here and I was not. He was also educated before I was. It's a simple matter of timing and geography. How was I to know father wanted to go into the carriage business; he'd always been in brewing."

"Regardless," snipped the youngest child, "the geography lesson's over. Thank God father knew he could not have made his new dream manifest without his eldest son. This is why he came for you. He loves you, Joseph," and she took his hand. "With William being so very ill; and Thomas in Pennsylvania with his new family studying law, and George...," her voice breaking when she said his name, "not being heard from since he put to sea;" - breaking because all she can remember George ever talking about was being a sailor, "father invested heavily in Robaré's talents. But he turned his head more times than he should have to his trickery."

Amanda's humanity towards Robaré's situation was also evident in her expressions and body language, but not towards him personally. She wished she'd never intrigued with him; causing him to fall so hard, and so foolishly. Whether it was her independence or her persona; she did not know, because if she had it to do again, she would've surely refrained from paying him the interest she did. But alas, she too was human and at the time in need of male companionship. The good that came from it, if it could be called *that*, was that she refrained from opening her legs to him; even when she was tipsy and desirous of a man to be inside her; successfully warring off his aggressive advances only to please him once with her hand. And at this moment, she couldn't be any more certain that Robaré would never be the man for her.

Enveloped within her sensitive, Tillinghast vulnerability, she took Joseph's hands in hers and looked at him. And with more sexual allure than ever, she uttered, "I understand, Joseph," and she squeezed his hand. "I do. I understand ..."

Under a **MOONLIT SUMMER'S NIGHT**, a different, yet equally elegant carriage rolled to a gentle stop along a village side street. Innes, the only operator, waited behind the reins at his front station. The coach's suspension was new and greased, but new or otherwise, the stirring inside caused it to squeak just the same.

With the shades drawn, Joseph and Amanda passionately moved about the cramped quarters. Clearly the aggressor, Amanda's hand was inside Joseph's trousers well beyond the point most would consider it time for the ring finger to be brandishing a wedding band. Joseph on the other hand was doing his best to contain his lover's advances and attempted to remove it, along with her hot lips from his already risen bulge, but like a bitch in heat, she wasn't about to entertain any notion of relinquishing her stone prize. So once again, Joseph acquiesced.

He rolled her to her back and lifted her gown where she willingly opened herself to him; holding her ankles especially wide, as if practiced for. As Joseph peeled his suspenders over his shoulders, Amanda hooked her bare heels into the back of his trousers and dug in hard; working them down past his knees. She cared not when the sound of popping buttons and tearing seams pierced the air. She then drew him all the way into her warm belly.

Atop the rocking coach, Innes dozed like a baby, but below, a male passerby out for an evening stroll with his terrier stopped to listen. A concealed chuckle from the man caused the dog to yap. This roused Innes who immediately recognized the actions of his lady and Mr. Tweddle.

"Off with you!" he shouted to the stranger. Yet Amanda's passionate cries prevented the man from departing. The dog yapped again.

"OFF WITH YOU!" Innes shouted, this time climbing down to do physical harm, but before the Irish watchdog could reach the street, the man and his lap-friend were well on their way, shaking their own backsides as they departed.

Looking **DISHEVELED** from his tumble with Amanda, Joseph entered his father's home through the front door and then closed it behind him. Shaking off the cold night air, he noticed Robaré reading in the parlor; candles burning and a brandy close by. But just as Joseph took a step, Robaré turned a leaf in his book and remarked in a smug tone, "You will never win her, Joseph." Joseph stopped, but unwilling to engage, tiredly continued upstairs to bed.

CHAPTER three
ALBANY

A WELL DRESSED African man in his fifties opened the front door of the Dunlop manor, "Nice to sees you again, sirs," said Sully. He then stood to the side so John Tweddle, Robaré and Joseph could enter. He closed the door and stepped ahead of the men where he began the process of escorting them through the enormous mansion. Although the Tweddle's had been here before, they still enjoyed the sculptures, paintings and art that accentuated the décor; especially John Tweddle. And though Fraser Dunlop possessed many fine qualities, taste was clearly at the top of the order.

Passing a closed oaken door, they could hear chamber music escaping from the other side. Unnoticed by his father who was busy respecting the art; and Robaré who cared less due to the pondering of where his next drink was going to come from, Joseph stopped to listen while Sully continued to lead the other two on. Joseph quietly slid the tall, ornate slap several inches and peeked inside. There, next to an overtly tall window hung with green velvet drapes pulled to the side and secured with gold satin ties, Amanda sat at an Imperial Grand Bosendorfer big

enough to bury an ox in. Without missing a note, she
waved Joseph in, but before he entered, he looked both
ways and upon the reception of his father's
condemning glare, along with Robaré's oblivious
arrogance, he ducked in and slid the door closed.

In the MANSION'S OPULENT, yet warm and
comfortable two story library, three towering ladders
on wheels fitted for book and manuscript retrieval sat
ready to be ascended.

　　　　And here is where the immaculately dressed,
Fraser Dunlop stood by his own colossal window
looking out on the lush gardens that enveloped his
estate on this beautiful summer morning. A knock
sounded at the double doors. When they were pressed
apart, they came to a stop at their jambs with a soft
thud. Sully announced, "John Wawker Tweedle and
Robear Pullin', sir." Robaré immediately took note
that the indentured man not only mispronounced his
name again, he also failed to announce Joseph,

whereby he discovered once again, that been he'd taken in by his little stepbrother.

When Dunlop called out in his usual full-bodied flair, "Ah, where's our young wheel-wonder?" John Tweddle stepped across the threshold. Doing so forced Robaré to follow and he said, "He'll be along shortly."

Sully pulled the doors together and stood quietly beside them.

"I see," said Dunlop knowingly.

But when Robaré noticed the man's grin, it only helped to confirm how much he hated the Irish.

In the MUSIC ROOM, Joseph and Amanda sat side by side at the massive instrument. Amanda began to play a beautiful interpretation of Beethoven's *"Moonlight Sonada: Quasiunafantasia"*, whereby the timing of the opening notes and the placement of her smooth and flawless hands across the ivory keys was easily enough to drive Joseph's face seductively into her neck, filling his head with the bouquet of her young and fertile scent.

a **HALF a MANSION AWAY**, John Tweddle and Fraser Dunlop examined large engineering drawings that had been prepared by Joseph. Robaré on the other hand was busy loving Dunlop's exclusive whisky; poured for him from his posh and well stocked bar by Sully. John Tweddle however appeared annoyed over Joseph's lack of business sense; that his son would rather play than work.

IN THE MUSIC ROOM however, it was Joseph now playing the giant piano, and Amanda whose hands were everywhere but on the keys. Not an accomplished pianist by any means, Joseph missed note after note as Amanda took her turn at gathering in her own basket of man-essence.

In the LIBRARY, the men shuffled through more drawings. Dunlop looked up from the near window size pages and commented, "Maybe he's misplaced himself? After all, it is a rather large house."

Robaré, who'd been waiting for an opportunity, chimed in, "I'll find him." And though John Tweddle had never approved of the two fighting; for unlike the past when Robaré usually came out the victor, he witnessed Joseph's demonstration of strength first hand and had a better idea of how an altercation might turn out should it become physical. And though it had been more than ten years since the two had fought;

truth be told, he didn't want to know, but he did know Robaré would ferret out the hiding boy.

Dunlop turned to Sully who'd been standing vigil behind the bar, "Go with the man, Sully – would you please. We don't want to lose two of them now, do we?"

"No sir Masser Dunlop," he said and he removed himself from behind the bar and walked to the doors where he began to part them. Only a few inches of clearance separated the library from the room on the other side when Robaré suddenly pulled them apart the remaining distance and whisked past the thin man like an odor. Sully stepped across the threshold, did an about face, but before excusing himself looked at his employer. Dunlop gave the dark man a confidential look. In return, Sully acknowledged it with his eyes and then slid the doors closed. Dunlop returned his attention to John Tweddle and expressed to his partner once again in his sincere and jovial nature; his love of carriages and the successful future he envisioned for their partnership. He asked John Tweddle to indulge him, and began proudly showing him some of his previously unseen and beloved possessions displayed within the massive repository.

PASSIONATE BREATHING quietly floated throughout the air of the music room. Behind a large, highly wrought dressing screen, Joseph's shirt was unbuttoned and its tails pulled out while Amanda's dress had been peeled to the floor.

Entwined, Amanda's words left her mouth on fire, "Why have you been ignoring me? --"

"It has not been my intention," whispered Joseph, every bit as hot.

"See that it stops," she averred, caressing her own breasts.

"I shall-" signed Joseph, on his knees, his hands wrapped around the girl's haunches, his fingers deep; relieved that his face was once again buried in his lover's fragrant blossom.

Amanda panted and attempted to ask, "When're you... ...going to ask Uncle for my hand? ..."

"Soon," murmured Joseph, savoring the strong redolence escaping from her soft, auburn mound. Suddenly the door slid and the disheveled couple froze. From the threshold, Sully and Robaré scanned the room; Robaré more so. Behind the screen however, one of Amanda's hands continued to press Joseph's face into her hot sex while the other held his fingers inside her.

"You fool!" loathed the Frenchman, "Don't you know the house in which you work? Where is he?"

"Cain't sazes I know, sir," the man calmly replied.

"Hmpf ..." puffed Robaré and he stormed away for the next room in the house; and there were many, but Sully, before sliding the door, noticed a slight movement behind the dressing screen. There, Joseph and Amanda were doing everything humanly possible not to burst out laughing. And before Sully departed, he kindly smiled, revealing several dark spaces where sparkling, white teeth once shone.

In the LIBRARY, Robaré had planted himself squarely in a bolstered leather chair where he'd been sulking over a crystal tumbler of whisky. On the other side of the room, Dunlop and John Tweddle stood between the Irishman's Herculean desk and a ten-foot tall window examining a cumbersome drawing under better light. The men's smoldering cigars lay at rest in a sterling ashtray as big as a dinner plate. The rising smoke and gasses naturally mixed with the sunlight entering through the window, thus causing the floating dust particles to illuminate and dance as if separated by an unknown force.

"I do apologize, Fraser," said John Tweddle sincerely as he rolled an ash off his cigar, "An engineer I am not, only an out of practice wheelwright. I will personally speak to the boy. You have my word."

"Don't bother, John. Please, save your embarrassment. You *must* remember what it was like – don't you? Being in love?..."

John Tweddle kindly smiled because he truly did recall what it felt like to be in love with his children's mother; the only woman he ever truly loved in deed, and heart.

The doors of the library came apart and Joseph's Cheshire cat grin was immediately met with the indignant stare that only Robaré could muster after being roused from a liquored-up stupor.

John Tweddle might be aware of the matter, but it didn't mean he was pleased, "Joseph! Come here," he said, "and show Mr. Dunlop why you're being paid!" Robaré opened his eyes fully and scoffed...

Later, as Robaré slept it off, Dunlop, Joseph and John Tweddle stood over another large drawing. At the same time Joseph's index finger on his left hand expertly pointed to a wheel assembly, he began to clearly explain what he'd designed.

CHAPTER four
TRIUMPH meets TRAGEDY

Seven YEARS LATER, deafening machinery noise was everywhere. In fact, it was inescapable. The only barrier that prevented the barrage of sound from consuming the drawing room and office-space above the factory floor was some paper-thin walls. The vibration from the steam powered engines driving the variety of machines was so definite; many of the plate-glass panes that allowed a view to the lower area were either cracked or completely broken out.

Joseph's left hand was now pointing to an updated version of a similar drawing he'd been describing, but this time a shiny gold wedding band was clearly visible. He was speaking to his mid-forty's foreman, Andrew McLeod. The two were leaning against a large layout table in the middle of the room discussing one particular area of a drawing that had been laid extra flat. Andrew was a tall, lean, levelheaded man and completely suited for the job as factory foreman.

Easily seen throughout the upstairs area were dozens of rolled up drawings that stood in every corner. These same rolled drawings were piled high on cabinets and stuffed into just about every conceivable crack and crevasse available. To offset this visible chaos, the walls had been lined in beautifully framed, pen 'n ink illustrations of people enjoying the many aspects of carriage ownership. One illustration in particular resembled the carriages at Cleary Glen. Another depicted a middle-class couple out for a jaunt in their two seat sport buggy, while a multi-pictorial collage displayed six happy passengers inside the company's top of the line model with extra baggage on top, all being pulled by four beautiful animals. Without a doubt, it was Joseph's art, and his engineering that shined.

In a more open space towards the back of the area, John Tweddle and Robaré had been taking a meeting at a voluminous roll top desk. Robaré poured a generous portion of cognac from a Louis the XIII baccarat crystal carafe into a water glass, but refrained to replace the glass stopper, thus allowing it to roll off the desk and onto the floor where it broke. The look of sadness on John Tweddle's face was unmistakable when he got down on his hands and knees and started picking up the pieces. This decanter you realize was a wedding gift when he married Joseph's mother; and though she'd given her Spirit to God, and her body to the earth three years ago, the old man was frequently stricken with grief; despite the fact he'd gone on to marry Robaré's adoptive mother, Clara Pulling.

Nonetheless, it was Joseph who was in charge at the layout table, "Remember Andrew, when the men turn the left assembly anti-clock wise, tell them just tight enough to compensate before they lock it, eh? We can't have Mr. Buntline returning over the same matter."

"Nor any matter," clarified Andrew.

"Nor any matter," said Joseph with a nod.

Andrew was Irish and proud of it, along with his aptitude. "It won't happen again, Mr. Tweddle. You can count on me."

Joseph gave Andrew a reassuring look along with a pat on his shoulder to indicate the confidence he had in the man he'd hired against the wishes of both Robaré and his father. Regardless of his heritage, Joseph knew that Andrew was fully capable of solving any problem placed before him.

Robaré on the other hand could care less that his stepfather was crawling around on all fours over the sentimentality of a glass bottle. He could only glare across the room at the respect Joseph gave to Andrew – and watch as his blood heated, his nostrils flared and his face wrinkled with the same acerbity that took him over as a boy.

Andrew jotted down a note and then turned for the door. When he opened it, the machinery noise blasted past him and into the offices. When he courteously closed it behind him, the sounds diminished to their previous din.

From the landing atop of the stairs, the entire factory floor was abuzz with activity. The latest in steam powered tools and machinery assisted in the heavier aspects of bending, pressing and shaping the family's coaches that rested in various stages of assembly; all of them neatly lined across the massive space with two to three men carrying out the building process of each carriage from beginning to end.

On the main floor, twenty-nine year old Ned Buntline anxiously stood next to his new buggy. He was a short based man with dark hair who'd been sporting a large handlebar moustache since he was old enough grow it. And along with it came the machismo to back it up. The chassis of his buggy had blocks under it and the wheel assembly was lying on the floor. Andrew's foot came off the last step and he walked up to the snappily dressed author of *Ned Buntline's Own;* a magazine that reaped its rewards from sensationalism, "Please forgive us, Mr. Buntline," said Andrew humbly, "It's all sorted now."

"Good," said the man.

Andrew was actually quite literate and had some genuine concern over the stories that Buntline had published, and asked him, "You're not going to write about us, are you sir?"

Buntline checked his pocket watch and looked up at the man and said, "I write fiction, but if it doesn't stay fixed, I could tell the truth; will that suit you?"

Andrew was completely aware of how powerful the pen could be and therefore replied, "O no, sir. No. That's quite unnecessary, Mr. Buntline, quite." And with that, the unassuming man went back to work on the reassembly process of the buggy's wheel.

Upstairs, as Joseph worked on another drawing, he suddenly heard the breaking of glass. When he turned, he saw that Robaré had slammed his glass of whisky down, cutting his hand in the process, "I will have no more of your scolding, Father!" he shouted, "Not for an instigator like Buntline, or any other person! I'm not an infant!"

At the sight of Robaré's bleeding hand, John Tweddle took out a clean, white handkerchief and kindly handed it to his stepson. Furious, Robaré snapped it from him and stormed for the door. With his hand crudely wrapped, he blew past Joseph and out the door like a cold chill, leaving the door wide open for the deafening noise to enter and consume all.

John Tweddle closed the door. Concerned, he stepped up to Joseph and said, "He's so full of drink, son. He won't talk to me anymore."

"He's been full of drink since he landed here, father. What can I do?"

"Look out for him. Please?..."

"I can't, not any longer. I have too much work to do. He's a grown man. Either he'll come around on his own, or he won't."

Suddenly an earsplitting scream cut through the air. From the factory floor came shouts of agony, "O GOD, HELP ME! HELP ME!"

Workers from all over congregated around a huge piece of machinery. More shouts came from the men below, "ACCIDENT!" "DOCTOR NEEDED!" "HURRY! ..."

Hearing the calls, Joseph and his father raced down the flight of stairs with Joseph in the lead. When they reached the crowd of men, they cleared a path to where a large steam powered press was stationed. There, Andrew hung, bleeding profusely; his right arm caught in the ferocious sprocket mechanism on the side of the machine. He'd been lifted off the ground; his encumbered arm and coat jammed into the enormous gears thus preventing the sprocket from turning.

"Turn off the steam!" shouted Joseph to the men standing paralyzed. Get a box under his feet - Now!" Joseph headed for the man. At the same time he shed a suspender, he grabbed a box from a man standing in shock. He dropped it next to the crate that had already been placed under Andrew's feet. When the steam ceased, there was a *whoosh* and the machine disengaged.

Joseph stepped up to the injured man. He worked to tourniquet the arm that was gushing blood from below his shoulder, but there was little room to work with. Through bone and flesh the arm has been pinched clean off by the opposing cogs of two wheels. Only Andrew's thick wool coat and the box under his tiptoes were supporting him.

He was in tears and fading, "I'm sorry, Mr. Tweddle," he whimpered, "I'm sorry ..."

"Quiet now," whispered Joseph.

The rest of the men could only watch. A few of them stepped out of the large door and threw up their lunch.

Joseph cinched his suspender as tight as he could around the little bit of stump he had to work with and said, "Hold still now," and then he cut the coat. As he did, Andrew dropped into the arms of several men who gently lower him to the ground, but before stepping down himself, Joseph reached behind the cogs and retrieved Andrew's arm that was still inside the coat's sleeve. Doing this caused more men to exit the building.

Ned Buntline watched in distress as Joseph retrieved the foreman's limb. This would affect him for the rest of his life, for he was just talking to the gracious man and was rude in doing so.

Andrew, who was now being comforted by Joseph and his father mumbled, "I turned my head, only for a moment, sir. I swear. Someone must have bumped the leaver.

Joseph looked around and then screamed, "WHAT HAPPENED?!...

As if Moses himself were parting the sea, Joseph stared each man down. One by one they separated, and there, at the end, Robaré stood with the blood-soaked handkerchief around his pathetic wound. He merely shrugged before alleging, "His sleeve must have gotten caught," and with that, stumbled away without a shred of remorse.

"WORTHLESS DRUNKARD!" shouted Joseph with tears in his eyes.

Joseph along with his father waited with Andrew and couple of others while a wagon was brought around to take him to the nearest doctor. This was a great deal faster than bringing a surgeon to the grounds. The rest of the men disbursed back to their work stations. The ones that had walked out to get sick were now returning. In doing so, they crossed paths with Buntline who feigned the collection of his wits, but then he too walked outside to heave way.

a **CARRIAGE ROLLED** beyond a set of iron gates and down a damp 'n shiny cobblestone drive where it circled behind an altogether different and unique Albany home. Moonlight helped to illuminate the exterior as Joseph, blood stained and shaken, exited the carriage and entered the house through the back door.

Amanda, radiant and pregnant rushed up. She cared not if she became blotted and said softly, "A messenger was sent. I am so sorry my love."

A Negro servant woman stood ready. She understood the gravity of the situation. It was all Joseph could do to bury his head into Amanda, "He had a wife and two sons," he sobbed …

An **AFRICAN MAN** poured Joseph and Amanda some tea while they sat together in their parlor. The mood could not have been any more sorrowful. Aware of the situation, the man sympathetically acknowledged the completion of the task, bowed back and quietly left the room. After he'd closed the door,

Joseph said, "I'm to travel to Buffalo in two days. Father just informed me."

"But why Joseph?... rebutted Amanda. "You're completely overworked - look at you."

"I'm needed there to oversee a shipment of interior woods back to the factory."

"But that's Robaré's job; even I know this."

"Too much invested," he said, trying to be clear; but his exhaustion was evident by his weakened tone. "After today's events, father wants Robaré to remain where he can be watched at all times.

"Can't it be sent down the canal?" she argued, "I heard they're widening it."

"Too many narrows," he said, "and too much ice this time of year. Besides, the arrangements have been made."

Amanda was about to contest again, but the unborn baby kicked, "Joseph, it's only wood for God's sake, Please ..." Amanda's womb was jarred again, but this time she noticed Joseph's pistol inside his jacket, "Joseph, you know how I'm moved towards illness at the sight of those dreadful things; especially since my father was nearly dueled down. Between the baby and the thought of you wearing it, or even worse, I feel unwell. Must you?..."

"Please, dear, I have enough to think about. Drink your tea if you're not feeling well."

Amanda knew that Joseph had been through much. The beginning years in business were hard on him. Along with the manual labor that was demanded of everyone except his father and Robaré; it also included endless hours at his drafting table creating not only engineering diagrams, but every other drawing from marketing and advertising, to signage, placards and stationary. Couple this with Robaré's ceaseless desire for drink and one could easily articulate that the past seven years had taken a toll on him. So Amanda prevailed upon herself that traveling to Buffalo was something her husband must do; if not to help calm his overall burdens, then perhaps to assist in clearing the memories of this tragic day.

"When? ..." she asked.

Joseph forced a sip of hot tea, "Two days if all goes to plan. There and back in a week, you'll see."

Amanda squared herself to her husband of six years and took hold of his hands, "Joseph, we've tried so hard for this baby. I need you here. Please my love. I know it's unlike me to ask, but I worry so; even when you're away for only a night."

"Don't, please," he said, "The doctors have informed me we still have more than a month. I'll return with time to spare." And with that Joseph kissed her on her cheek, "I promise."

CHAPTER five
BUFFALO

SIMULTANEOUSLY whilst thick, pillow-like clouds billowed from the stack of an idling locomotive, steam sprayed from between its iron wheels causing a massive cloud to erupt and rise from the engine's under-belly. A man atop a water tower, dressed for the morning chill, pulled hard on a rope and a large dripping water spigot swung away from the engine and its tender car. In securing the rope the man slipped, causing him to nearly fall to the hardened ground. Whether injured, killed, or dead from old age, this was a worker that would immediately be replaced by one of thousands standing in line for a job with railroads.

The whistle blew and business was quickly wrapped up. Railroad workers began to walk around making their last minute adjustments to doors, handles, latches and locks. The passengers yet to board said their final goodbyes to those not traveling. Couples hugged; securing their bond with a kiss on the cheek, while others offered up a bit more than a customary peck.

Atop a flatcar, Joseph made his final inspection of the high-priced interior woods covered by an oiled canvas. He climbed down in front of a mid-forties businessman with a bowler hat; something a-la-mode for the times, "Everyzing satisfactory, Mr. Tweddle?" the man asked; his thick German accent hard and seemingly unbreakable.

"Are you sure it won't warp?" asked Joseph.

With assurance the man nodded and answered, "As long as za blocks remain in place and za load stays covered. Look again at your first stoup." He then handed a document to Joseph, but Joseph had no firm surface to sign on, so the German turned around and offered up his broad back as support.

As Joseph began to affix his signature, he glanced beyond the thick hair erupting from the German's ear to see a small, wiry fellow in manacles and leg irons being helped aboard the only passenger car by two well dressed lawmen. One was in his mid-twenties and seasoned looking; but the younger of the two appeared fresh off the farm and almost too boyish to be a law-dog. Inches from the man's ear, Joseph quietly asked, "What happened?"

"Escaped killer," came the reply. "North-Vestern Police Agency tracked zem from Pittsburgh. Every man knows, '*zay never sleep*'."

The whistle blew again and Joseph quickly

crossed the "T" in Tweddle and concluded, "All right then, we're off."

The German turned around and Joseph handed the document back. He then hesitantly reached to shake the Englishman's hand, but so many transactions he thought. He couldn't recall if this particular Englishman shook hands or not. But Joseph spotted his indecisiveness and though he rarely did so, he reached forward and kindly yet firmly shook the German's extended hand; giving the man whom once hailed from Germainia reason to smile and feel that much more American.

THE LOCOMOTIVE blew its whistle and pulled forward. When it did, it jerked the tender car causing the couplers on all the trailing cars to lock, in domino-like succession. The journey had commenced.

The only passenger car was crowded. And looking through the windows from the exterior platform, travelers could be seen preparing for their nearly three hundred mile journey: adjusting themselves as comfortable as possible on the wooden bench-seats arranged to face each other. After the train started to move, they began to read and talk; but mostly they watched the scenery pass. This was a new adventure for many of them.

At the front of the car, the shackled prisoner had been positioned in between the two agents with all three of their backs to the wall. The agents also prevented any passengers who hadn't sat down yet from sitting across from them. One woman who was ready to seat herself, looked at the captured man, but was quickly dissuaded by the agents. Even if she'd received an agreeable nod to sit down, the caked on filth the prisoner had established as an additional layer of skin, along with the accompanied smell, made her dry heave and move on.

Joseph casually entered from the opposite end with a leather satchel. He too sat down with his back against the wall. As he did, his jacket opened; not that much, but enough for the prisoner at the other end to spot the pistol he had tucked behind a suspender. Joseph too could see to the end of the car where the prisoner and the agents were seated, but he'd already received all the information required for an analysis of the situation and therefore paid the captive and his jailer's no further mind. He therefore retrieved an apple and some papers from his satchel. He put the apple in his mouth and held it there. Looking at his papers, some juice drained over his lower lip and onto his trousers. The train jerked again settling in on its final cruising speed.

A nicely dressed man wearing a winter coat tailored with a high collar and a wide brimmed hat pulled low over his face entered the car from Joseph's end. Joseph was too busy to care or notice that he'd asked an attractive young woman at mid-car if he might sit in the empty seat beside her. The woman gestured yes and moved her belongings. This allowed the man to sit next to the aisle with their backs to Joseph.

Joseph finished up his apple. When he set the core beside him, an argument broke out between the man and the woman. "Indeed not, sir!" argued the woman in a raised voice. In silent rebuttal, the man leaned in and whispered something to her. She moved to slap him, but the man grabbed her wrist and struck her back with her own hand.

Joseph, along with some other passengers looked around. People did care, but other than himself and the agents, there were no other men on board that had what it took to make a difference, so the passengers only watched.

An elderly man across the aisle shouted, "Let

her alone!" but before he could finish, the stranger's outstretched arm backhanded him athwart the face, causing his spectacles to fly off and land on the floor in front of him.

At the same time greenhorn Agent Seth Yondell felt the need to help the woman, the prisoner needed to relieve himself, but lead agent; English born Timothy Webster, clearly said, "No, it's not our affair," and jutted his thumb over his shoulder for the young agent to take the prisoner out the door that was next to them. But Webster quickly remembered that direction led to the engine. This route he thought could escort an escape, so he motioned to the far end of the car; and the door closest to Joseph's left shoulder, "No. Take him that way," said Webster, "and be quick about it."

At mid-car, the man and the woman continued to sustain their argument in low tones. The man had her pinned against the window persistently pandering, all while his wide brimmed hat and collar obscured both their faces. Passengers were confused and began to whisper words akin to, *"Are they married?" "Where is a railroad employee to stop this?" "Is there not someone who'll help her?"* The man's behavior continued to blur the lines of decency, but those who watched; after seeing what happened to the old man, were afraid to actually engage in defense of the woman. *What if he's carrying a knife, or worse?*

Joseph looked around the rocking car and saw a few men wishing they had what it took to end such a thing, but that's where it stopped. He also saw the old man attempting to re-bend his spectacles to fit his face; all for a heroic act that could have cost him his life. Therefore Joseph resigned himself to help. He stood up and stepped into the aisle, but as soon as he did, the man stopped his assault, got up and walked toward the front of the car where he side slipped past the young agent and the prisoner who were now making their way towards Joseph. He then exited through the door next to Webster and was gone.

Joseph was about to console the woman, but then saw the prisoner moving toward him with Agent Yondell right behind him with a strong grip on the accused man's trousers.

Passengers, especially the women, repelled at the sight and smell of the man as he jangled his way past; eyeing their flattened breasts that protruded from their Sunday-best. Joseph also noticed that moving beyond the two would be a tight squeeze; and since the man had retreated from his assault, decided it was a wiser choice to return to his seat. After he sat down, the young agent and the prisoner moved past him and exited the back of the car. Joseph readjusted himself and began to review his papers again.

Minutes later, a uniformed conductor with a

healthy set of muttonchops stepped up to Joseph and in a concerned tone asked, "Sir, are you traveling alone?"

"Yes. Why do you ask?" replied Joseph.

The conductor pointed to the back of the train and said, "There's a man making adjustments to your cargo."

Joseph got up and straight-away exited the back of the car. He crossed into the baggage car and gave a pressing nod to the baggage handler he'd recently encountered when he dropped off his own luggage. He then continued to the end where he exited onto the rear vestibule. To his left, the prisoner who was being closely guarded by Agent Yondell was relieving himself.

That's odd Joseph thought; why didn't the agent have the man relieve himself on the rear vestibule of the passenger car? Why bring him the extra length of the baggage car? He then realized that perhaps it was respectful of the agent to prevent any of the passengers from witnessing the event. Yes, probably a good idea Joseph noted when he observed the putrid man gleefully watching his yellow stream catch the forty mile an hour wind where it immediately turn to vapor.

On the other side of the vestibule, Joseph leaned his body out and into the wind to see for himself what the conductor was referring to, but he couldn't capture a clear view of his freight due to some high cargo stacked at the front of the trailing flatbed car. So he climbed the brakeman's ladder for a better look over the top. Three-steps-up and there he saw the same man with the large brimmed hat who'd been harassing the woman; again with his back to Joseph, but this time he was loosening the tie down ropes on the oiled canvas of his expensive cargo. Suddenly the wind caught the cover and it flew away. "Stop that!" shouted Joseph, "What are you doing? Who are you?!"

The man continued his sabotage, but *his* hat too caught the wind and was gone. This forced him to try even harder to conceal his face.

"You there! Stop that!" shouted Joseph again.

Then without reason, the man discontinued his cloaking attempts. Joseph was shocked when the man turned and looked at him directly.

"Robaré?" he muttered. Joseph immediately contemplated how this could've happened. Robaré continued to untie the load and a second later, it shifted loudly.

"That's father's cargo! Are you mad?!"

The load shifted again. This time some of the beautifully milled pieces caught the wind and were gone.

The shackled prisoner finally got around to

finishing up and in doing so, noticed the young agent's attention had been diverted to Joseph who was arguing with the unseen Robaré. In a single trade-move, he pulled the agent's pistol and kicked the farm boy off the train. Unfortunately for the lad, the train was passing between a series of boulders. His body, accompanied by its forward momentum was smashed so badly upon impact; it forever arrested any hope his mother had of him returning home and marry Lydia Hopkins.

Joseph, from his perch atop the third rung of the brakeman's ladder, watched the company's costly cargo shift to the side and fall off the edge of the car. He couldn't believe what he was seeing. Then all of a sudden his legs were swept from under him and SLAM, he found himself face down on the vestibule; head woozy with a bloody nose and lip. The prisoner knelt before him. He wanted Joseph's pistol as well, but the train jerked and pitched the bound man against the railing. This prevented him from taking hold of the weapon. Disoriented, Joseph started to get up. The baggage handler, who'd witnessed the commotion, stepped in to help, but the prisoner had already regained his footing. He cocked the agent's pistol and squeezed the trigger, discharging a searing lead ball that penetrated the baggage handler's face just below his right eye. The man fell to the landing in agony; his jaw and ear splattered against the door jam.

Inside the passenger car, Agent Webster had heard the shot - and so did the rest of the passengers who became concerned.

On the vestibule, a delirious Joseph finally made it to his feet. As he did, the prisoner tossed the discharged weapon to him. Robaré, after hearing the shot, had also made it to the landing in time to witness his stepbrother catch the gun. He also saw the fallen employee who was now barely moving, but he had the sense to turn his attention to the piss-stained hostage. "What have you done?!" he shouted at the dreg, "You've ruined everything!"

Inside the passenger car, Agent Webster, followed closely by the conductor, moved beyond passengers who were now beginning to grab at his coat and sleeves, but when they started to crowd the isle, it made his efforts to get to the end of the car even more difficult.

On the rear vestibule of the baggage car, a disoriented Joseph pulled his own pistol and aimed for the prisoner, but the wiry man quickly ducked behind Robaré using his paunch as a shield. Standing wobbly, Joseph FIRED ...

Webster continued to work his way past the panicky passengers where at last he neared the door of the passenger car. There, he could clearly see the remaining distance through the passenger car as well as the entire length of the baggage car to where Joseph's extended arm FIRED his pistol.

"It's trickery!" shouted Webster back to the conductor, "Order the engineer to stop the train!"

The train jerked causing the front door of the baggage car to slam shut in Webster's face. This also prevented him from witnessing anything further.

On the rear vestibule of the baggage car, the prisoner had disappeared. His absents left Joseph in shock as he stood over two downed men: the baggage handler, who by now had taken his last breath and Robaré, who was on his knees with his hands around his own throat; blown out the back of his neck.

Joseph's trembling hands released both smoking guns and they banged hard on the boards at his feet. He knelt by Robaré, "O Lord, Robaré? ..." Robaré attempted to breathe, but only managed to gurgle from the blood in his airway.

"Let me see!" argued Joseph, and when he managed to pry Robaré's hands away, blood surged from the tissue damage and began spurting from an arterial wound, "My God! No! No! ... Father asked me. I know I refused, but you can't die. You cannot!

The train jerked. It had started to slow. Robaré slumped over and bled out. As he did, Joseph laid him down as gently as one might.

Too stunned to feel much of anything, he stood up and saw that Agent Webster had opened the door that had previously slammed shut on him. Ready to continue his pursuit, Webster met Joseph's eye; and in one blink of that same eye, Webster aimed his pistol and discharged it. The large caliber ball left the barrel at optimum velocity where it traveled the length of the baggage car and blasted through Joseph's left sleeve blowing off almost two inches of shoulder meat before spinning the bloody aristocrat not quite two revolutions to the landing.

The baggage car door slammed shut once again in Webster's face, but this time it latched from the inside. Joseph crawled to the middle of the car and collapsed. The prisoner, who'd just slammed the door on Webster, had been looking for a way out of his irons. Webster leaned back next to the door and began reloading his pistol, "YOU! IN THE SUIT!" he shouted through the door, "YOU'RE BOTH GOING TO HANG! I WITNESSED YOU SHOOT HIM!"

The prisoner, while continuing to search for a key to his freedom, laughed at Joseph and said, "Hear that? Looks like you kilt someone."

"You murdered Robaré!" shouted Joseph, completely out of his element.

"No, you did!" rebutted the restless prisoner, "but you can thank me later."

The train jerked again; slowing even more. Joseph, holding his bleeding shoulder, had managed to standup. He looked out the back of the baggage car and saw a brakeman on the vestibule. Their eyes met, but fearing for his life, the brakeman clambered onto the flat car where Joseph's cargo once sat and hid behind the tall freight at the front.

"See there, you're just like me," said the prisoner, smiling through blackened gums and rotting incisors, "Now we can be friends."

"I'm nothing at all like you!"

But the shackled man paid no mind to Joseph's rebuttal or his condition; and as desperation set in, only sped up his search for anything that might help him out of his chains. "They be comin' fer you now," he barked, "maybe more so."

Webster shouted again through the closed door, "COME OUT PEACEABLE! AND YOU'LL RECEIVE A JUST TRIAL!"

Conflicted, Joseph stumbled over the baggage and headed towards the rear of the car. The prisoner, still unable to free his bonds, gave up the idea and correlated his thoughts to Joseph's when he saw him standing on the vestibule contemplating a jump.

Making haste, the grimy man hobbled up behind Joseph and with conviction shouted, "Hurry up now! They're murderers too. They're fixin' on hangin' me before my trial, or seekin' reason to shoot me; now jump!"

Joseph looked across the terrain and saw meadows and distant woodlands. He felt the man pressing him from behind, but he held tight. He wasn't sure.

"Jump!" shouted the restrained man, "Jump!"

With the help of the conductor, Webster managed to open the door of the baggage car. As soon as he entered, he could barely see the brakeman's arm at the far end pointing from behind the freight to the desperate men preparing to jump. Webster raced for the end the car.

"JUMP! DAMN YOU!" shouted the prisoner, this time pushing Joseph with everything he had.

Webster fired his pistol at the men. The prisoner, from mid-flight, skidded to a stop in the weeds face down. Webster hit his mark. The ball-shot driving brain matter and bone out of a hole in the filthy man's forehead the size of a small bread-heel.

At Webster's feet lay two dead men; their blood draining between the floor boards, dripping onto the ties and tracks below.

Joseph on the other hand lit out as fast as his legs would carry him. He knew he needed to put as much distance as possible between himself and the train. Holding his wound, he could clearly hear the high pitch squeal of the wheels as the brakemen turned the handles, causing the train to slow.

CHAPTER six
BEYOND the POINT

After RUNNING FLAT OUT for what felt like hours, Joseph finally came to a stop. Breathing solidly, he tried to squat by a brook, but only toppled in causing his clothes to become soaked. He rose to his knees and stabled himself enough to cup his hands for a drink. His throat was hot 'n raw, but the water was cold 'n sweet. He watched the water mixed with the dried blood on his hands: Robaré's dried blood, and he began to shake. He asked himself, why? Why was Robaré on that train? Why did he destroy father's cargo? Why? What of the fine wood now? Did any remain?

He sat on the water's edge and then laid back. Covered in mud and blood; tears rolled from his eyes, down past his cheeks and into his ears, "My God," he muttered, "I was only returning home. What just happened? ..."

Ten minutes later, Joseph stood naked with his shirt, trousers and jacket draped over some brush for the sun to dry them by. Most of the blood had rinsed out; all except some pink in his white shirt and the heavy dark spots on his trousers where Robaré's head rested as he died.

Should I continue running he thought, or should I return? This wound on my shoulder is almost clotted up now. Either way I won't bleed to death. As he inspected it, he noticed a small piece of hanging flesh and he pulled it off; anything that might rot. A wince and some blood oozed. Something else he'd remembered from his book on exploring.

He heard the train whistle blow again, but this time he thought perhaps it was farther away, but he wasn't positive. When he looked, he saw vultures in the direction from which he'd jumped. Probably that murderer, he thought. Yes, I'm sure of it, but what if that North-Western man forced the engineer to wait so he could give chase? If I turn myself in, I could very well be hanged before trial; like that wretched man said. The agents were murderers themselves, and for some inexplicable reason Joseph felt his words as believable. The train whistle blew again and Joseph played out another scenario: it was self-defense - was it not? He thought it through again, and then again. The North-Western man must have known I was defending myself against their prisoner, but he saw me shoot Robaré. O my God, Robaré... If I can make it to Albany without being captured, I can attain counsel. But the agent saw my face, and by now has my satchel and papers. He knows who I am and can certainly describe me. What if he thinks I shot the baggage handler as well? What of the young agent? What became of him? How many days to Albany on foot - on horseback? I could lie and wait for the next train, but for how long? Could I run n' catch it even? If I can make Buffalo, I can attain counsel there too. My Lord, what of Amanda, my sweet Amanda? She'll be alright. Will she…? Yes. I have time before the baby's due. The family will look after her until I can sort this out.

RESTED and SATED, Joseph put his clothes back on. They were damp and wrinkled, but certainly wearable. He continued southwest along the creek and at one point became grateful that through all the carnage, he'd remembered the importance of remaining close to water should he become lost; another subconscious lesson learned from his book on exploring it seemed.

Hours later and some miles from where the condors were rigorously feasting on the prisoner and his brains, the rough terrain had transformed into open meadowlands dotted by clusters of trees and knee-high grasses cloaked by small fingers of fresh, running creeks. Joseph stopped again at one of them; it was time to tend to his shoulder. He ripped off some clean, dry pieces from his shirttail for a bandage and applied the squared cloths to the injury. He finished the triage by tying a wide-piece all the way around to compress the area.

With suspenders over bare torso and his shirt across the back of his neck to protect it from the sun, Joseph started out along the same small creek that had now turned into a stream. He asked himself again, Can I actually return, or should I - covered in other men's blood and looking like this? I'll surely be arrested. Would I? The news *has* traveled, but how far? How fast? I need food. The last thing I had was that apple. Soon it will turn dark and cold will set in. I need a dry change of clothes.

The stream eventually found its way parallel to a main road where people and wagons were traveling in both directions. West bound appeared most popular. Joseph counted four wagons going east to about eleven headed west; more people to get lost amongst he thought. Exhausted, he continued to walk this comparable path separated by tall willow stalks and thick shrubbery. He was grateful the trail was far enough from the road so not to be seen by most of the travelers; however now and again, a person, usually a child, would scurry through the brush with a bucket to fetch water. Ever cautious, Joseph kept to himself as he continued.

A Negro family carrying all they owned in their arms approached. Mom and dad looked away, but their two little boys appeared happy and smiled at the white man in passing. The parents grabbed the two and turned them away in hopes Joseph wouldn't pull a whip and beat them for an unknown reason. But Joseph too looked away at the family in passing, causing private gratitude between the Negro couple.

That AFTERNOON inside the nearest railway shack with a telegraph operator, Agent Webster wrote a memo:

TO: ALLAN PINKERTON; NORTH-WESTERN POLICE AGENCY, CHICAGO -

FROM: T. WEBSTER –

SUBJECT: ESCAPE ATTEMPT-

SITUATION: 3 DEAD: PRISONER IN TRANSIT;
RAILROAD EMPLOYEE AND ONE BYSTANDER-

OUTCOME: AGENT YONDELL MISSING - FEARED
DEAD. ORDERS REQUESTED -

Webster handed the memo to the
representative who started tapping out the message...
After Webster made sure it was properly sent,
he stepped out of the shack and looked over the
surrounding area. His eyes came to a rest on the idling
locomotive that had stopped so he could get off and
wire Pinkerton. He also saw some of the passengers
watching his movements through the windows;
however they didn't appear in a hurry, only curious.
Either way, it didn't matter because he wasn't going to
board just now anyway. Instead he walked around to
the other side of the shack, sat on the porch and put his
head in his hands. It was only last night he was having
dinner with the Yondell family at their farm outside of
Buffalo. And it was there he overconfidently informed
the young agent's mother and father, along with Lydia
Hopkins, Seth's fiancée, how he would tutor the boy in
the ways of law enforcement so that no outside harm
would come to him. At this instant he felt personally
responsible, as well as saddened and embarrassed over

his conceited remarks; as well as the tragic news that he must inform them of upon his return.

DARKNESS HAD FALLEN and Joseph, who was emotionally splintered, had been aimlessly walking the same path for hours. By the time he'd spotted a small camp fire far enough off the road to feel safe about an approach, he was shivering and hungry. Through the thicket he stumbled. When he'd side-slipped the last bit of briar, a Scotsman's voice shouted, "Who goes there!" and a callused thumb pried back the hammer on a big brass receiver into the cocked and ready position.

"Don't shoot!" shouted Joseph, "Please, I'm unarmed."

"Show yerself," the voice called back.

At the end of a hunter's long barrel, Joseph stepped from the brush and into the firelight, "I'm hungry, he said to the man holding the gun trained on him. I smelled your cooking. I can pay."

The Scotsman, a bearded trapper in his late-forties but looking far older, stood to the side of the fire. This allowed enough light to train his gun on Joseph's upper body. A wound from a weapon of this nature, and from this short distance, would surely end his running. In fact it would break his body so badly he'd probably not make trial to hang if he wanted to.

"Suspect ya are, by the look o' ya," said the man with a meek snarl; meat and grease hanging from his furry face. He lowered his double barrel swivel breach percussion rifle and chuckled, "Sure it weren't me trade yer smellin'?" and he nodded to a pile of stinking hides and furs that lay on the ground between two tired mules. Joseph walked in, dropped to his knees and warmed himself by the fire.

"Aye, no need to pay," said the hunter who returned to his stump by the fire. He looked at Joseph and decided to lay his rifle across his lap. With sticky-filthy hands he slid one tiny carcass off a twig-spit and handed it to Joseph. He then tossed the charred stick in the fire and said, "Plenny o' folk comin' by. Last squirrel, she's yers."

Joseph tore into the overcooked carcass no bigger than a rat and said, "I'm grateful to you sir. I am. Thank you."

The trapper leaned forward to relieve some of

the weight off his upper frame and started to pick his yellowish brown teeth with a frayed willow twig; a stem far too big to actually dispatch any of the encrusted formations; nonetheless, while he made the effort, he took a more vigilant note of the dried blood on Joseph's clothes. City feller, he thought. English too. Covered in blood; human maybe - surely out of his element. Too soon for a bounty if there were to be. Perhaps gun shot in that shoulder. But not my woe. I have trade fer market, but I'll disable 'em – or kill 'em if the need be.

When Joseph awoke from what felt like a thirty-second doze, the trapper hadn't moved, but time *had* elapsed because the fire was not as hot and his clothes felt warmer and dryer, "How far is the Ohio River?" he asked the man.

"Twelve days, less perchance," came the reply while sizing up Joseph's ability to actually make it that far in the condition he was in. "Follow the Erie shore south to Youngstown then on to Pittsburgh."

JOSEPH SLEPT soundly by the dwindling fire, but when the heavy action of the trapper's weapon cocked again and the burly man's sleep deprived voice called out, "Who goes there?" Joseph roused, bringing to life the pain in his shoulder and the stiffness in his body from sleeping on the cold ground. But as the trepidation from the previous day's events were about to set in, he looked up and saw a young woman in tatters. She'd appeared from the same bushes Joseph became visible to the trapper from, but unlike Joseph, she had something in her arms. She directed her meek Irish voice towards the man holding the rifle, "Spare somethin' t' eat?"

"No more!" shouted the wooly man.

"Please, mister. I have an infant," and the baby whimpered.

The trapper kept his large weapon trained on the woman-child and yelled, "There's no more! Go away!" He then directed his next words from the side of his mouth toward Joseph, "In these parts, highway trickery's common. The use of a female to lower a man's guard so her counterpart can rob or do worse is not unheard of."

The girl tracked back into the woods and Joseph sensed it was time for him to go as well, so he made his way to his feet, but the trapper stopped him, "Not you ... It hurts me to turn away the hungry;

especially me own. I did not say an untruth; there is no more."

Joseph could see the man regretted turning the girl away.

THROUGH the BUSHES and beyond the willows, the main road was busy with morning activity. Joseph however, lay curled up and shivering on the ground next to what was left of a barely smoldering campfire. When he managed to sit up, he felt the stiffened pain in his shoulder even worse as the skin had tightened around the wound and the events of yesterday immediately returned as vivid as if they'd just happened. And because there was nothing to distract him, like the young girl carrying the baby from the previous night, an abnormally high degree of anxiety set in. So high in fact, it well exceeded the most extreme uneasiness he'd ever felt, even while aboard *Helena*. But instead of dwelling on the fear, he picked up part of the same charred stick that helped to cook his last meal and moved the ashes around so he could warm his hands by the remaining embers. He also noted the trapper and his mules had departed. So with some safe time to himself, he emptied his pockets to take an inventory of his belongings; another important task his book on exploration told him to do if he should become lost. He slipped off his gold wedding band; the ring Amanda had given him on their wedding day and placed it on a rock by the fire. From his trousers he removed four, ten dollar gold eagles and three gold nuggets; nuggets that had made their way east from the first California gold rush at Sutter's Mill into the possession of Fraser Dunlop, who generously gave them to Joseph in exchange for a drawing he'd rendered on parchment of a wealthy white man kindly celebrating a snowy Christmas Eve around the tree with his Negro brood. The drawing was secretly purchased for Sully, framed and given to him as a holiday gift in 1849. Joseph always traveled with these nuggets to remind him of home and family. From his jacket he removed a small locket with a painting of Amanda inside. The locket looked much like the one he used to carry of his older brother who departed in delirium from scarlet fever at the age of two. This painting was Joseph's favorite reminder of his beautiful wife and mother to be, however when he felt inside his watch pocket, he said out loud, "Where's my watch?…" He searched all his pockets, twice. He looked around the fire and the surrounding area, "The trapper," he said, with anger in his voice. Once again, the ways of the land had come alive. In exchange for a meal and the abstention of any further discussion about his appearance; his gold watch, given to him by his father on his eighteenth birthday, lifted in the dead of night.

The SUN was HOT, but due to a light breeze and the unusually low humidity, the air was seemingly cooler. Joseph had been walking the same parallel path adjacent to the busy road since he departed the trapper's camp hours ago.

Suddenly he was caught off guard when the two men ahead of him turned up from the path and made their way onto the main road. Coming to a stop Joseph wondered, do these men know something I do not? Sure enough; dead ahead where the men turned up, a sharp drop-off to a narrow ravine. For certain, this was an impasse. Joseph looked behind him and there was no one, so he peeked through the brush and had a look for himself. The road was filled with wagons, foot traffic and those on horseback. He saw men, women and children from various walks of life, but this section of the roadway was different he noticed. The traffic; for some reason, was equally as busy on both sides of the road. There was almost as many traveling east as west.

If I turn back he thought, I'll again run into the same trickle of east bound travelers I saw yesterday. And that direction could get me spotted and possibly captured.

So for over an hour Joseph permitted time to pass. He sat to the side and let others go by him while he waited for a break in the line big enough to slip onto the roadway unnoticed. Here's my chance, he thought. Now! ... He pushed up and onto the main road - and as soon as he was past the point of any retreat, he again realized he needed to change out of his blood stained suit as soon as possible. Fortunately, he stepped up behind an unhurried covered wagon that was intentionally hugging the right shoulder of the roadway due to a wobbly wheel it was nursing. There were no other wagons behind it for some distance, so Joseph felt this was another opportunity to mentally rest easy for a spell. Regardless, his quick advance from the bushes took a young girl and boy by surprise. The two kids, who were no more than eight 'n ten, were sitting on the back drop-gate with their legs dangling. Barefoot and poorly dressed; flies infested a scrape on the girl's right knee, but she paid no attention to the insects and joyfully stated, "Mornin' mister."

"Good morning to you both," Joseph cheerfully replied, but still preoccupied with his surroundings over possible captors.

The children giggled at the Englishman's overtly crisp accent, "Where ya bound fer," asked the girl. The boy on the other hand, wearing a broke down beaver pelt hat and a dirty nightshirt, immediately elbowed his sister, "Shush nosey, that's nunna yer binness."

The girl having experienced the pointed joints of her brother's appendages from an early age felt nothing new when his elbow jabbed her ribs. "We're headed fer Californie," she said excitedly. "Pa's been sayin' there's gold; free fer the taken. Just bend on over and pick it up, like a rock. Others bin sayin' it too."

Joseph was enjoying the moment, anything to alleviate his concern, and he said, "Sounds like an adventure indeed."

"Nice meetin' duds," said the boy as he eyed the cut of Joseph's suit. But Joseph wasn't sure if the lad was actually capable of sarcasm, yet again was reminded that although his suit may have been stained, it was of quality textiles, tailored to fit and levels above the attire almost all of these road travelers were donning.

"Yes, they are quite nice. I agree," he proudly stated pressing his lapels out, "Nothing a bit of laundering can't remedy." This is also when he did a double take of the blood stains and frayed material around his shoulder. "Yes, in fact, I'm certain of it," he added with a chuckle, "I aided a friend in...-disemboweling a bear."

"Huh? ..." replied the kids in whimsical unison over the long word they'd not heard before, "What's that mean?" they asked.

"I helped him gut the bloody thing."

"O...," they said, and they looked at each other in agreement because they knew what that word meant.

"It's also how my jacket became torn," he said, nodding to his shoulder. Joseph then craned his head for a better look inside the back of the wagon where he saw a slender grandmother clock built into a tall case and a wide farthingale seat with curved legs that terminated into ornamental feet. But when Joseph became aware the children were watching him, he moved his eyes to the shaky wagon wheel and said,

"Would you like some help with that wheel?"

Right then the girl turned around and shouted through the inside of the wagon, "Pa! There's a man wantin' to barter!"

📖

As STORM CLOUDS GATHERED, Joseph finished up the repairs on the bad wheel. He motioned the wagon forward and the man behind the reins gently started a single mule team. The wagon rolled off some crudely made axel blocks that Joseph chopped from limb wood and banged flat. To improve the wheel's condition, Joseph carved down an ax handle along with a shovel handle as substitutes for two broken spokes. Moreover, he silently reminded himself how hard it was to be a wheelwright and became grateful his father had the funds for him to take up engineering instead.

He wiped his brow and leaned against the wagon. The children stood close. The little girl said to her brother, "He fixed that wheel good, he did."

"I know it," said the boy and he kicked some dirt on her foot, "I was standin' right chere lookin' at 'em, just like you was." The boy then coughed hard and brought up a lobe of phlegm which he promptly spat at his sister's other foot, but the girl was wise to his abuse and fully aware of the timing needed to step clear of the goo-ball.

The children's father, a late-twenties, sodbuster looking type climbed down from the wagon and stepped up to Joseph 'n said, "I'm indebted to ya, mister. I'm not inclined in the ways of bigger repairs."

Joseph thought this odd; and though he'd negotiated with the man briefly before he started the repair, came to realize he was similar to himself in ways, yet a great deal more out of his element and, with far more responsibility. "I recommend a new wheel," said Joseph, "It won't take you far."

"Not likely," the long limbed man replied, "We'll trade're out - 'n the animal too if need be, and make the remainder of the journey by whatever means the good Lord provides. Will Prine," announced the man and he extended his hand. A hand that looked closer to that of a concert pianist with years of graphite 'n grease between the creases and under his nails. And though Joseph was still not inclined to shake hands, he was getting used to it and therefore shook this man's hand - and did so firmly.

"And what can I do fer you sir?" asked Prine, looking over the aristocrat's stained suit.

The **ORANGE BALL of the SUN** had moved well below the wooded horizon and remaining light of the day was nearly gone. With foot traffic to a trickle, the crickets and the katydids came alive to create an orchestral-harmony by which the likes of any other organic sound would find impenetrable to the human ear. And except for an occasional rider, almost everyone had pulled over for the night. Campfires, candles and lanterns marked both sides of the road for long stretches where multiple families had grouped together to help ward off any latent highwaymen on the prowl.

This was when Joseph departed the wounded wagon. Dressed in work clothes with a bedroll over his shoulder, he entrusted the Will Prine Family to finish up their supper and fend for themselves.

The WILL PRINE FAMILY, doing just as Will had said they'd do; stuck to the roads and traveled southwest along the Ohio until once again the wagon wheel turned bad, but this time irreparably.

After the news had surfaced that gold was discovered in California, Prine, who self admittedly was indisposed in the repairs of larger effects, was bitten by the gold bug, and soon thereafter settled his affairs as fast as he possibly could. He left behind a good paying job as a gunsmith at the Colt Armory and his home on the Connecticut River where he was rightly established. He did this without selling the house or giving any notice to his employer because he feared being terminated before he was actually ready to depart. He then dragged his frail wife Jaroucha and their two children, Arthur and Emily, against their wills on his mighty quest for the colorful ore.

Unfortunately for the family, Jaroucha succumbed to pneumonia only thirteen days out. Upon her death, Prine enrolled his traumatized children to help burry their mother and his wife of eleven years in a shallow grave; building a monument with only eight rocks: all the harsh environment would allow them to unearth.

Add to this, Arthur, who'd looked forward to his tenth birthday with such anticipation, could only stand and watch as his sister and father planted his mother's corpse just 24 hours before *his* big day. Couple this with his father's insensitivity toward the tragedy; saying that sacrifices had to be made, and Arthur became so overwrought with grief that it sparked a case of juvenile epilepsy; at times causing the boy to aimlessly walk while convulsing.

Fortunately Prine knew his guns. He sold parts and repaired dozens in trade for the goods and services his family needed along the journey.

It was not until the Good Lord however, made it abundantly clear to Will; through a freak river crossing accident that took Arthur's life and handicapped the gunsmith by rope-burning his hands to the bone in an attempt to hold back a barge that was dragging the convulsing boy under, that if he were to continue his dream, he and Emily; the last of his blood kin, would have to make the remainder of the two-thousand-plus mile journey on foot.

Will Prine's carcass was left to the condors and the elements twenty-one days later on the planes of the Oklahoma territory after the gunsmith had slipped into a coma caused by his infected hands gone septic.

Emily was kindly taken in by a group of Latter Day Saints traveling west to the *promised land* in a large, well outfitted group that consisted of some forty wagons, buckboards and carts; most of them covered in dirt brown canvas that was as white as snow when they started their journey. There were also several heavily laden Murphy Schooners; each one drawn by twelve to sixteen oxen, hijacked from a freight company ironically in route to re-supply the federal troops in pursuit of the religious faction.

Three years later, after a lengthy courtship in the ways of *John Smith*, and within the limitations of a remote desert compound, pretty little Emily, at the tender age of eleven; with only a prairie bonnet and a dirty white dress, was married to a sixty-six year old, high ranking church official; a man already in possession of nine wives.

Emily bore three children all before the age of sixteen; with the first newborn arriving just two-hundred and sixty-eight days after her first cycle. Sadly however, while nursing her third baby, she was abducted in secrecy, repeatedly raped and beaten to death by rabid church elders when it was discovered the fourth fetus she was carrying was that of her lover; a younger, virile man who possessed not a single wife, yet they were in love.

In an attempt to kill as many of *them* as he could to avenge the life of his lover and unborn child, the distraught young man of only twenty, found his way into a covert church meeting but was immediately captured and charged as a cattle thief. He was hanged that same night.

For this particular Mormon sect, it was "un-Christian" to murder the kin born from the egg of a nonbeliever. So the elder wives separated Emily's offspring in the name of God. Any information surrounding the events became unbeknownst to the children and the innocent families they were imparted to: cast off and forgotten.

CHAPTER seven
MOSES ON THE MOUNT

Joseph looked more like a drenched cat than a human as he trudged through the pouring rain. Behind him the dimly lit settlement he'd just departed. Out of gold coins and his treasured nuggets, all he had left to trade was his wedding band and Amanda's locket. With his head hung low, he weariedly asked himself, "What am I to do? I can't continue like this much longer. I must choose, but I'm so tired. I need to sleep…"

The SKY was BLUE and the air was cold n' crisp. With his bedroll over his shoulders, Joseph squatted against a large rock formation and shivered. In the last few hours leading up to daybreak, he'd been lamenting over Amanda's portrait; and except for the heavy water droplets on the leaves above him, collected from the night's rain; droplets that were now rolling off and decisively tapping the ground along with the top of his body, all was exceedingly quiet. He looked at the locket and whispered, "What in God's name am I doing? I *must* return. Everyone's worrying themselves, aren't they? ... They must be. What of you my darling, and our beautiful baby? I'm so hungry, I can't think clearly." Joseph looked into the glistening trees and haplessly called out loud, "If there *is* a God, please help me! ..."

From the silence a shot rang out and Joseph jumped. He looked around and wondered if it was meant for him. Then as if released from a high, a large animal landed solidity in a puddle right before him. The impact spattered mud and leaves in every direction. The animal, a mountain lion, lay completely motionless and the echo from the musket report was heard, but just as fast, it was deadened by the saturated surroundings. "Bloody Christ," exclaimed Joseph, looking in every direction as best he could. But still he kept low, crouching by the boulder.

A man's voice, Kentucky born, called out, "Don't shoot, I'm comin' in." From the woods, Moses Lafayette (Hick) Shelby came a walking. He was twenty-three, wiry and doubly strong. In one callused hand he clutched an American made Sharps Model

1851 breech loading, sport rifle, and in the other, a wineskin leather bag from which he took a drink; squeezing it until some of the homebrew drained into his mouth. At five-foot-nine inches tall and a head full of thick, blond hair to the middle of his back, he was outfitted in a long-sleeved, doe skin pullover with a pair of buckskin lowers. This hunting rig of sorts; although dry, was covered in everything from blood and small twigs, to grass, leaves and tobacco juice - perfect for game hunting. While the hunter kept one eye on the big cat, he pushed the tobacco quid packed in his cheek to the other side of his mouth and then spat a stream of brown juice with the same accuracy used to kill the cat directly at a frog sitting by a puddle. The frog jumped.

"Don't shoot?" blurted Joseph, who slowly began to stand up, but still kept his palms flat against the rock formation, "Look what you just did!"

"Better it than you," retorted the hunter; brown juices now dribbling down his chin 'n onto his raggedy collar. He knelt by the cat to inspect his kill. He then looked up and coyly remarked, "Less you'd rather I'da not... ?

"No sir, Joseph quickly recanted after getting a clear look at the cat, "No, I'm grateful to you. I am. Thank you."

The man could ascertain from Joseph's tone

that he was genuinely grateful. "Yer English," he said and he wiped the dribble from his chin. The comment caused Joseph to become cautious again and to wonder if enough time had elapsed for a bounty to have circulated.

"City feller, eh?" the hunter asked rhetorically, and he rolled the animal over. He then looked Joseph in the eye with the same seriousness that killed the cat he announced, "Hick Shelby, but around home folks call me Hick, and that's *all* they call me by," and he grabbed the cat by it's hind legs and dragged it a short distance to a dryer spot where he pulled a knife from a waist scabbard big enough to fry an egg on, "Been trackin' 'er fer some colored folk. No one else volunteered, but they pooled fer a bounty," and he slit the cat from its navel to its sternum in one motion with the razor sharp blade. As the cat's entrails slid out onto the wet ground he remarked nonchalantly, "Kilt two picaninnis."

Joseph turned a naive shade when he heard the bluntly delivered information, "Regretful," he remitted.

"Why be sorry?" asked the hunter, "Eatin' 'll be fine tonight. Cat tastes mummm good, and this here pelt's worth at the least four dollars, maybe more." Hick began the process of dressing out the one-hundred-ninety pound lion and in doing so, glanced between it and Joseph and then chose to look beyond the Englishman's garments and took a keener note of his articulated language and mumbled, "Just cuz it don't shine, don't mean it ain't worth somethin'."

"I meant the children," said Joseph with a tinge of sarcasm in hopes to hear some sensitivity from the man over the children's demise.

"O, well that's long done," said Hick in a frankly fashion, "but I'm sure you'd be thanked by their kin over yer concern. As a matter of, I thank ya right now, sir. Ida never hit 'er if it weren't fer ya. We'll share in the profit too. And you might be?" he asked looking between Joseph and his immediate task.

"Thomas Tucker," Joseph said in a flash; moving farther and farther into no-man's-land with a lie big enough to get him killed or captured if he were to make the slightest error in judgment.

"Thomas Tucker, eh?" said the hunter in a sideways fashion.

"Yes, but you can call me Tom."

"Well, Tom Tucker, I thank ya. I shorly do."

"I didn't do a thing."

"Why shore ya did," expressed the woodsman, turned story teller, "You was a sleepin' under that there rock, ya see."

"I wasn't sleeping."

"Well, the feline shore though chew was; so she

come-a-crawlin' down to RIP YER NECK OUT! I'd say you did plenty. Got off a clean shot. Clear through 'er lung, see ..." and Hick rolled the cat over. Sure enough, a hole behind its shoulder blade from the large caliber projectile big enough to where he could stick two fingers in, and Hick did just that to make his point, as well as to dig out his bullet. Locating flat-back projectiles wasn't easy in this remote part of the country, nor was lead for that matter. After removing it, he dropped it into a small leather purse attached to his hip. This is where he saved them until he had enough to make it worth his while to melt them down so he could mold more.

Tom looked at the rock, and then at the mud covered lion weighing more than he did and wondered who should be thanking who. He then remarked, "You're a mighty Nimrod."

Hick stood up and snapped, "I ain't no Nimrod! You take it back!

Tom's assumption that Hick would like the reference couldn't have been more inaccurate. "I apologize," he said with reverence, "Nimrod was Noah's great grandson, the powerful hunter--"

"I know who his was!" barked the blood covered huntsman. Folks call me Hick, and that's ALL they call me by!"

"Understood," said Tom respectfully,

"Understood."

In England you see, Tom knew a number of men who'd hire Hick on the spot to help them stalk game, but after this display of misinterpreted words, he felt it best to leave well enough alone; especially considering the term for such a sporting guide - was a gillie.

an OWL HOOTED and the fire was warm. Hick savored every bite of his meal while Tom ate his with a tasteless frenzy; his first full helping of all meat since the night before he departed Buffalo. With his stomach full, he became tired. He dozed on a dry spot by the fire while Hick finished the lion's hide previously staked out flat on the ground. By now though, what Tom saw through the smoke and haze was the cat hanging on a hemp line between two trees; its front legs and paws stretched to either side and its head slumped forward.

Hick called Tom's way, "How'd ya become

injured?"

Tom roused from his slumber and intuitively knew he mustn't tell this man what he told the Prine children: that he'd hurt it while gutting a bear. So Tom called back, "Working under a wagon."

"Where ya bound fer," asked Hick, "I mean before this kitty interrupted yer journey?"

Tom sleepily rolled to his elbow and faced his wily inquisitor, "You are certainly probing," he said. He then looked at the stars above the fire and became utterly aware of the fact that if he were to continue, he needed to know exactly where he was headed. "South, along the Ohio River," replied Tom. "And what brings you to Pennsylvania - Hick?"

Between the smoke and the nightlight, Tom saw that Hick was hesitant to reply, so he made an effort to lighten the conversation, "What I meant was; is there more to why you've traveled here; more than an animal bounty?"

Tom's question struck a chord. Hick was still reluctant to answer it, so he continued to scrape the pelt, but then he gently nodded and said, "I reckon so. A mind to explore; the latest *Sharps Sportsman* and a reason to discharge it. There, ya happy?"

Tom appeared content with Hick's answer, so he again pondered the stars and contemplated the choices that had taken him to where he was and thought it interesting how a full stomach can change the way a man reflected on matters.

Hick scraped the hide and continued, "Been huntin' my whole life, and where I'm from, lotta new folk settlin'. Gittin' me cramped. So tell me Tom Tucker, what's England like, open and bountiful?"

"I'm sad to say, Hick, it's pitifully crowded and London smells of sewage."

So Hick changed chords and asked, "Have you been up in the sky; danglin' from a colorful bubble?

Tom thought, *colorful bubble?* ...

Hick could see from Tom's expression that his description needed clarification, "Yes sir. In a flyin' basket?"

"O..." said Tom, finally understanding, "No, I've not, but it does sound like an adventure."

And with that Hick moved onto the next subject of importance, "I'm also headed south," he said, "My people are in Kin-tuk-kee. And if you're inclined, Tom Tucker, yer welcome to travel along.

Tom knew that he wasn't within a realistic geographical range of returning to New York on his own, nor was he in possession of the ability or means to do so. Ironically though, he replied, "Thank you, Hick, but I'll be quite fine."

Hick raised an eyebrow and then looked to the top of the boulder. Tom's eyes followed his track to where the big cat held its purchase before falling to its death. "Uh huh, I can see that," he remarked subtly.

"Absolutely," Tom recounted, trying to sound confident, "I'm in no hurry. I'll be fine; really, but thank you."

Hick then stuffed his hand inside the head of the brainless cat and like a puppeteer, began moving its mouth. The cat said, *"Uh huh, I can see that too, but on the river boats, deck hands are always needed."*

Tom turned queasy over the thought of moving water and said, "River boats? ..."

"Yup," replied the cat with certainty, *"Headed our direction too."*

Tom contemplated the choice he was about to make, because it was a most important one.

"If need be," continued the cat as Hick now held its huge paw up and gestured with it, *"you can always return, but this way, I can teach you how not to get yerself kilt by the likes a me."* Hick lowered the paw and then reached around to the cat's mouth and lifted its droopy whiskers; exposing a set of fangs that would have surely done as the hunter previously supposed, ripped Tom's neck out', *"And if the likes a me don't git cha, perhaps a highway man will."*

Upon Hick's colorful description, Tom directly recalled what Robaré's throat looked like after his forty-plus caliber ball passed through it, creating irreversible damage, along with how easily the trapper lifted his watch in the dead of night.

"Hick," defined Tom, "you certainly possess the type of intellect needed to educate an individual.

And with the same hand he used to create the cat's snarl, Hick reached for his wineskin bag and tossed it to Tom, who drained a few drops in his mouth.

"*Yup,*" said the cat, "*no gittin' past that.*" And Hick pulled his hand out of the gelatinous cavity and began wiping it off on some leaves.

"I accept your invitation, Mr. Shelby," and Tom tossed the bag back. Not seeing that Hick was bent over wiping the muck from his hands, the hunter, hearing the bag in-flight, stood and caught it. Fully prepared to finish off the last few drops; he also saw that Tom was feeling some pain in his shoulder from the toss.

"Let's tend to that shoulder," said Hick and he started towards the Englishman, but then he stopped. And in a tone that once and for all positioned Thomas Tucker straight on the man that just saved his life, the hunter coherently stated, "Sir, folks call me Hick, and that is *all* they call me by."

Tom looked up from rubbing his wound; and eye to eye, clearly enunciated, "Understood Hick," I shant fail again."

TOM and HICK were the last to board a small mercantile barge in a quasi dry fashion. The rain had been falling steadily and the mud along the shore of this narrow tributary was thick 'n sticky. Once onboard the boat pilot gave the order and the two black men onshore tossed their lines to the men onboard and then pushed the barge as hard as they might into the moving current; themselves finally hiking aboard covered in sludge from their shins down.

On deck, dozens of slatted crates held two wild turkeys to a pen; all stacked and secured around the perimeter of the boat so they wouldn't fall over. A bearded man with one-leg and a crutch had found seat on the starboard gunwale next to a zealot bible salesman clutching his own personal waterlogged copy. Whenever something ordinary and of no consequence would happen, such as a log bumping the side of the barge, this religious man would quickly turn some pages and mumble passages as if a terrible ordeal was about to happen. But as the trip progressed, the salesman's words started to irk the one-legged gentleman who eventually began poking the man's foot with his crutch every time he opened his mouth.

Most on board however, wanted to be close to the woodstove that was belching everything but heat.

These persons had absorbed the rain to the point their bones were merely hangars for their dark and soggy garments.

Tom and Hick had found themselves a place to sit by the birds and Tom stretched his frame out and laid his head back on a turkey pen. He closed his eyes and felt the temperate drops hit his face. Sounds he'd never heard before came to life from seemingly everywhere: fish jumping, misquotes buzzing; the sound of a beaver felling a tree in the distance; river otters frolicking and the voices of men upriver and down working on other boats and barges. While native birds squawked in nearby trees, directly next to Tom, turkeys quietly gobbled as the steady, ardent rain laid itself down across the scape. It was a cacophony of new and enchanting sounds, and Tom liked it.

CHAPTER eight
WORTH and WORTHLESS

ON a VARIETY of flatboats and barges that carried an ample diversity of products, Tom and Hick worked their way down river; pushing into some of the most remote outposts by way of the narrowest tributaries.

Tom, whose emotional state was weak at best, performed only modest tasks and could barely pay his passage. Fortunately though, Hick willingly made up the difference in the labor between the two, keeping the boat pilots more than happy.

Upon reaching the Ohio, any township of significance with an acceptable mooring facility; and always at the judgment of the boat pilot, was compensated. Harbors never to be missed: Youngstown; Pittsburgh and Wheeling, along with many of the flourishing industrialized bergs that boomed along the gaping waterway.

When not onboard; and in times when food wasn't a priority, Hick patiently attempted to teach Tom how to shoot his sporting rifle, but Tom was still gun shy. He was all thumbs and had a difficult time focusing, so when Hick spotted a boar in the woods rooting around, the shooting lesson was temporarily over.

     Hick tenderly removed the weapon from Tom's nervous hands; knelt, cocked the hammer and aimed. Then soft as a feather, his trigger finger squeezed the curved piece of metal causing the hammer to release and strike the percussion cap - BOOM! These smooth and gifted moments preceding the discharge; though anticipated by Tom, actually made him recoil as if he were not expecting it.

     Hick stood up, "Did you follow that, Tom?" he asked, handing him back the discharged rifle. Tom nodded and silently took hold of it as smoke poured from its breech 'n barrel - the entire forefront, a cloud of white.

     Grateful Tom was for his new friend, because if it weren't for Hick, he would surely be dead, or waiting to die. And at this very instant, he knew to be fact.

WITH the BOAR gutted and quartered only a few feet from where it took its last breath; a blackened skillet borrowed from the boat cooked chitterlings on the fire that Tom had managed to build.

"Best we fry these chitlins outta sight and down wind," said Hick, looking around, "lest the others'll want some and we won't git our fill." He stirred the now cooked pieces and sprinkled some home seasoning on them from a small pouch. He then poked a sizzling bit with his knifepoint and handed the greasy globule to Tom, who put up his hands and turned his head.

But Hick insisted, "Take it. You need to eat. Besides, they're tasty." But Tom could barely look at it, especially since witnessing the way Hick prepared it. "Go on, take it. Take it, Tom. Eat, insisted Hick.

Reluctantly, Tom removed the hot, dripping blob from Hick's knife-point and took a small bite. Hick waited for a response, silent or otherwise. Surprisingly the expression on Tom's face changed from grimace to Mmm…, and then to surprise.

"Good, ain't they? Some folks don't like 'em at first." But Tom finished it and then reached for another.

"Now tell me, Tom; tell me about James Cook the great explorer – with your words."

WHEN THE DAY turned to dusk; and the boats, so many and so varied in size and cargo approached the shores and townships too small for a wharf, they'd tie onto the cypress trees that grew from the water. By extending planks from boat to boat, crew members wandered as they sought out old friends and made new acquaintances.

Where available, white men womanized, but in any case, they still drank 'n gambled. The free blacks and slaves though, always kept to themselves; camping to the sides of the vessels; yet always within earshot in case they were needed for a task.

Tom on the other hand, remained onboard most nights. Unable to mingle, he paced the deck; his trousers shredded below the knees and the shirt he traded Will Prine for was now a mere rag that he tied around his head to keep the sweat from burning his eyes.

This night, like many before it, Tom looked around to make sure no one was close and then snuck out the oval locket with Amanda's painting in it. "Hello my love," he sweetly sighed and he sat down on a portion of the starboard gunwale hidden by the wheelhouse, "My cowardly fear carries me forth, deeper south than I'd ever dreamt of running, or traveling into the frontier and glory of The Americas. How beautiful they are; gallantly pristine in so many stunning, yet delicate and attractive ways. I yearn to share this magnificence with you and our beautiful child. My heart aches for us to be together again, warm in our bed, under the covers, taking in your love. I hunger for the life I've abandoned, and soon I will return because… I'm not the same without you."

Tom became startled when he heard a crack, but when he looked, it was only the echo of a distant branch that had snapped off and was working its way through the coppice to the water below.

"We're a day down river from Youngstown," he continued, "a rising settlement that manufactures munitions, possibly for an impending war. O God, I'm so sorry I said this. I know how you hate weapons, … and now, I have experienced why. I detest myself for my haughty stupidity and going against your sound advice. I'm now reaping the harvest of my thoughts and actions. The decision to travel with a weapon on my person has completely wrecked me, like a ship on the rocks. I'm aware now the fear which embodied my meager existence somehow convinced me to bring the damn thing. Perhaps cursed, I've been traveling with a man I believe suspects I've done wrong, yet declines to ask for details. We're similar in many subtle ways. I feel him trustworthy, and like me, he steadfastly conceals certain aspects of himself, but we've quickly grown to be friends. It becomes harder by the day to hold up this facade I've created. For some inexplicable reason, I am now going by the name, Tom; my brother's name. Maybe because it's easy to remember, yet it weighs profoundly upon me. Most men appear to have left behind something old for an original, fresh start in this new and unaccustomed land. It appears to be deserving of most. Some are very proud, and some not so, but in my case, I cannot disclose all that I am proud of; nor whom I love for fear it will lead to greater and heavier untruths. Untruths I'd have to manufacture falsehoods to cover; which in all likelihood will lead me to the gallows if I were to say the wrong thing, thus causing us to never see each other again."

The **SUMMER NIGHTS** on the rivers bearing south had become as humid and intolerable as any part of the globe; so much so that no sane boatman would ever think to sleep below deck. As a result, except for the concords of the insects coupled with the men's snoring; from midnight 'til morn, all sounds softly blended with the prolific activity of the silent glow bugs. No visual difference really between the fire of the male and the female; so Hick advised Tom, but a well-known fact was when nothing else could be seen, the ever subtle qualities of their luminescent abdomens were what attracted or repelled their genders.

AT the FIRST SIGNS of LIGHT, barge after barge rang out. The small pirogues, or swamp boats carved from the trunks of cedar trees could also be seen paddling from the tributaries with their passengers and cargo to be transferred to the larger crafts. Vessels no longer went singly, but lashed together in teams of six to eight; entire flotillas on their way down the mighty Ohio.

Tom was more alert now and well beyond the point of feeling the need to contribute. He humbly showed Hick how to lap-joint two pieces of wood together and then showed him the process for mortise and tenon work; a simple yet popular building technique he'd learned as a boy that took him far in the world of engineering.

When the tributaries that led to the main river body became wider and deeper, so did the drafts of the boats traveling them, like the massive triple-decker cargo barges that transported everything from cattle and oxen; to flour, hemp, clothing and hardware. These colossal vessels pulled in and docked only at the ports large enough to support their size, weight and commerce. Yet if a vessel of this nature was within the vicinity of a smaller township, and the current wasn't too swift, sometimes the boat pilot would allow row boats from shore to tie on and conduct business. For piloting one of these often times over laden behemoths too close to shore risked the hazard of running a ground or becoming held in place by the mud. And if this were to happen, it would surely cost more in men than the township could muster to remedy such a blunder.

PORTSMOUTH, Cincinnati, Madison, New Albany, Louisville and Evansville; while Tom repaired anything and everything, Hick worked the deck; and laughed every time Tom ran to the side to throw his guts over.

FIVE weeks later, close to where the Ohio meets the Cumberland, two small boats were lashed alongside a sizable flat barge. Day had yet to break and not a single floating thing in this watery neighborhood, including sticks and debris was moving faster than the mile wide, dawdling body would carry them. The rain from the previous night had soaked the bypassing landmarks with a sultry and unhurried pace. But soon the sun would rise to brand these torrid surroundings like it did on most summer mornings: with a scorching iron.

More notable than the twelve slaves it took to control this barge, was the log-built cabin square in the middle for its fancy fare paying cliental to sit inside of so not to soil their eyes by the likes of a dark boatman; cliental who often traveled to the smaller townships that the larger and more fashionable vessels did not call upon. Remaining indoors under these oppressive conditions was unbearable, especially for the overdressed elite. So above board these hussy torts lingered, on and around whatever makeshift seats they could muster while waiting for the vessel to make port. This was also when fishing was made the most of as a way to pass the time.

At the back of the smallest boat, Tom and Hick sat on the gunwale with their lines trolling. An alligator gar lay gutted on deck; remnants of its head and entrails strewn about. These fish were too greasy and strong tasting for most, but a particular favorite amongst the black 'n slave population that lived on the boats or near the waters where these prehistoric river dwellers resided. This was of course more outdoorsman information that Hick imparted Tom's way. Because before Tom met Hick, he knew only what he'd read about concerning this land.

Along the shore, a murder of crows could be seen weighing down some long willow branches. As the boats passed, the crows lifted off one by one, cawing as they gained altitude, flapping and then finally circling over the slippery leftovers on deck.

"Crows," said Hick, "unlike their larger

cousin's the raven, don't soar all that well. It's believed this lack of facility; along with their smaller size causes their more scavenger-like tendencies".

Tom looked at Hick and continued to appreciate the wealth of knowledge he had about wildlife. Several of the crows attempted a quick touch 'n go for a fish treat, but failed as Tom whacked at them with a stick. He eventually grazed one causing it to nearly collide with the water's surface, and with this, he and Hick tossed the guts overboard and rinsed the deck with a barrel of river water.

Hick then kneeled against the edge and pointed, "Yonder's Smithland. It's also the county seat," and he took a nip of his newly acquired bourbon whisky; named after *Bourbon County Kentucky*. A bottle he had the good fortune of obtaining shortly before to two departed Cincinnati. "Lotta folk settlin' here, Tom," he continued and he replaced the cork in the rounded canteen style bottle, "Rich soil too I say. Paducah's even got a market-house where folk can back in their wagons and slave labor'll load ya out; fire brigade too. There's a real fine market in N'awlins, right on the mighty Miss. Best shrimp, crabs, crawfish and oysters I ever ett – big celebrations there too, but she's too far south to travel fer a meal, or revelry. Not to say I haven't thought of it a time 'r two; especially when I found myself tirin' 'f the vittles 'n critters these parts provide."

"Really...?" asked Tom inquisitively, "What's a crawfish?"

"Ever ett a Lobster? Tom nodded because lobster was ample in areas on the eastern seaboard.

"Well I never ett one," said Hick, "only seen drawings 'n read about 'em, but I ett plenny-a-crawfish. Like a lobster, but only about this big," and he spread apart his finger and thumb. "Story goes, they started out as lobsters from yer neck, but after they made the swim south to the big gulf, they ended up losing weight. After ya boil 'em, you twist off the tails and pinch-out the meat. I ett two buckets 'f 'em once."

"Really?..." replied Tom again.

"Yup," popped Hick, more drawl added for each ounce of liquor he consumed. "Not that either destination would do us some good. Paducah's on the other side of the Ohio, over by the Tennessee; almost two days there 'n back on fresh animals. N'awlins is at the mouth of the big gulf. That's another river journey. I'm around the bend - there in Dycusburg," and he pointed again and spat. "Salem's there and Pinckneyville's yonder on the Cumberland; and across from them's the virgin land I told y'all of. We call it *The Cumberland Valley*. My family's a stake in the ferry crossing so I come 'n go without payin'."

Tom stood up and looked at the pastoral places Hick had been pointing to. He shielded his eyes from the water's glare and gazed at all the glorious shades of green with new hope. Geographically he was a thousand miles from anything having to do with his prior difficulties, yet something innately told him he needed to make a decision one way or another concerning his return to New York. Either way, it was not going to be an easy choice. Because as each day passed, Tom's impending option was made more difficult by his love of hard work, the hot sun and the slow 'n steady rhythm of this newly acquired *live and let live* way of life; a way of living that was temperately warmer and far more colorful than anything he'd previously been exposed to. And if it wasn't evident before, it certainly was now; that the maelstrom of the south's sweet nectar had him in its tender, yet firm and sticky grasp.

"Any big bears?" asked Tom, continuing to shield his eyes so he could look as far as he could.

Hick laughed, "You mean Grizzly?"

"Yes. Grizzly..."

Hick could see Tom's sincerity, so he stood up and adjusted his pole to ponder the question, "There's a few I reckon. Not this close to civilized folk though - why?" But as soon the question left Hick's mouth, the boats bumped together causing him to slip on some remaining fish slime and tumble forward. Tom however, grabbed him ahead of falling overboard, yet not before his bottle of whisky shattered on deck.

"Good wage spent on that liquor!" shouted Hick, "Glass containers 'er hard to come by! I was saving it fer when I got home... Dang..." And Hick sat down and started to weep for a spell; feeling the loss of his liquor like a child feels the loss of a toy.

Tom left his friend to collect himself and returned his attention to the area's magnificence. Since he hailed from the commonwealth that pioneered the industrial revolution now filling the skies over his tiny British isle with soot and filth; vestal was the only word that came to his mind as he looked.

"The Cumberland Valley, you say?" asked Tom, feeling the need to be certain.

"After we dock at Smithland," said Hick while hitching up his britches, "I go east." Tom on the other hand, still looked uncertain. "I normally return sooner," continued Hick, "Four months is a sight long fer me to be away. I was also figgerin' you'd'vc sorted out your thoughts by now; I was hopin' anyway. Listen Tom, you've turned into a good boatman, no doubt there. You could even make yer way to pilot, sept for yer illness on the water. And fer as often as it overtakes you; I still cain't figger how you keep anything down long enough to shit. So I feel I ought warn ya; waters ahead can turn mighty rough as these barges make their way to the big gulf; especially this time of year. Didn't wanna-larm ya too soon, that's why I kept it to my self, but when a storm, or a twister comes from nowhere, bein' on the river I reckon's no different than bein' on the sea. Mind you, that's only what I heard; never been on the sea, but water's water and you mix blustery air with it and yer gonna call to yerself some ailing. I reckon I might even loose a meal 'r two.

Right there, Tom appeared queasy over Hick's vivid explanation and gave the nod, "Smithland sounds like a plan."

"Fine then. Cain't wait to cut this fur off my face. Dern scratchy it is."

Indeed Hick's long and disheveled reddish blond beard had grown to look and become quite cumbersome; at times finding the need to cut it away with his knife, leaving uneven patches of growth.

Tom on the other hand had less growth overall, but there was still plenty of hair to get in the way at the rate his beard grew, especially seeing that he was used to a clean shave every other day; a shave conducted by someone other than himself. You see, even aboard *Helena*, others had the duty of shaving the higher class passengers. And a qualified barber was something Tom had a great appreciation for, as well as something he'd demonstrated gratitude in favor of; always privileging the skilled harvester with more coin than asked for in return for services rendered.

Tom sucked up his queasiness and said, "Hick, I continue to find it remarkable that you've given no consideration at all to the field of education."

"Nope," cracked Hick, gloating as he too stared at the greens and yellows of the area, "Never will neither. Yonder's Smithland," he said and he spat a stream of brown sap into the lime green water.

When the boats rounded the eastern bend of the Ohio, just past Dog Island, dozens of barges, flat boats and even row boats could be seen sitting idle at Smithland, the doorway to the Cumberland tributary. Anything not docked was moored off shore or tied to the trees. Everyone waited their turn to load or offload their cargo. Fortunately for these two travelers, the dock master felt the cargo of gunpowder and grain stored beneath their backsides should be offloaded first and thus directed the boat pilot, Frank Doyle into a berth that was just vacated by a southbound long-barge carrying tobacco, hemp and coal.

The slaves onboard tossed the docking lines ashore and Hick, outfitted like the hunter he was; in a clean doe skin shirt, buckskin lowers and bull hide moccasins, lost no time hopping off. Naturally he was accompanied by his *Sharps Box Lock* and this time an

altogether different shoulder bag that contained his
personal accoutrements.

Tom on the other hand looked like a cross
between a woodsman and a teacher; unshaven yet
filled and proper. Never caring much for the feel of
animal skin against his own; Tom still enjoyed the
simplicity of a white cotton shirt, dark trousers and a
pair of lace up ankle boots. He was however, wearing
an old beaver pelt hat that he'd traded a slave boy for
in return for the knowledge of how to write the words,
I love you on a piece of paper with a graphite stick; an
item he'd discovered in his jacket when he was taking
his inventory. He also carried the weapon he'd
recently procured: a *J. Henry* .44 caliber, cap 'n ball,
Indian trade rifle with a full stock and thirty-five
inches of barrel – a very long gun; and a weapon he
wasn't used to shooting by any means. But Hick
suggested it because of its favorable qualities: being
built to last, the ammunition came easy and it was
acquired at the right price; won by Hick after a fellow
hunter wagered him that he couldn't drop a bull elk
with one shot from seven-hundred feet with his
Sharps, which possessed a shorter barrel. If Hick
would have lost the bet, he offered up the killing and
dressing out of two smaller elks for the hunter. Hick
still knew it was a good gamble even if he were to lose,
because his skill-set allowed him to dress out two

smaller animals faster than one large bull. Hick was confident and the dialogue ended when he picked his mark, knelt and fired.

Tom and Hick were heading off the dock for dry land when Hick shouted back to the pilothouse, "Thank ya, Cap'n Doyle! Please take my blessings to yer kin."

Built like a tree stump, four-foot eleven-inch Frank Doyle waved goodbye to the two unlikely looking companions. Shortly thereafter at the age of fifty-four, Doyle killed a man with his bare hands thrice his size and half his age in a fit of madness when he discovered the man cheating at cards. The bigger, younger man was clearly chousing the other players to call his defrauding bluff, and it was Doyle who called the hand. The man's death, followed by his hasty burial on the Monongahela was never spoken of again except in folklore where the story was embellished to the proportion of David and Goliath.

Doyle went on to work as a boat pilot for another twelve years until failing from a cerebral hemorrhage while drinking and played cards; all while he ironically waited for a hundred custom caskets to be offloaded from his vessel; himself being buried in a no frills, plain pine box.

With over fifty years on the eastern and southern rivers, the only indulgence Doyle religiously looked forward to was having his bald and shiny noggin shaved by a barber at every opportunity. To look at him after he'd taken off his cap was akin to looking at a hardboiled egg-half atop the crags and furrows of a sun richen face. When asked why he did this, he said it helped him sleep better during the often times insufferably hot nights; as well as it prevented parasites from burrowing into his scalp; and a scalp with hair was a chore he simply didn't want anything to do with. This was because when he first began working the rivers as a boy, "The Indians," he said, "were fierce in some places, and losing one's hair was a sight easier back then." So he shaped a thought that if he didn't have any hair to lose in the first place, it would make the Indian's job that much harder; and as the years passed, it was something he got used to, and liked.

This one and only luxury he allowed himself, which helped to bequeath a sizable estate to his third wife and two lovely daughters of twelve and fourteen; whom also met with an ironic demise when their stage coach was robbed and they were raped and left for dead by six highwaymen; finally succumbing to fire and torture by Indians, was all for not. The events coming to conclusion just nine days after making their fateful decision to travel west from St. Louis to San Francisco with their estate in liquid form.

After fifteen years of marriage; and against the sound advice of those Doyle paid handsomely to see that his loved ones stayed safe and funded for the remainder of their lives on earth after his passing; Doyle's widow, a woman he unwittingly granted free rein to, was determined to have matters her way, which ultimately gave just reason for her pen-lover of six years to never hear from her again.

BY and LARGE Smithland was chaos; created mostly by trade. Far and wide every kind of freight imaginable was moved to and fro, largely by slave and free black labor. Add to this bedlam, voices of multiple nationalities conducting business. These languages and accents swapped tall stories, jokes and of course, commerce in Gaelic, German, Italian, English and French, along with some Hebrew, Dutch and Portuguese, not to mention a variety of Native dialects. Pointless to say, arms and hands flailed endlessly in their attempts to communicate more effectively.

Before Tom's second foot stepped off the dock and into the mud, a man's voice called out, "Brother!" Hick 'n Tom looked up to meet the eye of James Washington Shelby, a twenty-six year old farmer sitting on a tobacco barrel firmly engaged in the process of whittling down an insignificantly small willow branch with an exceedingly large, Scottish dirk knife. The blade of which completely dwarfed the small stick; and the act of doing so almost appeared silly. Because for as brilliant and tactical as Shelby was in some ways, he was simple and innocent in others, genuinely emoting over the sight of his younger brother, "I missed y'all, I did! I'll take an oath to it."

Hick took hold of Tom's sleeve and gave it a tug, "C'mon," he said, "it's kin."

Upon reaching Shelby, Tom sized-up the ordinary looking chap for his ability to fight and capture; something he did with every man he encountered since being on the run.

Shelby rose up from his tobacco barrel and with his knife in hand, bear hugged Hick and whimpered, "It's good you've returned, brother," and his eyes welled up.

"No need for an oath, James," replied Hick with sensitivity, "I accept yer feelin' as true."

Then without so much as a glance, Shelby found the knife's sheath lashed to his trousers and directed the steel into the leather.

"What brings you off yer farms?" asked Hick. But before an answer came, Shelby jumped atop his barrel and suspiciously looked around. Skillfully balancing he whispered, "Folk bin sayin', river's gonna rise."

Hick glanced at Tom and then back to his brother, "Not in the next forty year it ain't, James."

Shelby slapped his knee and jumped. In midair he said, "I knew I could count on you," and he landed like a cat; after which he straightened himself for an introduction, "Who's yer friend?"

Less cautious now, Tom said, "Thomas Tucker."

"Yer English," said Shelby, as if genuinely surprised, "Dern ..."

Hick shot Tom the same look he'd sent scores of others; the look that affirmed his brother's derangement.

"Yes, sir," said Tom with conviction, "I am English."

Oddly, Shelby turned his observations across the street. He lowered his head some to scan between the wagon wheels and the animal hooves where he spotted a proudly dressed Augustus Alley; newly appointed, late-thirties city constable. Alley, with one foot in the stirrup, prepared to mount his nervous and uncut red-dun from the boardwalk adjacent the shipping office. He threw his leg over the saddle, locked his other foot in and immediately reined the animal hard into the public zone. This caused pedestrians and wagons alike to be cautious of him. A wagon almost lost its load and the lawman's own horse mislaid a foot in the mud causing its boorish rider to nearly be thrown.

"Brother?" said Shelby, scarcely moving his attention off Alley, "I'm despairin' over a minor debt.

"You've despaired over small affects before, James," said Hick in an attempted to unwind the clearly agitated man. "Remember in school; you was good at cipherin'. No need to give up hope over an undersized quandary."

Shelby created another pregnant moment when he shifted his gaze to a huge, humble looking slave getting glove-slapped about by his twenty-something, overly dressed female owner; obviously of means, "I am utterly ashamed that you are now *my* languid nigger!" she said in a voice louder than need be. "I ought march right back to that auctioneer and demand my gold be refunded. I have never in all my days witnessed such indolent work practice. I was assured by that barker your credentials included bein' able pick up and carry as much as two men your own weight. And look at you... Look I said! You can barely put one barrel upon your shoulder. What will mother say when she's learned I picked a lazy one? ..."

Another tear formed in Shelby's eye. To say the least, some of the barrels weighed more than two-hundred pounds. And at this moment, Shelby felt sincere shame for being of the same shade as the black man's new handler.

Then as fast as it began, a warm resolve passed over Shelby's face, "I'm happy you've returned, brother," he said again, but this time with more sincerity than the first two times. "You are a good sibling and a fine man. And you Mr. Tucker have discovered unintended fortune in Lafayette as your friend." Hick promptly looked around to make sure no one heard his brother say the "L" word whereby Shelby concluded, "and you will not likely discover exactly how fortuitous you justly are sir, until shortly before your passing."

Tom could only stare at the young farmer in astonishment. What kind of fortune teller is this man he asked himself; making the hair on the back of his neck stand up with a single spoken sentence, but Shelby gave no thought to who was listening or looking at him, nor to any of the other things he'd said or done. He simply sat back down and resumed his whittling.

Tom looked to see that Hick was still trying to

recover from hearing his given-name spoken in public by a man he would never intentionally assault. Tom also noted that however remarkable the Shelby differences were in deed; both men, without a doubt, came from physically healthy stock and contained a strong resemblance to the apparent family blood line.

ONE BLOCK parallel to Court Street, a train of wagons loaded with a diversity of freight were expressing their way to the docks in an effort to get there sooner than another.

Tom and Hick, while minding their own business, walked well to the side of these folks that had somewhere to go in a hurry. Given that these two men had just come from some fairly spare surroundings; they appeared content to simply witness the commotion. Then from behind as they walked, a large, heavily loaded wagon piled to the sky with freshly milled lumber rolled dangerously close. Not as big as a prairie schooner mind you, but certainly worthy of killing or maiming a man if a wheel were to pass over him. With no span remaining to avoid being struck, Tom and Hick jumped into the roadside ditch lined with summertime berries and briar.

Atop the lumber pile sat a girl and a boy maybe all of six and eight who were getting bounced about and on the wagon's final spring; the one that caused Tom and Hick to jump, the kids were nearly popped over the side themselves.

The mule team that was making matters difficult for the driver was finally brought to a stop, but still the animals continued to be overly aggressive towards each other. Tom, as best he could, removed himself from the ditch, and with stickers wedged into him everywhere, grabbed a hold of the closest animal's harness and attempted to calm it down. The animal snorted and pitched about, but when Tom finally got a look at the driver's face, he quickly looked away. Never had he seen a female amid such fire.

Behind the reins glaring down at him sat an eighteen year old girl dressed in men's work clothes and a distressed beaver pelt hat. With an open flame in her eyes and a red-hot drawl as thick as glue she shouted, "Whoa now! I can handle 'em. Turn 'em loose!"

But Tom continued to hold the aggressive animal's head away from the second mule that it wanted to do harm to and shouted back, "You knocked us into the drain!"

"I didn't, "came a sharp rebut, "Now let go!"

"You should be a foreman!" barked Tom, still holding the unruly animal.

"I am a foreman!" she shouted and she snapped the reins, directing the horsepower forward, thus forcing Tom to release his grip on the harness. The girl regained control and without anything further, continued on her way. The kids, still atop the load, waved and smiled at the two men, but while floating the ribbons over the animal's withers, the feisty female reached back and promptly settled them down.

Picking briar from his seams, Hick walked up to Tom and said with a sideways grin, "Meet Sarah Adaline Jones."

"Bloody Christ she's aggressive," said Tom, now removing his own unwelcome prickles.

"True enough," agreed Hick, working out a particularly difficult sticker that had positioned itself on the inseam of his pant thigh, "And she don't like men much neither."

Tom took note of a bleeding scratch on his neck and then looked one more time at the swayback wagon headed for the docks; children on top, playing contently with a loop of twine and said, "Who'd even want to meet a woman like that? ..."

THE HUMIDITY in Smithland this particular
afternoon was high enough to cause the average man
to ring a quart of sweat from his shirt alone. Down the
street from the Livingston County Courthouse, Tom
and Hick had been relaxing under the porch eve of a
small general store; their backs comfortably against the
wall enjoying the simple pleasure of a piece of hard
candy. And though Tom's never been much of a sugar
eater, it's an uncomplicated pleasure, and one that
appeared God given for getting a man's salivation
glands working.

This community store, like many of the others
throughout the township, carried the basic provisions
of salted meat, eggs, flour and grain; while some of the
others provided harder items such as spades, picks,
gun powder, knives, mining supplies and weaponry.
And ironically for as swollen as Main Street was, this
particular lane was rather barren of traffic.

When a late-fifties slave woman referred to as
Black Lily approached the store with a large basket of
eggs atop her colorful headwear, three Hodge Brothers
rounded the corner from an ally with three mixed
hounds; every one of their canine ribs showing
through their droopy, rubber-like skin as if they'd
never had an entire meal to satisfaction. The boys,
mental defectives, were a mixed breed themselves.

With a shadowy mouth of rotting teeth, sixteen

166

year old Dart Hodge constantly scratched. More notably was his stubby hand that protruded from where his right forearm would normally bend at the elbow, but there was no forearm and no elbow joint, only seven inches of bicep and a webbed hand. Not good for much except holding things for others and swimming in circles perhaps.

Keech Hodge on the other hand was the nineteen year old, toe-headed, self-proclaimed leader that was nothing but mouth and trouble. With oily-thin dishwater hair that was always to be in his eyes and skin like a dried up corncob; he wore a zigzagged scar from the right corner of his mouth, up past his eye and above the top of his ear where no hair grew. Sadly though, Keech was born with a curse: he was a boy who just couldn't help being mean.

Loren Hodge, the oldest at twenty-two, was big and slow. He stammered with an impediment so severe, scarcely a person within earshot could understand a word he said, and therefore said little. He walked with a grievous limp due to being born with his left leg five inches shorter; and therefore compensated the lame shuffle he'd developed by securing a wood block to his one and only lace up ankle shoe that he wore without an under-sock. The sole of the shoe was worn clear through and the stitching nearly gone. And if it weren't for the block tied under it, the sole would completely flap 'n flop about making the shoe useless. So except for Loren's one shoe, the brother's remaining five feet were bare; and their stinking shirts 'n trousers were scarcely suitable as rags.

When the dogs spotted Black Lily, they started to bark frantically while turning circles around her. The brothers began to hoot 'n holler it up with Keech acting as instigator. If they could get the woman to drop her eggs, it would be a prize for the boy's ego and a meal for the animals. But for as much ruckus as the dogs created, something out of the ordinary prevented them from actually touching her.

Then as calm as a warm, summer's nightfall; Lily lifted the heavy basket off her head, and in a lightening move, spat a dollop of black juice at the hounds. Barely a second elapsed between the mixture leaving her mouth amid the spaces between her teeth and the animals scattering.

"Those hounds appear to know her," remarked Tom casually.

Paying no mind to Tom or Hick, Black Lily stepped up and into the store.

"O, they know her alright," said Hick as he slurped more of the goodness from his sugary marble, "Burnt the eyes out 'f the fourth mutt with that peculiar juice she just spat, like ... ?

"Acid?" said Tom, second guessing the word Hick was looking for.

"Uh huh," Hick was sure of it, "But more powerful-hot than anything the rest of us chew; her own private concoction. Her holder, Ed Marsden, allows her to preserve the little bit 'f self-regard she has left with it; to a degree that is, with animals and such."

Then from across the street at the *Blacksmith & Hardware Supply*, Sarah Jones came a strutting. She'd pulled her loaded wagon with the children on top to the side and parked it down a half-block where they awaited her return. When the brothers spotted her at mid-street they began to gawk. A hound came around from behind and started sniffing her ass, but Sarah sidestepped the mongrel and in a blur, slapped its mouth so hard the drool that was dangling from its jowls splattered across the brothers.

In passing, she ignored the boys, but Loren chose to engage and stammered, "Hey, HE, HE hey, mi, mi, missy. Did ya, lu LOOSE yer dress?"

Dart snickered, "Maybe her and her pappy traded under-bustles."

In stride, Sarah remarked, "And maybe a lunacy commission should be appointed fer y'all ...

But Dart had absolutely no idea what Sarah just said, so he smirked like he always did when big words came his way.

Sarah stepped onto the porch, yet before crossing the threshold, paused ever-so-briefly to shoot Tom a look of interest; a look intended to piss Keech off, and it worked.

Keech saw the gesture and tried to look proper, but quickly became untuned, "Hey Lafeet! he called out, "Who's yer fancy lookin' friend?"

And without a word, Hick leaned over the porch and located the perfect mineral stone: a nice, sharp one. "Ask him yerself, Keech. And stop calling' me by that name - horse's asshole," whereupon he flung the stone. The rock missed Keech by an inch, but it didn't miss his brother and banged Dart square on the bridge of his nose. Keech however remained completely oblivious to the airborne compliment and kept *his* eyes on Tom. Dart began rubbing the knot that had now erupted from between his eyes and shot Hick the stink-eye, but Dart knew better than to make any kind of move whatsoever towards Hick. That's because last year, Hick caught Dart suckling the cock of Bo Spencer's lap dog behind the First Baptist Church on a Sunday morning. Not that church, or Sundays for that matter, ever meant anything to Dart other than where to locate a suitable animal that wouldn't bite him. Besides Dart liked the smaller canines opposed to the larger ones his brothers preferred. After being discovered, Dart got down on his knees and begged

Hick not to tell anyone what he'd seen, especially his daddy. Hick agreed, but only after the scoundrel promised to never call him the "L" word again, ever. The accord was sealed in spit and shook upon.

Evidently though, by some intuitive yet conceivable power, the stone chunked at Keech was Hick's way of affirming that he wasn't about to let any of Dart's kin get away with such an act either. This, while at the same time honoring his word to Dart; an accord that Dart clearly knew to be in effect.

"Well, Fancyman?" Keech solicited, directing his stare even more intently at Tom.

"My name is Thomas Tucker, and from what I gather, you are Mr. Keech? It is an honor to meet — "

"I ain't Mr. Keech!" the boy inveighed, "My name's Keech Hodge!"

Tom grinned at Hick over the absurdity of the exchange, but Hick only shrugged.

"My sincere apologies to you, sir," stated Tom, "We don't want any trouble."

"Well, y'all found yerselves some, Fancyman! That's my sweetie yer layin' yer eyes on!"

Inside the store, Sarah and the shopkeeper watched through the window. They both smiled as they overheard Tom, as modest as it might sound, attempt to carve the bullies down. "And a fine looking woman she is, Mr. Hodge, countered Tom, "You should be proud that she belongs to you - and you alone."

Keech puffed up with pride and Sarah also liked what she was hearing, and her face revealed it. Hick took a swig off his newly acquired bottle and then tucked it away in a safe place on his person as he prepared for the inevitable.

"Don't care for you layin' yer eyes on her," snarled Keech; spittle draining from the numb and unfeeling corner of his mouth. He then took a hard false-step towards the porch. This action caused Tom to reach into his pocket and uneasily pull another piece of candy, but he dropped it and it fell into a porch crack. Tom's concern over the possibility of a fight became evident.

Like gold, Dart spotted the candy and gibed, "He's a lookin' mighty jittery, Keech. He musta not a heerd ya."

Loren only chuckled ...

Keech recurred, "Hey Fancyman, I said --"

"I heard what you said, Mr. Hodge," pronounced Tom, cutting him off.

Keech also puffed up, "Well? What do ya have to say about it?"

Not fully prepared to tangle with the brothers, Tom reluctantly got up and stepped into the street. As he did, he had to step around ol' Bobby, who was slowly riding bareback down the middle of the lane. Every single day, ol' Bobby, maybe all of thirty, rode his horse from one end of the town to the other; always appearing as if he was truly searching for something. Folks refrained from paying him any more of their mind because in the past when somebody'd asked him why he rode from one end of the town to the other every day, he'd just look at them, kind of irritated like, and say the same thing, "I'm lookin' fer my horse, dern ya."

Inside the store, Sarah grabbed hold of the shopkeeper's arm. She dug her fingers in past his shirt and prepared for her own adrenaline rush. She hadn't seen a good fight since the free black, Bill Temple was stopped mid-day out front of the school house and accused of being a mule thief by four farmers that lived across the river in Salem. Bill fought his way clear of a lynching for more than an hour. He'd fought so long and so hard; fracturing frames and choking men to near unconsciousness, that the farmers figured he was just borrowing the animal; like he'd stated, with his previous owner's permission, returning it more than a week before the men had even confronted him. By end results, the lynch mob thought it a whole lot harder to hang an innocent man than an actual mule thief; consenting to the notion as they hobbled away licking their wounds.

Because Bill Temple had previously fought Mandingo style; traveling from plantation to plantation with various owners and winning a number of bouts to the death, he'd miraculously negotiated his freedom. He also knew what it took to hobble his accusers without destroying them. Tired of fighting and living in a slave state, he made his final trek north to Pennsylvania, a state that had been free from slavery since 1790. But even there, with sixty-five years of abolition behind its people, he still received a sizeable share of trouble, but nothing like what he and his brethren were being subjected to in the southern areas of the country.

Sarah was a young girl at the time and she watched it all happen from the porch of the school house. She even took a licking by the teacher when she refused to come back inside, only standing there, feeling the rush of what it must be like to fight for a thing you truly believe in, like your life.

Keech met Tom eye to eye and Hick moved in behind his friend, back to back and the brothers stepped in close. When they did, a boat whistle blew and the events before Tom's eyes went blank. He was immediately transported back to the Buffalo Train Depot and the morning Joseph Tweddle climbed down from the flatcar. Signing the document the German had just handed him; Joseph glanced up to see the shackled prisoner being helped aboard by North-Western Agent's, Webster and Yondell.

The whistle blew again and when Tom recognized the sound was coming from a river boat, he returned to his senses. "Mr. Hodge," he said, "I do apologize. It was not our intention to upset you, or your brothers. Will you forgive me for looking at Miss. Jones?"

Hick was a bit mystified and ready to say something because he'd like nothing more than to whoop some ass, especially with the butt of his Sharps against the skull of a Hodge brother or two, but he also figured Tom had a plan when he saw the brother's mouths agape – wide enough to reveal their decomposing protuberances.

This is also when Keech began to nod ever-so-slightly. For never in his life had he won a fight without having to actually fight, "Now that's the kinda talk I like heerin', yup. Well boys, should I let Fancyman off?"

Forgiveness it appeared, based on a previous experience mine you, hadn't anchored itself in Dart or Loren's consciousness, nor Keech's for that matter, but Keech *was* sweet on Sarah and therefore began to simmer. He also had the brainpower, little that it took, to recognize that if he cooled down, he and his brothers would not be underwritten an embarrassing defeat in front of Sarah if they were to fight Tom and Hick; a result that contained a high degree certainty.

But inside the store, Sarah looked disappointed. She slowly released the shopkeeper's arm; nail marks to prove it. Not to worry; secretly folks had always wanted the best for Sarah, but Tom's reluctance to stand up to the brothers made her wonder why the new man in town didn't have more going on in the war department.

Little could Sarah possibly know that Tom was beleaguered by women while practically living in Victoria's Court. He also had his fair share of skirmishes and fights; going fisticuffs with many-a-man over who would lay an unwed maiden; with Tom winning most of the bouts due to his intellectual ability concerning the spoken word. He nearly always allowed the other man to leave with his dignity while still taking the prize.

But the brothers quickly ceased their snickers when Tom argued, "However Mr. Hodge? If we ask Miss Jones to step outside, she *will* agree with you, will she not?"

"Agree... ?" rebutted Keech, feeling uneasy all of a sudden, "Agree to what? ..."

"That she's your sweetie. That is what you said, was it not? Or did I hear you incorrectly?"

Having fallen from his element, Keech

disputed, "What kind of backwards shit-talk's that?"

Dart and Loren continued to listen in dismay as the exchange now started to sound more like a foreign language.

"Think about it, Mr. Hodge," stated Tom firmly, "if you have the capacity. O, and if you don't like other men *layin' their eyes* on your pretty girl, then I highly recommend you locate an unattractive one, and you'll be guaranteed to never have this problem again." Then like a well-timed stage act, Hick stepped onto the porch, grabbed Tom's rifle, backed up to him and handed him the weapon where Tom said, "Good day to you now."

Cautiously the two friends started to walk away in tandem. Tom strode forwards while Hick walked backwards; his Sharps in one arm aimed high while keeping an eye out for any trickery the brothers might try to hatch, but there wasn't any, only their parched and filthy faces completely flummoxed by the ordeal.

Sarah stepped onto the porch, and along with a few bystanders, looked over the back of the brother's heads - everyone watching Tom and Hick while they walked away. She then took a mental note of a different emotion altogether. Earlier it was the eager anticipation of violence. But this new feeling appeared to be contrasted by resolution. It was also coupled with a novel sense of hope; all rippling down her spine, and she liked how she felt.

CONSTABLE ALLEY received an ironic surprise when he brought his high-strung animal to a skidding stop in front of James Shelby who was still sitting on his tobacco barrel. The abrupt halt by the lawman, which spattered a significant amount of mud across the young farmer, was his way of getting Shelby to react, but he didn't react, and Alley found himself taken aback when the man kept to himself, content to be watching slave labor all the while whittling another small willow branch down to the size of a toothpick.

Alley, a man with contempt through and through, shouted from atop his tall mount, "Gotta levy a new debt, Shelby!"

Right then, Shelby jumped atop his barrel and balanced like a circus performer; this time putting the famous Dirk knife on display while shouting, "You! Constable Alley, are the King 'f *Lickskillet*, while I am the "King 'f Diamonds!" And without regard for Alley or any other person, Shelby skillfully brandished the Scottish made war blade used by his daddy's Uncle Isaac to kill many a man - the hero of three wars. "Set foot on my land Augustus Alley, and I'll steal your life!" the farmer promised.

Alley's horse spun, kicking up more mud, but Shelby showed no sign of backing down. Suddenly two of Shelby's slaves raced up from behind him and helped him off his barrel, whispering to him what he seemingly needed to hear in order to calm down. And as the dark men walked their incensed owner away, Alley barked, "Pay up then!" and with that, one of Shelby's slaves; the smaller of the two, fearlessly turned around and delivered a look to Alley that clearly announced only a foolish man would take this petty dispute any further.

TOM AND HICK made their way along Main Street; and after the events of their last mishap, became more than aware of how well to the side they needed to walk in order to remain clear of being injured. This is when Hick declared in earnest, "I do say, Tom, Keech is one mean fucker. Best be mindful round 'em. Stuck a red-hot poker up a cat's ass; two, three times - a cat belongin' to Ol' lady Talbot. It was her *familiar*. Cooked the innereds right up it did."

Tom casually looked the town over and then remarked nonchalantly, "Sage words, Hick, but I'll not fault those boys for their disliking of cats, however I might for how they smelled."

Hick only chuckled, "That's mighty proper of ya, sir. Hunkey-doria some might say, and real polite too, but Ol' Lady Talbot shore faulted 'em. She was a witch, and a seer. Even owned a glass-armonica – like the kind Ben Franklin invented; summoned spirits with it too. That feline folks say was part of her spirit. Some say they'd seen it change into other animals, shadow-people too. You get a look at that scar he sports?"

"I did," said Tom.

"Good, cuz that's where the feline caught 'em with a cycle knife when he wasn't lookin'; inside his mouth. Cut 'em up past his eye. Almost took his ear clean off; scalped the side of his head. That's why he drools like a dog. It's a wonder his head can do any of the things it's spose to."

But Tom's attention was elsewhere when he said, "If you ask me, it sounds like the Talbot woman's the one to watch out for."

"Sounds like you didn't hear me proper, Mr. Tucker. Lady Talbot was across town. Plenny o' folk made plain to her whereabouts at the time Keech got cut."

Tom stopped, looked at Hick and said, "Then perhaps her witch-cat, or what-have-you, should have changed into a bird and flown away."

"Maybe so," said Hick, keeping up his seriousness, "but the cat got the poker and the ol' lady disappeared - she did. Folks looked and looked - fer a long spell - includin' me. And I couldn't find 'er."

That's when Tom started to look a more interested. He knew first hand that Hick's tracking skills were top drawer, and Hick could sense Tom's interest so he continued his argument, "Talk is, Doc Sanders guilted Keech's daddy outta most everything he was worth, which wasn't much, in trade so Keech could eat and talk again. Made 'em start over. After that, the ol' lady went missing."

"Over a cat?" asked Tom, "None of that makes sense."

"That's cuz the whole family's inside blood; generations of it. Sickened minds; all 'f 'em. They can murder and not feel it, so it don't weight on 'em like normal folk - which usually gets 'em caught. And it wasn't just any ol' cat."

"I'll be careful. I promise," said Tom in a tone intended to curb Hick's enthusiasm.

"Good," said Hick and he justly nodded.

"Inside blood you say… ?" asked Tom, "You mean inbred?"

"The big'n, Loren, he come outta his daddy's sister, Mary Ethel after his daddy was lovin' on her. She's dead now. No tellin' who Dart come outta; animal I reckon. He's the scratchy one with the stub fer an arm. Keech was born to a travelin' whore, that's why he's the smartest 'f the bunch, but he's still fulla stupid, and anyone can see that. His daddy took a likin' to the whore after she was with child. Could be why he kept him instead of feedin' 'em to the hogs. The whore left town, makin' *her* the smart one."

"Who they have relations with, Hick," refuted Tom, "is not my concern."

"Well, 'Mr. Dandy Fancyman," said Hick in confidence while spitting, "If you're a likin' Sarah Jones it is. Immortal behavior might not be wise. Keech Hodge is sweet on her. You heard 'em."

"Why would any person think I was interested in that woman," flicked Tom, "because I'm not. Besides, she doesn't like men. That *is* what you informed me of, is it not?"

"I recall, and I'm also gonna recall what you just said the next time she lays her sireen eyes on you. She might not like men all that much, or so it appears because she rarely varnishes her opinion and's never actually been seen with one, but she's double-hard not to look at, and even harder to remove yer eyes from once their set in place – *fine as frog's hair.*" Tipsy, Hick removed his bottle and continued, "Wholesome as she is, Sarah Jones's always been the girl we all secretly dreamed of marryin', but good luck with that notion," and he took another swallow while sending a knowing look to Tom.

"Murder?" asked Tom, more inquisitively, "And without acquiring any guilt or conscience over it?"

"It's also what ain't in the blood, Tom," sputtered Hick; one eye solidly on the Englishman as he upended his bottle.

KEECH and LOREN dozed in the apathetic shade of the general store while two of their hounds did the same under the porch steps. Dart however sat cross legged while digging for Tom's lost candy with a twig in his good hand as the third hound rested at his side, helping him by turning its long, slobbery tongue sideways into the narrows between the planks in hopes of a sugary taste. With every few attempts by the dog, Dart popped it on the nose with a different twig he was holding in his stub, but this action certainly wasn't enough to dissuade the starving hound. It wanted the candy as bad as the boy did.

Directly in front of where the brothers slumbered, a Jenny began to bray as loud as a train whistle. This unrefined howl immediately caused the brothers to rouse.

With sweat pouring from under its saddle, the animal was being tied to the store's hitching post by six-foot six inch, two-hundred-ninety pound, Big John Farley; late-fifties, a ragtag of a farmer who was attached at the hip to his beloved mule *Honey*.

Specifically noteworthy of Farley's worn appearance was his excessively long nose hairs that integrated, meshed and braided their way into his bushy mustache. It was a completely incorporated affair: a work of art. The salt 'n pepper mustache though, was far thicker and longer than the ten days of

184

stubble growing from the rest of Farley's burley and weather-beaten face. And though it may have been a work of art, it was in no way clean or fine. Dried snot and dust, combined with other matter made for an unsightly welcome, but folks were used to it and paid no mind when Big John came around, in particular if he was in a mood to buy. And for as formidable as his presence seemed, Farley wouldn't even harm a roach. And at this moment, could care less that Honey continued her earsplitting assault, especially against the Hodges.

"John Farley!" shouted Keech, "Shut that animal up!"

By now, Honey's bray had driven Loren from his dream state, forcing him to cover his ears. Even the hound that was helping Dart went astray. Farley, who was hard of hearing, whispered in his animal's ear, but Honey kept it up.

"SHUT IT UP!" screamed Keech, but this only caused Farley to shout across at Loren, "Shut yer stupid brother up! I cain't hear the secret Honey's tryin' to tell me!"

"Huh?" sputtered Loren; uncovering his ears, "What su, su, su, SECRET... ?"

Dart chirped, "Secret... ? Tell *me* the secret."

Farley scratched his nose and then pinched into a nostril and jerked out a few hairs that had been causing his nose to itch. He then trundled onto the porch and over Loren's big frame to enter the store where he shot Dart a dumb like a fox look. Only then did Honey finally settle down. With hate in his eyes, Keech ironically stared at the crossbred animal. He then removed a length of twine from his hip pocket, leaned across and tied one end to the post that held up the roof over the porch. Dart and Loren watched as he tugged on it to make sure of its security. Keech gave the nod, and Loren, who was still on his ass, rolled his fat head through the door. Inside, Farley was paying for some eggs that were just being wrapped in newsprint by the shopkeeper.

"Ja, Ja, Ja, John, Fa, Fa FARLEY!" called Loren, "Cu, cuuuu, come qui, ick! Somethin's wra, wra, wrong with Ho, ho, HONEY… !

Naturally concerned, Farley, eggs in hand, immediately exited the store and Keech jerked the twine; catching Farley's foot. The man's big body, along with the eggs, toppled forward; his plunge terminating in a face-plant next to his mule. The boys roared with laughter and the hounds finally got theirs; tearing past the paper to lap up the scrambled mess all the while growling over territorial rights, because getting fed by the likes of a Hodge would never happen. In fact quite the contrary; the fourth mutt that lost its sight from the juice that Black Lily spat was slaughtered and eaten shortly after the incident.

Dart and Loren held Farley's legs while Keech straddled his level torso, but this was no easy task. Farley was a big man, however the fall had winded him and therefore not rightly capable of immediately fighting back.

With his fungus infested toes, Keech pressed Farley's face into the mud; so much so the old man had to fight to breathe, and then he jeered, "Next time, John Farley, do like I say!..."

"Yeah, do like he says," echoed Dart.

By the time the boys allowed Farley up to his knees, he was a completely humiliated man. A man who only a year earlier, promised himself, and Honey, a vow of nonviolence after he'd detected an inhuman state within his own personality; an unhealthiness that would have him harm animals and then miraculously seek out help in the nick-of-time in order to make him the hero, and a savior.

On the morning before his promise, he discovered within him the same perversity to harm a young boy; just a toddler he'd come across while walking alone on the road. He also knew *The Good Lord's Benison* was the only power that could save him from this terrible affliction. So right where he stood, he got down on his knees and swore to never again harm another living thing. He even included flies and misquotes in his declaration: insects he detested. Because for as wrathful as he felt this very moment; debased beyond scope, plastered in the mud that was mixed with the shit 'n piss that Honey just took, he would refrain from hunting down and secretively choking the life out of Keech Hodge for the sake of comeuppance. For he knew he would *not* get him to a doctor in time to save his life. "No Lord," muttered Farley with tears streaming down his face, "I will not kill this boy…"

On Smithland's LOADING DOCKS, Sarah Jones stood before Cran Vardner affixing her name to a document. She then handed the paper back to Vardner who said, "Please deliver our kindest sympathies to yer ma and kin. The Misses and I still feel terrible over yer pa's passin' like he did."

"I will, Mr. Vardner," said Sarah, knowing the man meant well, even though it had been more than three years since her father had died. "We're also grateful to y'all for extending deferred payments on the equipment we procured," she said, "It was mighty helpful, thank you, sir."

Vardner nodded and replied, "All right then," and tried to assist Sarah into her empty wagon, but she politely declined, easily climbing up next to her Uncle John's children who were now on the bench seat beside her.

DART had finally mined Tom's candy from between the planks with enough finesse not to have disturbed Loren who'd gone back to sleep against the wall of the store. Obviously not wanting to share any, he looked around and saw that Keech's attention was also elsewhere, so he popped the hard nibblet into his mouth, and with his tongue and fingers, positioned it perfectly between his last two upper and lower molars and bit down. When Keech heard the tooth crumble, he laughed out loud and without looking, reached down for a piece of dried horse shit and threw it in his brother's face for his efforts, "Yer stupid," he chuckled, "More stupid than him," and he nodded to Loren who was snoring soundly.

on **COURT STREET**; Tom and Hick were relaxing against a dogwood tree; sluggishly enjoying the shade it provided. They'd been watching the commotion between Farley and the Hodge brothers on State Street, but since no gun shots or screams were heard, they decided to leave matters alone. But as soon they closed their eyes, a fashionable new buggy driven by a well dressed couple pulled to a chattering halt on the sun baked earth. With almost military like precision, Hick stood up, but Tom elected to remain seated in the shade; he could care less. Besides it was too damn hot to care about anything, much less a buggy driven by someone who was clearly absent of the skill needed for the operation of such. When the buggy stopped, Ned Buntline, accompanied by a young and stylishly dressed woman, relaxed his stature from behind the reins. This was a man who'd always had a keen and a dangerous nose for a story - regardless of the facts. Tom noted Hick's respectful behavior and decided to rise as well, but much slower. "Hick," called Buntline, "How are ya this glorious day, sir?"

"Just fine Mr. Buntline," replied Hick, always excited to see the writer. "Beautiful animal, sir. You're a fine judge of horse guts."

"Why thank you sir," countered Buntline with sincerity. And though Buntline was only six years Hick's senior, the hunter showed immense respect because he felt Buntline had earned it; even if by iniquitous notoriety, and he wasn't in town all that often. "You look to be travelin'," said Buntline, "just get in… ?

"Yes sir. Procured me a new sportin' rifle and hunted some bounty with it; northeastern areas this time."

"I see," said the writer; leaning over to have a look at the gun lying on the ground by where Tom and Hick had sat. "What're you shootin' now, boy? Should I presume the latest? …"

"Yes sir. Accurate again," replied Hick, "*Sharps '51 breech loader.*"

"A fine looking weapon," he remarked, shifting one eye on-and-off of Tom, "and a fine hunter 'n trailer he is too. I should know. Ned Buntline's the name;

and you *might* be? …"

"No possibilities about it sir," stated Tom firmly, "My name is Thomas Tucker."

"I see. And you *also* might be English?"

Not caring for the author's persistence, Tom openly sized the man up; in particular his buggy, "You are rhetorically accurate, sir."

"Good, good, good," said Buntline, always loving a proverbial spar, "I know everyone in town and most folks beyond. I'm a writer, promoter and a sovereign traveler." Turning to his woman, he looked deep into her almost black eyes and affectionately asked, "Is there somethin' about Mr. Tucker we should be aware of my love?" where upon he turned and looked directly at Tom.

"I don't believe there is, Mr. Buntline," said Tom, now choosing to ignore the man and resume his previous seat against the tree.

Buntline took a deep breath and exhaled with feigned disappointment, "Mr. Tucker, have you ever been to Albany?"

"No sir," replied Tom in short; looking up at the woman who was clearly a station or higher above the man she was sitting next to. "On the other hand, if I should elect to travel to Albany, I will immediately advise you upon my decision; whereby my bags will be packed and ready for your staff to pick-up," all said while looking at the woman whom at first had turned away, but was now actually looking and listening to the Englishman with interest.

Buntline took the exchange in stride, but also noticed his woman looking at Tom with a bit more worth. Therefore he raised an eyebrow and said, "Well then, we'll be off," and he tipped his hat, "Hick ... Mr. Tucker... O, and Mr. Tucker, if at any time you should care to repudiate anything you've said you can find me through *The Gower House*." Buntline then leaned into the lovely female and popped the reins over the animals back. Without a look, he carelessly entered the roadway nibbling on her neck; his horse bumping against a rider on horseback who shouted, "Watch out now! Mind your team!" and he spurred his mount ahead giving the absent minded lovers a wide berth.

As the buggy rolled away, Tom's discomfort was noted by Hick when he heard him say, "Now why would I retract what I told him?"

"Ya know, Tom," said Hick, "I figger whatever you keep private belongs to you--," But before Hick could finish, Tom cut him off, "Indeed it does, sir," and Tom started to walk away.

Hick's always allowed a man his own mind, especially seeing he's had his most of time. And because he and Tom were friends, he did show a tinge of feeling about the remark and the push behind it, but he soon shook it off. To give Tom his private mind was only right.

he soon shook it off. To give Tom his private mind
was only right.

THE TWO MEN walked along Adair Street and once again, a wagon rolled dangerously close. Yet this time it pulled to a safe stop, but not before they were still forced to skip to the other side of the drainage ditch. The driver, Sarah Jones looked down at the two and said sharply "Well? ... Git in."

Tom, more than surprised, looked at Hick who only shrugged as he started for the back of the empty wagon. Sarah shooed the kids off the seat and into the back as well. They had always enjoyed Hick's company and the weary hunter was not about to give up a ten mile ride he might otherwise have to walk; the distance needed to reach the family ferry that crossed the Cumberland River to Dycusburg where he lived. As soon as he got in, the youngsters immediately won him over into showing them a new string game.

Tom on the other hand hesitantly climbed up

front, but before committing to sit beside the hostile woman that nearly killed him just a few hours prior, he stopped to check her profile, but before he could get a clear look under her hat, she snapped the reins causing his ass to drop hard into leaf sprung seat.

DEEP in the CUMBERLAND VALLEY, Tom silently took in the flourishing abundance of the area, whereas Hick remained stretched out in the back of the wagon with the kids playing Jacob's ladder over his prone body while he slept.

Sarah drew rein and brought the wagon to a smooth stop, but when she applied the brake, the small jolt caused Hick to wake up. Sleepy-eyed he said his good byes to the children and clambered out. Tom also started to get down and as he did, tipped his hat, "Miss. Jones… Thank you for your consideration, and the ride. It saved us quite the walk."

Sarah pointed hard in the distance; and with a nervous outline to her already thick drawl, managed to say the words, "Grace Devers!" Tom however, upon reaching the ground, wasn't sure what she'd just said, but did notice she was blushing and was starting to fluster some. With both of them lost for words, Tom saw the possibility of aggression on Sarah's part, so he prepared himself, but instead of an attack, Sarah took a deep breath, collected her thoughts and stated with level precision, "Yonder's the ferry! Two days, *Grace Devers!*" She then knowingly glanced down at Hick and shouted, "Giddap!" and the horsepower once again moved the men to the side. The good-natured children waved goodbye, but their new game was what interested them now.

Hick stepped up to Tom and conveyed, "Well, if that don't prevail over all?"

"Pray tell," responded Tom with a pseudo southern accent, "what's prevailin' now, Hick; a cheddar filled breeze flutterin' about with more counsel on the feminine gender - I reckon? ..."

"She shore likes you boy," said Hick, smiling from ear to ear while side-slipping Tom's bad accent along with his "fart" comment.

"She didn't say but two words the entire way," snipped Tom, looking again at the departing wagon, "Besides we're both not interested, remember?"

"Two words, that's all it takes," said Hick, pulling out his tobacco pouch, "*Grace Devers*, nicest paddle steamer to Nashville."

Tom scratched his beard, "So that's what she said? ..."

"Yes sir. And I also recall what you said."

DYCUSBURG was a small river port settlement uniquely laid out so that her two main streets dead ended at the Cumberland River.

A whistle blew and Tom appeared a bit insecure as he stood by the gang plank of *Grace-Devers*; a beautifully adorned paddle steamer lavishly fitted with every fixture required to entice her city bound cliental to purchase passage. In part, Tom's self-conscious stature was due to the obvious difference between his white, clean shaven face and the rest of his sun darkened complexion; something he'd never seen in a mirror because he hadn't shaved since Buffalo. His grosgrain ribbon was long gone; lost inside the first couple of days of running, along with his shoulder length hair; choosing now to keep it shorter, yet still able to tie it into a ponytail with a rawhide strip: an accessory that helped him blend in better with the rural surroundings.

Not overly concerned about time since being on the run, Tom noticed a man with a watch chain hanging from his vest pocket. He thought about the time piece his father had given him; subsequently lifted by the fur trapper and he asked the fellow for the time, but before the man could pull it, Tom glanced up and saw Sarah approaching in a small buckboard.

"Thirty-one minutes after the hour of nine" the man proudly stated looking at the hands on his watch, but Tom's attention was elsewhere. "Thank you," replied Tom keeping his eye on the wagon as he watched it roll closer.

Dressed in a fashionable, yet modest peach colored sun dress, Sarah's long red hair was neatly tucked under the hat she'd saved nearly two years to buy; finally obtaining it for a mere fraction of its value. Not from the catalog she'd intended to order it from mind you, but through a hardware merchant who'd oddly discovered it amongst a shipment of weaponry he'd ordered. Not the exact sunhat she'd coveted, but sufficient in style and close enough in size so she could feel good about the money she'd saved. This was because the merchant actually gave it to her when he saw how pretty she looked in it, and more so after she'd slipped some flowers under its ribbon.

"Whoa *Terry*," called Sarah, pulling her favorite filly to a controlled stop in front of Tom. Tom ran his hand along the animal, "Miss. Jones," he said, strategically placing the horse between himself and the spirited woman.

"You shaved," she said in a matter of fact tone, "Call me Sarah." Tom offered his hand, but Sarah, unaccustomed to formalities, had to think for a moment, but then took it.

When she climbed down, Tom took note of her horny and callused hands. He could also see that the insides of her forearms were heavily scratched with a sizable scabbed-over scrape from the heel of her wrist to the inside of her elbow; just below the garment's short cotton sleeves; sleeves she'd hemmed up due to the heat and humidity of the region. Regardless of what others thought, Sarah was not about to be uncomfortable in a situation meant to be the opposite. Her life was hard enough; and the few months of labor that Tom had on his hands and arms, by contrast, didn't begin to equate with the toil Sarah had on hers.

On BOARD *Grace-Devers*, her whistles blew followed by the casting of her lines. When the steam power delivered the necessary muscle to her giant paddlewheel, the hull vibrated and she began to move.

Acutely aware that words might spoil the impression, Tom and Sarah, who were equally filled with nervous butterflies, said next to nothing: only muted pardons and tactical pleasantries. Ruining the moment was the last thing either of them wanted to do, so they simply stood along the railing and surveyed the purity of the surroundings as the steamer departed the area.

Splashing their way towards Nashville, the couple warmed up to each other at the same time they casually strolled about the top-deck by the wheelhouse. Sarah enjoyed being treated like a lady; and why not, it was the one thing she'd placed her complete concentration on until the untimely death of her father and the recent illness of her mother; an event which pushed her to quit school in order to keep the family business afloat. Thank the good Lord her older brother David and her sister Mary stepped in to help with their four younger siblings, because if she had to do it alone, either the business or the family would have suffered, but more than likely, both.

Tom continued to be taken in by the painted landscapes that Kentucky had to offer; just as he had when he first laid his eyes on her lands only three days ago. Although Sarah didn't know Tom, she did notice he appeared to be more distant than where his eyes were actually set. She also felt the sexual tension rising up in her loins 'n belly. For the one thing she knew that Tom didn't; *Grace-Devers* could take as long as four days, baring breakdowns and cargo transfers, to complete her roundtrip to Nashville and back.

Inside the ship's busy restaurant, black men in white uniforms cleared and set tables for their white patrons; some of which were impatient gambler's who couldn't wait to lose their holdings to the card sharks one deck below. Therefore rudely staring the servants down in hopes their table magically cleared itself so they could be seated sooner was all they could do. And for as bad-mannered and arrogant as these white folk often behaved toward the Negro help, they also knew to never raise a hand to them or they would suffer the consequences of the boat pilot: the all mighty lord and master while the ship was in service on the water. Tom and Sarah sipped on cocktails from a window table and watched the vastly separated farms and fields as they passed on by. When a large barge passed on the port side of the ship, it caused the paddle steamer's smooth motion to suddenly become affected. In no time Tom looked queasy, but Sarah, completely unchanged by the gentle sideward tipping thought to herself, Dang it! I did it again. I'm too dern forceful. This poor man becomes unwell on the water. Now he probably thinks I'm a real mule-hole fer influencin' him on this journey.

"Sarah, will you excuse me please?" asked Tom getting up from the table a bit wobbly. Sarah nodded 'n held the tablecloth and the drinks while Tom stepped away thinking to himself; It's confirmed, I'm a bloody *skirt* for becoming ill so easily.

Tom made his way to the restaurant door that led to the ship's rail; a familiar place he'd spent many-an-hour wishing to God he were dead. Yet to retch and vomit was an activity he'd still rather not have strangers witness. Aboard *Helena* you see, nearly everyone became sick from her motion at one time or another, even the captain, and to witness a passenger or crew member with their head hung over the side only brought the two closer at some later point, but this was not sea travel, and Tom didn't see any other passengers who were sick. So with his stomach on the rise, he recalled reading how some of these larger river vessels had actual facilities for relieving one's self. Dry heaving, he quickly asked a passing steward for such a facility. The dark man kindly turned him in the proper direction and guided him along a short corridor to a state-of-the-art washroom. Once inside; not having breakfast, Tom hung his head over the pot and coughed up the little bit of whisky in his stomach. He also knew he mustn't allow these kinds of intoxicated interactions to continue, no matter how small the drink. He accurately sensed that under Sarah's repose, her possession and ability to dredge from him that which he must not say was completely possible.

📖

KNOWN TO BE SELF CONSCIOUS about her smile, Sarah grinned from ear to ear as Tom escorted her down the gangplank on a short stop to Nashville. Conversely, Tom liked Sarah's smile just fine, yet refrained from commenting on it. By American standards, Sarah's teeth and smile were actually quite pleasant to look at. The English consequently had different ideas about dental hygiene; but in Tom's case, his teeth were good and strong; if not by heredity, then certainly by the fact he'd never troubled with sugar in his tea, or sweets in general for that matter, so caring for them had always been rather easy.

With his land legs back, Tom naturally brightened when city life was anticipated. Nonetheless, he was always concerned with accidentally saying too much; giving reason for further inquiry. This concern contrasted by Sarah's reluctance, willing or otherwise, to engage in idle chitchat was first on Tom's mind; and why he was enjoying her company. Another was that he was unquestionably attracted to her. She was small, curvy, strong, and possessed a most balanced and proportioned backside. Not one ounce of fat; and not one shred of deceit on Hick's part when he'd informed him that Sarah was doubly hard to take one's eyes off of; face or features once her gaze had been set and, that she was *'fine as frog's hair'*. Lastly, Tom had not been this close to a woman since loving Amanda the night before he departed Albany. So in short, Sarah's innate attractiveness, together with her unwillingness to speak without having something definitive to talk about, was to say the least, a breath of fresh air to Tom.

Not to stray too far from the steamer, or a getaway path if need be, Tom and Sarah enjoyed a barefoot walk along a wide stretch of the Cumberland River.

"Come 'n sit," Sarah said and she led Tom by the hand to a dry place in the sand. Tom mentally questioned the order, but still accepted her hand and sat down. Sarah came around behind him and scooted in close. She stretched her legs out alongside his so that Tom could see her ankles and calves. They were white and covered in soft, corn-silk like reddish-blonde hair. While this action naturally forced Tom to visualize the lush garden where this tartlet's golden leg hair terminated, he began to feel a pair of hands manipulate his neck and shoulder muscles. Sarah's own action caused her feet and toes to wiggle and cure akin to a kneading cat and she knew this was *swim or die.* Either this man understood the value of such an action, or he was inept as the others. The others being, anytime Sarah saw an opportunity to please a perspective suitor with her limited knowledge of the sensual arts; learned by way of a book she secretly ordered through a madam she'd made the acquaintance of, it was taken advantage of. However she always performed these acts, innocent as she felt them to be, as far away from where she lived as possible. This was because her mama eloquently taught her that, *"makin' honey where wasps live always led to problems"*. Her daddy though, wasn't as articulate and would plainly say, *"shittin' in yer own kitchen always leads to a smelly mess."* So between the two, Sarah gleaned a clear understanding of what a blossoming young woman could do, and where not to do it.

To please a receptive mate; and to be pleased in kind had always been an important aspect of any happy life she might hope to attain. And though Sarah was only eighteen, she knew full well she would not remain ripe forever. There were too many stubborn women falling un-triumphant to prettier females who knew how to beguile a man with what they possessed between their legs.

She also learned early on that men were intrinsically uncomplicated and strongly felt there were two simple ways to keep one from straying. First, make sure he stayed fed and that he liked your cooking over any other woman's; and two, keep his manhood and his nostrils desirous of his woman's touch and scent; with the latter being the most important: for she'd learned that touch and smell was most important. And where this burgeoning relationship currently stood; the couple's pheromones were interacting quite nicely as they sat close.

Out of sorts some with Sarah's beckon, Tom soon melted into her skillfully strong hands. So much so that he couldn't help the bulge from rising in his pants and the wet spot that followed as she kneaded the flesh and muscles around his neck like biscuit dough. Sarah noticed Tom's response; and his quiet dissolve made her happier than he could ever know. The look on her face, while pleasing him was a sensation her facial muscles had been waiting to feel and experience; a sensation that informed the rest of her body and soul that she'd found a man who knew how to receive the touch of a strong, yet loving woman. Sarah was deeply satisfied over this seemingly simple act of open reception on Tom's part.

But Tom was not always like this; however loving Amanda as deeply as he had, had taught him the importance of accepting the strengths a woman had to offer. He soon discovered that a woman needed this as much as food or air. He also learned that a man; who could be vulnerable, was a man that women found difficult to resist.

TOPSIDE, while Tom and Sarah leaned against the starboard railing and looked across at Dycusburg; her houses and businesses resting along the southern edge of the Cumberland, the mariners of *Grace-Devers* began the docking process. Lines were cast and her rigging was secured. The paddle steamer finally came to a complete stop and the two sighed with relief. They were back.

CHAPTER nine
1855

HICK stepped from the door of Cobb's Mercantile onto the board planking. He was back in his home town of Dycusburg and dressed in new garments. He also had an up-to-the-minute copy of Walt Whitman's, *Leaves of Grass* tucked under his arm like a bible; a book he'd eagerly anticipated the publishing of for some time.

While admiring his reflection in the store's window panes, two scruffy twelve year olds: Isaac Martin and Enoch T. Potts stopped to comment: "Lacy new shoes, Hick," said Enoch sarcastically, "Goin' to a meetin'?" Isaac on the other hand chose to remain silent. And though these boys were streetwise and uncombed most of the time, they belonged to local families. And for as neglectful as these families might sometimes appear towards their children, they weren't breaking any laws and they still held a measurement within the community.

"Well, well," sparked Hick with the look of play in his eye, "If it ain't Isaac Martin and his pet toad, Enoch T. Potts. Sure as a duck shits, Enoch, if you'd quit cher pilferin', you might one day save enough to buy yerself a pair; so to cover those toad like members sproutin' out below yer ankles."

Enoch paid no mind to the epitome of common sense and slithered toward the mercantile to do just that: slip inside unnoticed and pinch a piece of hard candy. But as he passed, Hick tripped him and he banged his head on the shop's door at the same time Morris, the forty-something, apron wearing proprietor opened it. Hick took a nip from his small bottle; direct from *Oscar Pepper's Distillery*; one of his favorites when he was on the home front. He then placed his hand on the Martin boy's shoulder and drew him back to watch the fun. Morris grabbed Enoch by the scruff of his neck and trousers, lifted him up and tossed him down the rough planked walkway where he skidded to a stop on all fours. It was a good-sign the planks were running perpendicular to the direction the boy was pitched otherwise Enoch would be working slivers as big as toothpicks from his hands and knees for weeks.

In the midst all this, Pete Skimerhorn, an early-sixties farmer and part time pastor at the newly built Baptist church in Pinckneyville, along with his wife Rebecca, pulled to a stop in their buckboard. The Skimerhorns watched as the Potts boy picked himself up from the splinter infested cross planks with the anticipation that Morris would run after him, but Morris, in respect of the pastor and his wife, refrained from the deed he'd love to exercise. Therefore he only shouted, "Run boy, run! It's almost day!"

Morris then turned to Isaac who was still in front of Hick with his head hung low. The boy's eyes eventually looked up, revealing as much hope and prayer as he could muster that Morris, known for his temper, would abstain from chucking him down the slivered walkway like he did his friend. In any other circumstance he certainly would, but Hick had a firm hold on Isaac's shoulders and Morris knew better than to remove anything from another man's possession without first asking, especially Hick's. So Morris opted to scold the boy with less contempt, "Don't you get any stupid ideas, Isaac Martin, or folk'll be shoutin' that nigger talk your direction. Now you git!"

In an attempt to thank Hick before Morris changed his mind, Isaac looked up at the man that kept him close and then quickly turned. As he did, Morris kicked hard for the boy's back side, barely missing it along with Hick's face; sending his shoe skyward where it banged against the overhang and landed next to Hick. Hick chuckled as Isaac shuffled away, grateful Morris' boot failed to make contact. For the last time it did, he returned home with a black 'n blue mark so big the boy had to falsify the facts to his folks; saying that he'd gotten dim and walked too close behind a pregnant donkey.

"Mornin' Pastor," said Morris, "Mrs. Skimerhorn," tipping his faux hat.

"Mornin', Morris," said Skimerhorn, but the pastor's wife, Rebecca, just acknowledged Morris with the nod of her head. She didn't care for Morris, or the way he treated children, no matter their behavior.

Hick cheerfully announced, "Mornin', Pastor," and removed his new, short brim hat. He placed it over his heart and addressed the Pastor's wife, "Ma'am..."

"Mornin', boy," Skimerhorn said with infectious solicitation.

"How are ya, Hick?" replied Rebecca.

"Feelin' mighty fine ma'am. Acquired me some new Sunday attire; long overdue." But Hick wasn't sure about his new hat, "Y'all like it?" he asked, adjusting the head cover for the couple, but mostly for the female in the crowd.

"I like it just fine," said Mrs. Skimerhorn.

Hick then cheated his body some towards the Pastor who turned embarrassed and said, "I don't know Hick, it's just a hat fer goodness sake."

With that, Morris gestured his departure and returned to the inside of his store. Hick turned to find one more piece of window pane to admire himself in; something he was rarely in the right circumstance for. And though he looked rather naive doing it, he still did it without any sense of shame.

"You look ready fer a meetin'," remarked the Pastor.

"Ah now," said Hick while gazing at his reflection and holding his new book, "You know how I feel about that sir. As much as I like yer new cleric building; my God ain't in no church."

"I know, I know," said the pastor in a way that told Hick he had no intention of pushing his religious viewpoint any further, "I didn't stop fer that. Now listen boy," he continued and he leaned in close, "I don't wanna stir an uprisin', but Big John Farley's gone missin', and it feels suspect. He's been tradin' with those Natives on the mountain again."

"Ah Pete," said Hick, still admiring his image, "He'll turn up."

The pastor took off his hat and said, "I know he's a few lines removed, but I'm all the kin he has."

Innocently Hick turned and faced the Skimerhorns; his thumbs proudly pressing-out the lapels of his new jacket, "You know *Honey* always gets him home, and keeps him warm."

"O Hick," chaffed Mrs. Skimerhorn, turning her head in disgust.

The Pastor however, knew how Hick was and paid no mind to his wife's imagined upset, but he did shoot a hangdog look towards him in hopes to retrieve some understanding from the master tracker.

"Alright Pete," said Hick giving in, "If he don't turn up, I'll set out fer a look."

"Thank ya, Hick. Thank ya," whereupon Rebecca patted her husband's shoulder. She's the kind of woman who could be grateful for a man like Hick when he was needed, but would rather not let him know it. Especially if it meant losing any control of her ma - the one thing she would never allow to happen.

CHAPTER ten
TILINE, (Tileen)

Under a GIANT PECAN TREE, Terry stood at rest while harnessed to Sarah's buckboard. Tom, who'd been laying face down on an Indian blanket, propped himself up to his elbows and with both hands cupped, began to practice his mourning dove call, "Coo ye coo…, coo coo…." And when he heard a shotgun blast, he didn't even flinch; even after leaves and twigs fell on him. Sarah stepped up and dropped a squirrel next to three others and a rabbit. She then set her *hammerless needle-fire shotgun* down; still a rather new weapon; given to her by her late father because she was the only one who had the willingness to learn it's features, as well as how to load it properly in order to hunt small game without obliterating the entire animal.

Tom quelled his calls. He flipped to his back and cheerfully mocked, "What's for dinner my darling?" Sarah sat down cross legged with Tom's head close to her lap. While looking at nothing in particular, she began massaging his neck 'n shoulders and as soon as she did, Tom lowered his head and melted.

She then remarked, "I like how you smell when

you come home from a huntin' spree with Hick.

"Like horse shit and pine needles?" replied the tranquil man.

"No," said Sarah, and she bent over at the waist and burrowed her nose into Tom's armpit, "Mumm... like cinnamon and sugar. Manful 'n virile," she murmured, and she sat back up, "Intoxicatin' ... ... Makes my head - woozy..."

Sarah always liked the sound of her own voice, especially when it came to sex with Tom, so she worked her way down his physique, past his shoulders and onto his chest. Tom always softened when Sarah got drunk on his scent. She'd manipulate her strong fingers into him. In turn, this made him feel breathtakingly powerful while not having to lift a finger. Just lie back, smell bad and enjoy it.

Smiling big, Sarah said, "You shore knocked Uncle John over when you so politely asked him if you could marry me. Whooey! He didn't see that one comin'."

Tom rolled to one elbow and looked up at the woman, "What do you mean? We both knew he expected it; especially since your mother just passed. He was completely open to the idea. Besides it was the proper to thing do."

"Maybe so," she chuckled, full of vim, "but it was still like a ball-shot to his head when he heard the words."

Sarah's remark all of a sudden brought up the shootings on the train for Tom, "I see," he said.

"Tom... ?"

"Mmm...,"

"When can we move in together?" she asked, "The cabin's almost done and I'm the only one left of my direct kin not married or moved out." Sarah then reached over and grabbed a sumptuous handful of Tom's ass.

"You've already moved in on that," he said, swatting her hand away unconvincingly, "besides, you sneak over every night."

"I don't sneak over – anymore..." she responded.

"Moreover," he continued, "you practically live there."

"So what if I do. Uncle John don't care."

"He doesn't now," said Tom, "but he did. And we're both lucky you didn't end up my shotgun bride. You do remember – don't you?"

"I recall," she said, smiling fondly, "on *Grace-Devers*?"

"Yes," snipped Tom, "on *Grace-Devers*. And I'm sure you remember how conveniently you refrained from informing me that our one day trip was in truth a four day excursion. Listen Sarah, I know we're of an acceptable age difference, but when we met; for as lovely as you looked, you appeared far younger. We could have been asked a lot of questions. Could we not have requested a bundling-board or something in order to gain some insight into our compatibility? How on earth did I allow you to take me on a four day boat adventure? I'd only known you for three days, and I abhor boats and traveling on the water."

"Cuz you didn't know it took four days, that's how. And how was I to know you didn't like boat rides? Would it have mattered?"

Tom was about to respond, but before he could, Sarah adjusted his head downward and leaned in close. She took in the scent from behind his neck, in turn causing her to start kneading the flesh of his ass through his trousers, "Are you regrettin' it?" she asked; her voice, low and seductive.

Tom was near his place of abandon and sighed, "Well, I ..."

"Are you penitent over me pullin' and sucklin' on yer hard prick for those four days?" This last inquire was timed perfectly as she dragged her fingers up the back of his pant leg to locate the bulge he was lying on. When she gently parted his legs and diddled her fingers deeper, Tom moaned deeper. "Are you regrettin' me working my fingers into your tired, knotted muscles like this, 'n makin' 'em let go? Are you repentin' my actions Mr. Tucker?"

"No Sarah, I'm not," answered Tom firmly, his words muted some by the blanket, "but we can't move in together until we marry, and I can't be having your cunny in that way either. If you become with child, we'll have people pointing fingers at us for as long as we live here."

"Fine," said the woman, but a girl has more than one hole ya know.

"People're talking and have been for months," upheld Tom. Then he flopped over to his back and looked up at her concerning her last comment. Because for as aroused as Sarah's words and actions make him, he absolutely knew he mustn't yield to her wooing ways before they get married; ways that could get him captured and perhaps hanged.

Sarah allowed the words to pass, but continued to engage temptingly close, "Tom?" she asked with even more seduction.

"Mmm..."

"Who 'm I marryin'? ..."

"Sarah... for the love of Christ --"

"I certainly hope so," she wryly exclaimed...

"For the hundredth time, you are marrying the only man *I* know of who can love you the way you need to be loved.

"I know you love me good, Tom, but I cain't help but feel there's a part of you locked away in another land."

Tom reached up and pulled Sarah in close. He took in some of her neck and hair scent and softly said, "There is more to me my love - and you. This is what's grand about marriage; is it not? Growing old together? Discovering all those amazing little things about each other - over a life time?"

Seemingly satisfied, Sarah cooed, "I reckon...", and she stretched out alongside Tom where together they looked up through the dark, majestic branches that contrasted the light blue sky, "Absolutely heaven," she said. Sarah then cocked herself to an elbow and began diddling the hair around Tom's navel. Skillfully she worked her hand under his waist line and gently took ownership of what she claimed to be hers. Tom closed his eyes and breathed in the clean, sweet air of Kentucky. Sarah on the other hand, unimpeded, scooted down for an intimate encounter with her granite-like possession.

INSIDE THE OFFICES of the *North-Western Police Agency* in Chicago, meetings were taking place, documents were shuffling from desk to desk and the general atmosphere was authoritative and expectant. Secretaries, clerks, and agents alike, were all moving about with something important to do.

Inside an executive office with a marginal view of the city's promising skyline, the *'We Never Sleep'* (big eye logo) could easily be seen through the frosty glass on the door. Agents Timothy Webster and his current partner, Agent Kate Warne; a mid-twenties, slender built woman dressed in stylish yet comfortable attire and donning short brown curls were sitting in large chairs across from a mid-thirties Scottish born Allan Pinkerton. Pinkerton, an able bodied man with a full beard less the mustachio commanded his operation with an iron fist. He closed a brown file folder and in a thick, barely discernable brogue stated, "When the political climate changes, I'll send word," and he passed the folder to Webster, "New York still has it out for him, and so does this firm."

In turn, Webster briefly looked at the file, but already knowing what it contained passed it to Warne, "I still have it out for him, sir," claimed Webster, "We'll capture Tweddle. You can be certain of it."

Hick GALLOPED a beautiful two-year old openly towards the giant pecan tree. In a cloud of dust, he reined the animal to a hard stop and surprised an entwined Tom 'n Sarah when he shouted, "John Farley!"

Tom sat up and flipped the blanket over Sarah's beet red ass. Embarrassed, Sarah quickly pretended to be brushing bugs off her and Tom.

"Brute Muley just found 'em" shouted Hick," Come quick!

With the Indian blanket wrapped around the couple, Tom and Sarah worked their way up to sitting.

In control of his nervous mount, Hick again called, "Forgive my startlin' y'all," and he spurred the animal, setting out as fast as he rode in.

In a **QUAINT and SHADY HOLLER**, unpinned hogs and chickens roamed freely within the proximity of a one room cabin and a distant backhouse covered with some six inches of peat moss on its roof and a moisture sodden door. Locals had been arriving on horseback and wagons for the past two hours, and the few that lived close by or had no transport could be seen walking in.

On the side of the cabin, Farley's mule, *Honey* was hanging from the branch of a Catalpa tree by her hind legs - skinned. The only hair remaining on the carcass was on her head 'n tail and a few inches around her hooves. Her excessive weight had caused the thin yet strong tree to torque over, akin to a cane pole with a fish on. Her eyes had bulged out from the inward pressure of the fluids attempting to escape and the buzzing of insects along with the fetor of exposed meat strongly prevailed. A few inches from her nose was a pool of blood with the texture of warm pudding; and the curious talk of 'who?' was quickly being passed around by the locals. Tom and Sarah could be seen arriving in their buckboard while Hick brought up the rear on horseback.

On the other side of Farley's cabin stood a poorly built, square-box that surrounded a well hole. There, six men peered over the sides into the darkness below. Suspended over the hole was an improvised conical of wooden supports with a rope and pulley for lifting water, and if necessary, heavier objects like buckets of mud or rocks should the well fill in.

Four additional men had hold of the rope and they began to pull. A few seconds into their draw, two arms reached over the side of the box and up popped Leo Brewer gasping for air. Covered in muck from head to toe, he leaned his torso over the wall and dry heaved his guts out, "Lordy! It's bad," he gurgled, barely getting the words out.

Tom and Hick joined the men on a second rope that was still at the bottom of the well. Sarah however, elected to stand back as these healthy souls heaved-ho. The wooden supports over the well hole strained and the lashings around the pulley frayed, but eventually John Farley's body appeared, feet first, wrapped in the bloody rug of Honey's hide. All persons gathered were taken aback by the mordant stench that accompanied the putrefaction of the big man's enveloped remains; so much so that the men holding the rope, including Tom and Hick, began to lose their grasp; having to catch themselves before the nearly five-hundred pound package dropped the sixty-plus feet back into the hole.

Others came forward to help, but mostly to watch while they held their noses and mouths. Efforts to prevent their retching were to no avail. Both men and women alike stepped to the side to get sick in the bushes. Some couldn't move fast enough, throwing-up where they stood.

As the men grappled with the draped corpse so to maneuver it over the wall, Sarah worked her way through the crowd and up to Tom and Hick. She too had her mouth covered and her nose pinched to prevent the smell from causing her to retch, but it didn't work either. And though Sarah's always had a strong stomach when it came to skinning and cleaning game, the line appeared to be drawn when it came to the carcass of a man pulled from the bottom of a muddy well, all while wrapped in the hide of a not so freshly skinned mule. Therefore, before she could reach them, she too headed for the bushes to pitch her lunch. Tom on the other hand seen and smelled so much death aboard ship, that to see John Farley like this didn't affect him that much. Also, not knowing the man personally helped, but to see the giant wrapped up like this *was* disturbing, and therefore it did cause him to gag some, but the solid ground beneath his feet appeared to be the antidote. For if he were to have witnessed a sight like this on the ocean; or on any water for that matter, all bets would be off for holding in his guts.

After wiping the spittle and snot off her face with her dress, Sarah finally made it up to the men and blubbered, "Mercy Tom, it looks like Injun work.

Tom scrutinized her words and the scene for a few moments and then shook his head, "No. I'm certain they know better."

Protests in favor of and against a 'punishing party for the Natives could be heard from those gathered.

Hick walked over and whispered to Tom, "You thinkin' what I'm thinkin'?"

Sarah overheard Hick and leaned in, "Just what *are* you two thinkin'?"

A local man spoke up, "Let's track 'em!"

Another man's voice shouted, "There's an encampment on the ridge north o' Salem!"

With hysteria mounting, the slaves that were ordered to come along had quietly moved to the back of the crowd. They looked nervous, and by rights should be. A few of the elders had witnessed incidents like this before. If the crowd couldn't be satisfied with a death, virtuous or otherwise, an instigator would set out and lynch a nigger or two before supper and call it 'justice'; regardless of who owned the guiltless man; all so the moral and unblemished could sleep better at night.

A woman shouted, "There're only women and children on that ridge!"

Another man yelled, "God hating Savages!

Burn 'em all!"

Tom stepped onto the tattered porch and raised his hands for the crowd to stop, especially the overheated men, but they weren't having any. And with each distorted curse they became more 'n more agitated. BOOM! … Everyone jumped and turned towards the blast. From the porch, Tom looked over the back of everyone's heads to see Sarah, her shotgun pointed skyward with a cloud of white smoke in the air, "Y'all listen to my man now!" she shouted.

Robert Mathers, a weak-minded troublemaker chose to engage, "We don't have to listen to no women."

Voices, mostly the men's, agreed in loud protest. So Sarah set her gun down and reached for Hick's sporting rifle. The hunter watched the heated woman; about the only person he knew of capable of getting away with such an act without serious injury, inspect it, cock it and fire it - BOOM! … Dead silence … Then in one fluid motion, she pitched it back to him, grabbed up Tom's Indian trade rifle, cocked it and pointed it up. This weapon however, was much heavier, so Hick finally called out, "Y'all best listen now!"

Locals had seen this kind of behavior before from Sarah, so the crowd simmered some. Sarah's long time motto had always been, 'a club for the dumb'.

227

From here on matters would only get worse and everyone knew it. Without compunction, the lighter side of Sarah A. Jones would walk right up to the loudest mouth in the bunch and slap it shut just as hard as she slapped the hound that was sniffing her ass on the day she met Tom. This; sadly or otherwise was the self determined force that many of the women in the crowd wished they held. "All right, Tom," said Brute Muley, "Tell us what's on yer mind. We need to git to it." Muley's words were acknowledged by the crowd, so they simmered and waited.

"Alright, Brute, alright," agreed Tom, "That's fair."

Tom stood tall and Sarah watched to make sure they all kept their mouths shut. She had lowered Tom's rifle and thanked Hick with a wink for speaking up. She didn't know how much longer she could hold the heavy mussel air born before looking stupid - and this Hick knew.

"I know I haven't lived here as long as most of you," Tom began with, "but I believe you know me.

Tom's stature and constitution alone was enough for these folks to listen with a more tuned ear, nevertheless the crowd did sputter some.

"You know me to be of sound mind and Spirit. So when I say to you, the Red people on the ridge had no part in this, I need you all to trust my words."

Tom looked at Blanch Mathers, the woman who shouted in defense of the Natives, but the crowd grumbled strongly with disagreement. Even so, for as strongly as they were at odds, there was still something innate within the majority that did not want to commit a similar act of horror upon another. So except for the two or three that talked tough, these people were mostly farmers, not soldiers, and the few that did spout off were cowardly in nature and usually committed their acts out of sight; which lowered cause for those in attendance to disbelieve Tom's words. "Blanch is correct," argued Tom, "I've been to the Native encampment and there is no healthy man or two capable of this act."

Blanch elbowed her husband Robert in the solar plexus hard enough to render him temporarily out of hot air. She also shot a fast look to Sarah who missed nothing, and in turn sent the Mathers woman a knowing glint back.

Leo Brewer, who was standing soundly to the side due to the repulsive reek radiating off the mud on his clothes called out, "Hey Tom? Who then do you think committed this?"

The crowd respected the question. They stood waiting, and so did Leo who was about to fall over from the weight of the sludge that covered him.

Yards away, yet within earshot, Dart and Keech

Hodge watched from behind a thicket.

Tom calmly continued, "We all need to study this death carefully. No passing humbugs. No innocent lives sacrificed. We do this so that those who perpetrated this act are the ones that hang indeed of the act."

In the back of the crowd, the slaves began to relax some as Tom appeared to be getting through to the crowd. Although these dark subjects had no schooling, they certainly understood what it meant when the words, "No innocent lives sacrificed" were spoken to an imminent lynch mob, and the mob actually responded.

Blanch Mathers asked, "What's a humbug, Tom?"

"Rumors, Blanch; hearsay. In this case, false words that cause the loss of blameless life."

Robert Mathers whispered to his wife, "I knew that." But Blanch had come to the conclusion that her husband of seven years didn't know very much at all, and that he tended to be a follower rather than a man who adjusted himself to the common vein of humanity: a man that would never operate alone, but weak enough, that within erroneous company, combined with poor timing, might act with righteous indignation and take an innocent life for an unproven crime. For this, among other insurrections, Blanch would file for

the dissolution of their marriage inside the next
eighteen months. A Kentucky judge denied her
petition on the grounds that her unhappiness was not a
strong enough argument. So she took it upon herself
to secretly travel to Philadelphia where a distant
relative resided - never to return.

The crowd took Tom's words into serious
reflection. They trusted Tom. They always had; from
the moment they first met him.

In the bushes, Dart whispered, "Lordy Keech,
they're gonna lynch us fer this. Why'd we come back."

"Cuz I wanted to cut the ol' fucker more,"
rebuked Keech, wiping his knife off on some leaves,
"We kilt no one, so shut yer hole, I'm thinkin'." But
Dart was scared, "Them folk're too mad to care he was
dead before we showed."

It was obvious the brothers felt concern and
would clearly like nothing better than to have the town
folk blame the act on the Natives.

A voice in the crowd spoke up, "Do you know
who did this, Tom? Are you suspect to who kilt Big
John?"

Dart and Keech listened intently. They both
knew they had to remain still or the likes of Hick or
Sarah would hear them and it would all be over but the
uproar.

Tom answered with certainly, "I believe we've

all seen John Farley's killers in our daily passing." He then sent a covert look to Hick and in turn received a stealth acknowledgement back.

The crowd turned aghast when they heard that murderers such as these could be living amongst them.

Keech pushed the point of his blade quietly into its sheath and whispered, "Lafeet and Fancyman – Daddy'll want us to take care 'f 'em.

CHAPTER eleven
NORMAN HODGE

DARK 'n DANK; the only words that correlated perfectly to describe this holler and the dwellings that barely stood within it.

At the narrow opening to the area, fallow and some tall, green weeds camouflaged rusty farm debris standing along side piles of dry rotted lumber where wild cats could be seen roaming for any unsuspecting vermin or a possible snake.

Under a rat infested cabin laid a mud trough where dogs cooled out, chickens pecked, mosquitoes bred and hogs rooted around the timber stilts.

Nailed to the sides of the cabin, along with the chicken coop, the outhouse and a small barn that doubled as a place where the brothers performed their unkindness upon animals and each other were sawmill slats; split and otherwise, held fast with horseshoe nails. The nails, mostly bent over due to the inaccuracy of the individual that had swung the hammer, created an artless form that covered nearly every opening; large and small, inside and out.

Two soiled and gritty looking identical twin

girls in their early-teens sat on the porch wearing nothing more than flour sacks. One was undeniably pregnant and agitated with expectancy while the other appeared cross-eyed and unresponsive. They were holding hands as best they might when taken into account how severely webbed their hands were.

A second later Loren Hodge lurched out the front door of the cabin and landed face down in some pig shit. The boy's fifty-two year old bull terrier of a daddy, Norman, stepped onto the porch. Dressed solely in pantaloons that were shredded below the knees and hitched up by suspenders that had never seen soap; he bit and frothed like a rabid badger, "You fat chunka shit! Why I kept you I cain't figger! Shoulda fed yer bloody mess to the hogs when my sister pushed you out - like a turd!" The twins sat unaffected by the man's anger. "If them two ain't back by sundown," roared Hodge, "I'm a gonna slit yer sack and feed the big 'n to yer hungry sister!"

Loren only stared at the pig shit and shook. Farsighted like he was, he could clearly make out the maggots crawling on his hand, but he dare not say a word, or meet his daddy's eye. He knew he'd do it. He committed the same act on Dart while the boy was sleeping off a moonshine drunk one night; slit his sack, cooked the nut and fed it to the now pregnant twin. She ate it like a chewy gizzard and swallowed it before

Dart knew what happened. She was starving and Norman, who orchestrated the ordeal, laughed so hard he herniated himself. "You bring 'em back!" he bellowed, "fer a beatin' and a fuckin', you hear me! Or else I'll cook yer oyster! Both maybe!"

With that, the old man clamped onto the cross-eyed girl's arm and without looking back, dragged her inside and slammed the door so hard the nails that were holding the hinges to the jam loosened even more. The pregnant twin remained seated and between the periodic and uncomfortable movements of the baby, simply stared beyond the apathetic void, awaiting her turn with the devil's nephew.

CHAPTER twelve
PLOT Holes 'n Knot HOLES

ON THE GROUNDS of the Dycusburg Cemetery, Tom and Sarah strolled amongst the vastly separated grave markers and tombstones. This area felt to be a rather new consign to plant folk in; perhaps created by visionaries for an impending war.

Near the center of the grounds, two men with shovels were just beginning the process of digging a hole. Seemingly beyond that were some family monuments along with a few granite slabs, a hand full of crosses and some rock piles dotting the landscape. It was there, close to the tree line, that Hick was conducting a shooting match with a few other men. One by one, each man took aim, fired and by the look on his face, missed his mark. It was a fair distance from where they stood to where their targets rested; melons atop sticks rammed into the ground.

Tom and Sarah walked up to the group holding hands. It was Hick's turn to shoot, "C'mon, Tom, you 'n me together. How 'bout it?"

Tom was going to wait his turn, but looked at the others for their permission. Without argument, the others happily gestured, 'Go ahead', and they chuckled, 'This should be good'.

"Alright," said Tom and he picked up his J. Henry from the Indian blanket it was laying on. He loaded the receiver with a paper cartridge, pushed a .44 caliber projectile into the barrel and then pulled out the rod and rammed the package home. He completed the procedure by placing a percussion cap on the head of the hammer. Almost like soldiers, Tom and Hick dropped to a knee, cocked their guns, aimed and fired. As soon as they did, the surrounding air was filled with a giant cloud of white smoke. Four-hundred feet away however, two melons exploded at the same time like heads on horseman. The men that were leaning on their weapons like spade handles; the ones that believed this was going to be nothing more than a drinking party, now stood tall, fully awed by the display of plain-speaking, no nonsense marksmanship.

As it turned out, a number of these men came to Farley's service not because they knew Big John, but because they'd heard Hick Shelby was putting on a shooting match. They wanted to witness firsthand the potential of his marksmanship. The potential turned out, that in the end; Hick took money from every man in attendance, except Tom.

A man called out in jest, "How do we know the balls didn't cross in mid-flight and Hick didn't shoot yer melon, Tom?"

"Because," said Tom smiling big, "I loaded my *Henry* with a wad. Hick shot them both. Go see for yourselves." The men laughed hard and that's when Hick leaned into Tom and whispered, "Thank God for windage 'n muzzle riflin', cuz it'll be over fer them brothers just that fast."

Whereas the locals milled about looking at grave markers, shovels continued to throw dirt from Farley's plot. The men doing the digging were deep enough now to where only the tops of their heads could be seen.

Conservative folk, the majority of which were elderly women dressed in black, congregated together. These were the children of God who attended out of obligation to save the soul of John Farley. For without them and their silent prayers, the big man's essence would never locate the path to where Saint Peter waited to judge him.

Down another path; a trail more tangible in nature, Pastor Skinerhorn and his wife Rebecca approached in their wagon. Tied down in the back was an unadorned rectangular pine box that contained the remains of John Farley. Ned Buntline followed in his buggy, but his lovely counterpart would not be in attendance. This didn't set well with Ned. In fact, it down right exasperated him that she was so faint-of-heart about matters that he himself considered quite the norm: like death. But alas, he loved her dearly and in order to conduct the brand of relations he preferred, he allowed her the lead she required; relations surrounding his desire to be held accountable for his dastardly behavior in a rather subordinate manner.

As soon as Skimerhorn pulled to a stop, several men took to offloading the coffin, but because it was so heavy and built without handles, they quickly lost their grasp, allowing the front-end to bang hard on the ground. Skimerhorn turned his head for a moment and then paid the slip-up no further mind.

A number of women gathered around Rebecca Skimerhorn to offer their condolences. She played the part of the grieved relative well, but anyone who knew Rebecca, knew she never cared for John Farley one bit. This was because Big John never cared for the way Rebecca controlled her men, including her first husband; Farley's best and closest friend Charlie West; who, out of nowhere, began drinking heavily when Rebecca started to exert her control over him to live a more stay-at-home way of a life.

When the two married, under a joyful banner, Charlie was under the notion that Rebecca was content to be the wife of a trapper, who incidentally, made a first-rate living as such; having the good fortune to broker his best pelts and furs to the more prestigious outlets in the big cities. But after a while, according to

Farley, when Charlie would come home from a trip, Rebecca stopped wanting to have relations with him, even when he refrained from taking a bath. At first Charlie found this odd, but over time her rejection of him became heart wrenching. This was because when the two first became intimate, Rebecca couldn't get enough of her man, his warm sense of humor or his gamey scent, *especially* after he'd come home from an expedition. And though Rebecca was a barren woman, it never stopped her desires for a stiff and virile man; tearing into the timid trapper at every opportunity like a cornered animal.

One day in particular, Charlie confided in John Farley that *'my event'*, as he termed it, was the best and greatest thing that had ever happened to him. To have a woman that cherished and appreciated him, along with a way of life that was diametrically opposite to city living, which Rebecca tended to like, coupled with someone to return home to, and relate with, was as Charlie put it, *'the very thing that made my extended trips away from the area merit the effort it took to simply keep living.'* So when Charlie, uncharacteristically, took to drink, putting himself into a coma nine years ago with his demise coming a month after that, John Farley was so sadden at his inability to save his friend from a shattered heart that he began to hurt animals; coming to *their* rescue so he didn't have to feel the helplessness that was consuming him.

Big John saw plainly through Rebecca's manipulating ways and this was the reason she disliked him. He also knew why Rebecca stopped having relations with Charlie; and Farley, never one to back-bite, made no bones about saying what he knew to be true straight to the woman's face. Her superficial blockade toward the big 'n honest man was as transparent as a trout in a fresh water stream.

PASTOR SKIMERHORN, while petting his horse, could see that the men had Farley's box under control, so he walked back to Buntline who'd chosen to remain seated in his buggy, "What brings you to Crittenden, Ned, surely not John Farley?" asked the pastor amicability.

"At fault on the first count, Pete," replied the writer with a scale of condition in his tone, "I came concernin' the disbursement of the deceased's estate.

"On what grounds?" asked Skimerhorn with

surprised.

"Yer kin there," said Buntline, nodding at the coffin now being laid by the grave plot, "borrowed money from me - when he was alive."

"Fer what reason?" demanded the preacher.

"I haven't the slightest on what he spent the funds, but here's proof," and Buntline produced a piece of paper.

Skimerhorn looked at it, but needed his eyeglasses. He turned and looked for someone who could read, "Tom!" he called.

Tom could see the pastor waving him over, so he excused himself from Sarah and the others.

Rebecca noticed an exchange that may require her attention, so she too politely excused herself from the group of cloaked women and made her way over to her husband of eight years.

Skimerhorn handed the paper to Tom and asked, "Will you read this fer me, Tom? I failed to remember my spectacles at the farm."

In truth, Skimerhorn never remembered his spectacles. Actually he refused to bring them anyplace because he wasn't actually literate, leaving this task to Rebecca. But if he was, the words would have been too blurry due to his progressing cataracts.

"Of course, sir," replied Tom who silently read the paper and then looked up and said, "It appears

John borrowed twenty dollars from Mr. Buntline last winter. He affixed his mark."

"Where? ..." he asked.

"Here," answered Tom, and he showed him Farley's mark; a circle with a squiggly line through it: a most definitive blot.

Skimerhorn focused his good eye on the smudge, "Yes, that's John's mark," he muttered. Rebecca then held her hand out for the document, but Tom knew it wasn't her affair, so he pretended not to see it and handed it back to the pastor. In turn the old man passed it to Buntline who said, "I'd like to be humane, Pete, and I'm sure your awareness of the debt is sufficient evidence of its need to be repaid."

"Yes, it is. Thank you Ned, for understanding."

Buntline was trying his best to be sensitive, so he tipped his hat and remarked, "I know a good man; a stone carver who takes pride in his work."

"Quite alright, Ned," replied Skimerhorn, "but thank you. I have a sycamore slab in the barn. I'll tend to it shortly."

Rebecca then took a firm hold of her preacher's arm and guided him away from the clever storyteller. She wanted to know more about this matter and why she wasn't informed sooner. Twenty dollars was a sum she would not easily part with. Skimerhorn felt the squeeze of Rebecca's clamp and was reminded yet again of the hell he would have to pay: hell for being related to the only person, dead or otherwise that was privy to his wife's sullied secrets.

"I'll leave you to grieve your loss," uttered Buntline and he set his hat back atop his head, but he was speaking to the couple's backsides as Rebecca led her blind man away. Before he snapped the reins though, he gave Tom, who was also walking away, a long and curious look. He then called out, "Hyah!" and his buggy started to roll.

a **MAN** employed by the local undertaker started to hammer more nails through Farley's coffin lid. This familiar sound was a call to the idle mourners to gather around the hole.

On the cemetery path that led to the main road, Buntline spotted Hick walking in from his shooting match, so he pulled to a stop and said, "Reports tell me you've been inquiring where to hunt those man-eaters?"

"Yes sir," replied Hick with a grin, "Tom wants the hide to lay on, by the fire with Sarah. After he marries her o' course."

"Of course," held the author with a smirk, "Nice touch."

"I thought so too," remarked Hick.

Buntline may be thought of an intelligent by most, but he lacked creativity when it came to the romantic side of his union, and therefore appreciated any information he could garner about this mysterious world: anything to help him understand the woman he currently loved.

Buntline removed his hat and wiped his brow, "I heard there's a passel of 'em north, out of Marion."

"We were just over Marion way," said Hick, scratching his ear and looking towards Marion County.

"Wrong Marion," retorted Buntline.

"The township?" asked Hick, looking the other direction."

"Yes sir."

"How do you hear about so much, Mr. Buntline?"

"It's what I recall that counts, boy," he answered, thoroughly sodden with sweat. "Just because folks gossip, doesn't mean I recall every word they whisper."

It's a hot day and Ned would rather not be

wearing his hat, but vanity had always caused him to suffer rather than allow his bald spot to be revealed. After he wiped the inside of his hat with his handkerchief, he placed the lid back on his head and said, "Careful boy, those animals tend to become especially hungry; chiefly in autumn. If you go, go now."

"Yes sir. I reckon I will."

Curiously Buntline remarked, "I shaped you up for the kind to be interested in a possible bovine hunt; westward so to build yerself a pair of those buffalo shaggies. Was I wrong?"

Hick had thought about making a westward trek but not to hunt - specifically. It was because of his eloquence toward women with red hair. He'd heard there were some lighter skin Mexican red-hairs residing along the Texas border; and in some of his lonelier states, considered going there to bring one back, but because of his family history and upbringing, his imaginative engagement concerning the ordeal stopped with the fanciful thinking. But this was also a *private fact*. And for as much as he respected Buntline, he would never disclose this for fear it would be written about, and the relationship would change for the worse he feared, so instead he remarked, "I thought about a pair 'f shaggies sir, they *are* a sight, but after doin' me some assessin' on the subject, I felt travelin' that far west to shoot one wasn't meaningful enough. Especially seein' there's thousands of 'em just standin' in herds like cattle. Don't seem fittin' to skin one and leave the carcass to the scavengers. I like eatin' what I take. The hide's actually too thick fer anything other than foot wear or saddle makin', and the hair'd git snagged 'n tangeled in stickers 'n such that we have in these parts. Besides I don't care much fer desolate land, or discoverin' the need to defend myself agin' Native folk who feel I'm trespassin'."

"I understand," said the writer. "You're not goin' fer grizzly alone are ya, son?" he asked, genuinely concerned.

"No sir. This is a two man expedition. This time I'm bringin' the groom," and he nodded towards Tom who was over by the ceremony that was about to get underway.

Buntline glanced Tom's way and replied, "Well, I'm sure by the time you return; you'll both know the difference between buckwheat and bear shit."

"Yes sir, that's a fact. I reckon we will."

"Alright then," said Buntline, looking more at ease, "You shoot yerself one, and I'll see ya the next time I'm lookin' atcha." Ned popped the reins and his buggy began to roll.

Hick STEPPED UP behind the crowd mourners and looked on as the last nail was being pounded into Farley's coffin lid. When the hammer hit the nail for the last time, a pine-knot the size of a tea saucer fell inside the box exposing the big man's ragged and bushy face.

Skimerhorn pulled a few tattered pages from his jacket; pages that once belonged in his family prayer book. No matter how distant his kinship was to Farley by way of his dead brother's wife; and never to say an ill word to anyone about any person, the pastor always kept his sermons and eulogies brief and to the point. Because for as much as Pete Skimerhorn was the reason Rebecca stopped having relations with her husband Charlie West, the pastor knew if she could do it once, she was capable of doing it again; and though he may be getting on in years, Rebecca frequently, and with creativity, made a point to have regular relations with him. Nonetheless, because he never sired a child with her, he'd always detained a strong and prevalent sensitivity concerning her improprieties, thus feeling self motivated to create a secret last-will bequeathing his holdings to the State of Kentucky if he were to die first.

"We commit John Farley's body to the ground," pronounced Skimerhorn, *"Earth to earth; ashes to ashes; dust to dust. Let the Lord bless Big John and keep him; Let the Lord make His face to shine upon him and be gracious unto him."*

Folks giggled because Farley's grimace look could be seen through the knot hole, but Skimerhorn; hardly able to see the box, let alone Farley's expression, refrained from allowing this to stop him, *"Let the Lord lift up His countenance upon Big John and give him peace. Amen."*

The crowd politely acknowledged their own subtle *Amen's* followed by a few more titters. Then without fuss, Hick, along with five other men; three on each side of the box, picked up the rope-ends that were stretched under it and lifted it up. Three more men slid out the planks that were holding it suspended over the hole. Lowering the crude tomb; the man next to Hick, a gangly Swede spoke up, "Shouldn't we nail a plank over that cher hole?"

Hick strained not to laugh fearing he'd let go of his end, but he did call out, "That hole?.. Ol' John's too dern big to squeeze out that tiny gap."

People laughed and again the rope bearers almost lost their grasp. The congregational folk in black however, had no sense of humor. Hick's remark coupled with the ensuing cackles caused them to walk for their wagons sooner than they might have. To them, a joke over death was sacrilegious and in no way a laughable matter. Yet to those who knew Big John, they also knew he too would have laughed over the sight, and therefore cared not if they departed early.

At the same time a fiddle player drew his bow across the strings to create the first few notes of the Irish sailing song, *Fiddler's Green,* three young men and a pretty girl commenced to harmonizing the lyrics. No sooner did the music begin than a foot pressed a spade into the dirt piled beside Farley's plot. This time however, earth was being shoveled in.

OUTSIDE the Hodge cabin, Loren had been balancing on his good foot while his blocked-shoe pushed a worn out spade into the squishy, septic like soil. Norman had been standing on the porch of the cabin watching the boy with his arms crossed. He'd also positioned himself directly in front of Dart and Keech who were sitting on a bench with their backs to the wall. He was purposely obscuring their view by keeping *his* filthy, hairy back to them. Both boys with suspenders over bare skin, suffered cuts and bruises abounding their neck and shoulders. With their faces only inches from their daddy's pock-marked mid-line, they were also shivering due to the morning temperature.

In the near distance, the pregnant twin sat naked on a rock beside the inclining outhouse screaming with contractions. She too was shivering.

Norman pulled his suspenders over his brawny frame, scanned his tiny world and shouted, "No more mouths to feed!" sending his rage toward the birthing girl, "Git rid of it!" He then looked intently at Loren whose sole purpose in digging the hole was not to get beaten again, but Hodge's next words were clearly meant for Dart and Keech, "Its good ol' stupid ass there has the big mouth he does. Taught 'em right, I did; tell me everything first or we might all be swingin' right now." Then like a lightning bolt, the ol' man backhanded Dart so fast it lacerated his lip, knocking another tooth free. Keech on the other hand didn't even flinch at the attack. Dart spat out the bloody tooth in several pieces. It was rotten anyway.

"Y'all see that hole?" discharged the old man, spittle and food bits spewing from his cesspit like mouth. But the girl screamed again, interrupting Hodge's limited train of thought. Frustrated he roared, "SHUT YER GASH!" He then returned his mind to the boys and cunningly chided, "Yonder's yer new home," and he stepped aside so they could have a clear view of

Loren's progress. "I ain't gittin' strung up fer a killin' y'all did."

Keech had seen his daddy *crafty-mad* before, but this time he was genuinely concerned. Therefore he spoke up, "But Daddy --" However as soon as the words left his mouth, the back of Norman's abrasive hand; at the speed of a viper, crossed the boy's crusty face, causing blood to flow from the wound inside his ear; the same wound he'd been nursing ever since Lady Talbot's ghost-cat cut him with a cycle knife.

"Shut up! Don't matter!" snarled Hodge, "You take care 'f that Shelby boy and that English feller. I don't care to wait till winter. I want it done. You do it or I'll bury you both, alive - on top 'f the other.

The boys dared not say more. They knew he'd do it. So they sat and stared. Dart watched the twin who'd just passed a live fetus; now moving to bury it where she had the last several babies she bore: in a hole behind the outhouse. Keech continued to watch Loren do his best to walk the tightrope between digging too fast and too slow. Either way, a losing proposition: too slow and Norman would beat him again; too fast and the hole was ready for a body.

CHAPTER thirteen
A little BIT o' TRUTH

On the FRONT PORCH of Tom's cabin, Hick was leaning back in a chair against the wall. He then took a pull off a half-gallon size crock sitting in his lap. After swallowing, he exhaled thick white fog. Hick was misty, and this particular autumn morning was about as cold as he could remember it being in Livingston County.

The small cabin that was recently completed by Tom, Hick, Sarah and a few of their neighbors, rested on a naturally graded, yet gentle bluff where some acres of land made their way to the southern edge of the Cumberland River. These acres bore the remains of a moderate planting of tobacco and corn that was now turned under. At the side of the cabin were the remains of a healthy household garden that grew: cabbage, collard greens, kale, spinach, salsify, turnips, tomatoes, parsnip, potatoes and soybeans; enough for some to be stored in the small root cellar dug out behind the cabin for winter rations.

Two readied pack mules laden with supplies stood lashed behind a pair of saddled horses beside the barn. Erected across from the barn was a tiny, ten-by-ten shed with a door as its only opening. Tom exited the shed and secured a railroad lock to a hasp on the door. He started for the cabin where Hick was now filling his Spanish wineskin from the cider crock. Although an antique, the wineskin was a fully functional container handed down to him from his grandfather, and the one he always took on hunting expeditions. When Tom reached the cabin, he unlatched the front door and checked on Sarah who was snoring loudly in the wood-frame bed he'd built for them. When she heard the door open, she roused and turned over. Satisfied, Tom closed it and sat down in his own chair, "Thank you, Hick," he said with sincerity.

"What fer this time? ..."

"For all you've done and everything you've taught me."

"I didn't do nuthin' you didn't decide on doin' fer yerself," said Hick, securing the wineskin and handing the jug to Tom who took the smallest of swigs, "Besides, yer a quick study."

"Perhaps, but you showed me another way to live," said Tom, locomotive steam forging out his nostrils from the 180-proof apple mash moonshine that Hick just distilled; his own special ferment.

Hick thought for a moment and then said, "I only know one way to live, Tom," his eyes set well beyond the fence line where a fallen-down mud hut lay in the distance, "I learned it from my daddy." When Hick reached down for the jug, Tom asked, "I know you're sensitive about being referred to as, *you know who*, but... ?"

"I am," came an earnest reply.

Inside, Sarah was up now and the morning tea was on. She moved the curtains aside and noted Tom 'n Hick on the porch.

Then in a series of matter-of-fact moments; Hick recorked the jug, squared his chair and clearly stated, "The General came through Smithland in '25. Daddy was soooo taken by 'im, that he named me after 'em'; *Moses on the mount* too. I'll wager you didn't know the General was a terrible sailor, didja," he sustained, moving off the subject. "Not to say he wasn't a great man, cuz he *was* a great man. No telling how many times he crossed that ocean. But Lordy he was constantly sick every time he got on the water. Like someone else I know. There, you happy?"

Actually this did please Tom. To discover something previously unknown about his friend gave him something to smile over. Because in the five years these two men had been close; and without believing gossip, this was the one piece of information Tom wanted to hear from Hick himself. "So you are related to Kentucky's first Governor," he asked. Tom knew the answer, but still hoped to open the conversation some. "That explains those fine attributes you possess."

Tom also knew Hick well enough to know he seldom answered rhetorical questions, but Hick exhaled a foggy breath of remorse, reached down for the jug and replied, "Ain't rumor. He was my daddy's Uncle Isaac. I only wish the rest of the family understood. Seems most 'f 'em've forgotten how to let a grown man follow his own heart. All sept James o' course," and he took another nip. "Since James went senile before his time, the rest 'f 'em been on me 'bout bein' the next family politician. It's complicated bein' round 'em when they're talkin' politics 'n business; subjects I don't have a feelin' fer."

Tom nodded and recalled the first day he met the hunter, and how he'd ironically thought the same thing. "But what's wrong with politics? You have an especially good sense for what's fair and right."

"Nuthin', but it ain't fer me, Tom. I'd have to change the way I talk, along with my natural waya bein'. I'd forever be miserable. I wouldn't be able to wait fer an elk in a hickory, or fall asleep by a crick with my cane pole, or pick a quail out of a flyin' bevy, or catch bullfrogs at night, or... ...or take a trip like this with my friend; huntin' fer bear, so he can lay on the hide by the fire with his woman; after he marries her 'f course."

"Of course," replied Tom, catching Hick's eye; both men turning away in time to see the last part of each other's innocent smirk. "Besides," continued Hick solemnly, "my life thus far hasn't brought me many friends, so to be a politician, I'd have to find reason to carry those I don't care fer on my back. Truth be, I don't know any folk, or kin that don't judge or condemn me in some way; sept you Tom..."

Sarah opened the cabin door and stepped out with two steaming cups of tea. Modest she's never been around the comfort of her own home. Scantily dressed in Tom's white shirt and Sunday jacket; her messy red hair rested on the curve of her spine just where her rump began to rise; a look to cause most any sane man to audibly aspirate when seeing her, which Tom always did. She handed one hot cup to Tom and the other to Hick. Hick paid no attention to how Sarah was dressed and accepted the tea like family, "Thank ya, Sarah."

"You're welcome, Hick," and she brushed her bare feet off against the door jam and scooted back in out of the chill. Inside, she wrapped herself with a patchwork quilt and sat down at a window seat. She drew her knees to her chest and with her own cup of tea, looked out at her men.

Tom said to Hick, "Well my friend, no one on

this parcel's going to force you to do or say anything against your heart."

Hick poured some *shine* into his tea and bluntly asked, "What about you Tom? What's been makin' you follow my waya livin' all this time?"

This was a question Tom didn't want to answer. Asking Hick his own personal query in a moment when he felt the hunter's guard was down apparently worked; but now he had to pay the price for Hick's honest reply.

In an instant, Tom reflected upon his occasions in England with Margaret; the time he'd spent with his brothers and sisters, as well as his nights with Amanda and the years alongside his father and Robaré building the business. He then contemplated his current existence with the woman behind the door, the man asking the question and the effort it took to balance the vast difference between the two realities. He looked Hick in the eye, speculated the hangman's noose and stood up.

At her window seat inside, Sarah watched Tom and Hick step off the porch onto the cold ground and walk over between the ten-by-ten shed and the cabin. The area around their feet was a frosty, crystalline white. And her inability to hear their words made the natural busy-body in her unhappy, "Dang, slippery hunters," she snubbed.

With open remorse, Tom said, "I had it all, Hick: the perfect life; a thriving business, a loving family and an angel to come home to. We were expecting our first." Tom's words triggered the nerves around his old shoulder wound. When he rubbed it, he thought back to that day on the train when he stood holding the weapon that controlled his destiny. And how that despicable man ducked behind Robaré and used his body as a shield, tricking him into discharging it and shooting his stepbrother to death.

All these visions crossed Tom's mind in a couple of seconds. "I killed my stepbrother," he said with deep regret; seeing himself standing over two fallen men. In shock, he dropped the guns and when they banged on the boards at his feet, he left the spell. Feeling his shoulder twitch again he continued, "I was on my way home - to Amanda. I can still hear the North-Western man shout, "'You're both going to hang!'"

"Both? ..." asked Hick.

Tom stared north across the frigid field between the cabin and the Cumberland. He then looked east towards Dycusburg and said, "Robaré wasn't even supposed to be on that train, Hick. Although he wanted to go, father ordered him to remain home. He couldn't be trusted with anything. And for as much as I despised his behavior, he was one of the most intelligent men I'd ever known. I respected him for this, but over time, his excessive drunkenness had sadly taken nearly every reasoning faculty he possessed."

Tom sustained his look across the field, and as he did, his underlying hope was that Hick had absorbed his words about Robaré's sickness; a few of them anyway. Hick took a drink of his tea and had fun exhaling his foggy breath, yet still remarked with sincerity, "I'm sorry for your loss Tom, but that's over now. God's granted you another life. Best put the old one behind you and get on with the one you're livin'." Tom turned from his river scene and said, "Don't you understand man; I killed more than an ordinary person. I took the life of my father's preferred. I'm tired, Hick. Tired of running, and tired of my ongoing mendacity."

"What's mendacity mean?" asked Hick.

Inside the cabin, a frustrated Sarah studied Tom and Hick's every gesture. Hick motioned to the ten-by-ten shed, but Tom flatly declined his petition. Sarah grumbled, "Just what're you two huntsmen hatchin' up this time?"

CHAPTER fourteen
NUNNA DUAL TSUNY

TOM and HICK turned their horses off the uneven path they'd been on for the last hour and headed down through some brush where they popped out onto a wide, deserted pike; sections of which were almost completely overgrown from non use. This smoother surface gave the men and the animals an opportunity to rest.

Hick thought now was a good time to get in some reading and he pulled his copy of '*Leaves of Grass*' from his saddlebag. While each horse walked with a mule in tow, Hick quietly began interpreting to himself. Tom on the other hand was bewildered and compelled to ask, "A main artery? Where does it lead? I've never seen such a wide path in none use."

Hick looked a speck bothered that Tom would think to interrupt him while appraising what he personally considered a celebrated piece of American literature. Nonetheless, he indulged him with an answer, "Back's Tennessee," jutting his thumb, "and yonder's Oklahoma. Called *Nunna Dual Tsuny*."

Tom spurred his horse. Catching up he asked, "And what's *Nunna Dual Tsuny*, exactly?"

Hick resigned his notion to read. He put the book away and answered, "*'The trail where they cried'*; and Jesus too," emoting a tear himself.

"Where who cried?" asked Tom with a sincere desire to know.

"An entire nation. Oh how they loved this land.

"Yes, right," said Tom, quickly understanding the fragments of conversation he'd heard over the years concerning the forced relocation of the Cherokee, Chickasaw and Choctaw nations amongst others. "I recall now. O Lord, I can tell there were many."

"My education might be limited," continued Hick, "but it did teach me that all men are created equal. And that we're all endowed by our Creator to have certain privileges: life; liberty; and even if it outwits us, a warrant to track happiness - where ever it might lead. Those politicians made more than an error in judgment. They made a mistake we'll one day pay fer; in one way or another." Hick turned his horse, "C'mon, bein' on it can bring bad luck."

"Bloody Christ," whispered Tom, looking around in astonishment. Hick led the team off the road and through some brush onto a smaller parallel trail; much like the one Tom first traveled shortly before he came into contact with the Will Prine clan.

SOME Distance back, Dart, Keech and Loren chewed
and spat sacrilegiously while walking the *Nunna Dual
Tsuny*. With Dart and Keech in the lead, Loren brought
up the rear leading a swayback nag packed
haphazardly with some supplies and two well spent
Springfield, smooth bore muskets. The wooden block on
the boy's shoe was giving him trouble while refusing to
stay in place. Loren tripped and fell. Skinning his
knee, Dart and Keech laughed and so did Loren. Then
while bent over, he scratched a swollen itch on his
other knee; the one a wasp had stung him on
yesterday. Scratching it, he looked intently at the
swelling and then softly spoke akin to a four-year old,
"I wa, wa, wa, wanted to make ho, ho, ho, Honey;
before I too, took its bra, brain out."

With the HORSES and MULES tied to a cluster of willow stalks, Tom and Hick quietly walked along the water's edge. On the other side of the stream, less than a hundred yards away, they spotted a grizzly sow fishing the shore.

Further back, three armed Hodge boys watched and waited. Keech whispered, "If we make this right, boys, we'll have ourselves bear meat and a hide to sell, all before the end of day."

Upon Keech's words, Dart became addled and he eyes got as big as saucers, "I never hunted bear, Keech. Let's make shore it etts 'em up first. A hungry bear is sometnin' I'm greatly afeard over.

Loren remarked, "We can che, check fer 'em when we gu, gu, Gut it. They'll be ins,s,s,Side," he chuckled, "all cha, cha, Chewed..."

Loren's comment did help Dart feel less nervous, so Dart sputtered, "I get the Englishman's boots." Loren stammered, "I get his haaaaa, hA, hat.

But before either of them could sound another utterance, Keech backhanded Dart in his shoulder, "We cain't take nunna their belongin's, stupids. Wanna hang?" Both boys shook their heads in earnest.

From BEHIND some TREES, Tom and Hick watched the female grizzly grab up a ten-pound rainbow, paw it to the earth and strip the meat from its bones in a single pass.

Hick leaned into Tom and whispered, "She's too far fer you to get a clean shot. I'll cross over and circle behind."

"No, said Tom, "I'll go this time. It's my turn to flush. Just get the kill."

"But it's yer hunt, Tom…"

Tom was happy with the experience alone and Hick could see this. "Alright then, answered Hick, but don't cross that line between upwind and down, or she'll get to chasin' you. And remember, these bears can easily out-light a man; and don't even reflect on clamberin' up a tree."

"'*Put your faith in God, but keep your powder dry,*'" said Tom with confidence.

"You just think of that?" asked Hick with a grin while keeping one eye on the bear.

"Cromwell, two hundred years ago," answered Tom. And with that, Tom gave his friend a look of acknowledgment as the supreme hunter with more outdoor experience in his little pinky than in every digit the former engineer had connected.

With TOM SAFELY ACROSS, Hick waded into the stream with his Sharps overhead. Half way across he spotted a second bear lumber from the woods where it too entered the water and started to fish. However this one was significantly larger and luckily only thirty yards away - easily within range.

Hick froze. In all of a few seconds he recalled every animal, dangerous and otherwise, he'd ever stalked and taken; and this giant man-eater being this close, was the one that was now making his adrenalin level shoot higher than all the rest put together.

With the water pushing up against his shins, he carefully watched it, but suddenly the animal directed its nose up and looked around. It had caught a scent. Hick thought it might be him, but when the bear turned back for the woods, he knew it was Tom. Hick cocked his Sharps, drew a bead and squeezed the trigger, but it failed to discharge. As fast as he could, he cleaned the fire hole, set another percussion cap, cocked it and took aim, but the animal had disappeared. "Tom!" shouted Hick, "Tom, look out!"

On the other side of the stream, Tom was unable to hear Hick's calls due to the articulations of the water. Unaware the second bear was moving towards him, he proceeded.

The Hodge boys, having already made it to the other side, kept their distance as they followed Tom, but through an opening in the brush, Keech spotted Hick who had almost made it across, "Here comes Lafeet," he whispered to his brothers, "Git back!..."

The boys crouched down and hid. As Hick slogged from the water into a small clearing, he lowered his gun to the ready position and cautiously looked for any signs of Tom or the bear. From behind, Keech snuck up and cracked him in the head with his rifle butt. Unconscious upon impact, Hick connected with the ground face first. Dart emerged from a hole in the bushes and kicked him once for old time sake.

Keech set his gun down and proceeded to drive a knee into the middle of the hunter's back. Vertebra popped. He then pulled his skinning knife and grabbed a hand full of Hick's long blond hair. He put the big blade to his scalp, leaned in close enough for a kiss and chortled, "I haven't decided; should it look like Injuns, or bear?

A SHOT rang out. Dart and Loren jumped, but Keech being less skittish remained steady; however he did release Hick, but still looked around. He picked up his musket and stood with his brothers. Another musket ball whistled past their ears breaking some nearby branches and then the SHOT was heard. Leaving Loren where he stood, Keech ran for the water and Dart sprang into the woods holding the second musket in his stubby hand.

Suddenly the bigger of the two bears emerged from the brush. It was wounded and on the run. Loren, too slow to respond, watched the bear approach, but before his adrenalin level rose high enough for him react, the bear hit him like a train, galloping over him and down an open path. Keech, with his musket in hand, dragged himself from the water and into the clearing. He could see that the bear had stopped and was breathing heavily. He cocked the old smooth bore, took aim and pulled the trigger, but everything was soaked and instead of the loud discharge, there was only a 'click'.

A hundred-plus feet away, Dart had come to a stop. From his vantage point he could see the bear beyond Loren who was crouched down retying the wooden block to his shoe. Dart located a suitable limb to rest the rifle on. He cocked it, took aim and shouted, "Loren! Keep down!" but Loren couldn't hear him and as he made an effort to stand, the boy's shoe twisted again causing him to crumble forward. This happened at the same time a sixty-nine caliber musket ball exited the barrel of Dart's Springfield accompanied by the appropriate sound. The blistering hot lead walloped Loren square in his big ass and exited his left thigh. The impact of the projectile was so immense; it propelled the boy's two-hundred-forty pound frame forward against a tree, impaling him through the abdomen with a sharp deadwood limb. This all happened in the time it took the average man to blink twice.

"Jesus, Lordy!" cried Dart.

The three-inch diameter limb that had exited Loren's lower back held him tight - pinned against the tree, upright and standing.

Dart dropped the gun and ran to his brother. Keech however, only stared at Loren's frozen figure, hugging the tree as if he was fucking it.

Tom's shouts could be heard from the brush, "Hick! Hick man, you there?"

In pursuit of the bear, Tom emerged into the clearing. He assessed the carnage and quickly moved to his friend, "Hick! Hick, man? You alright?"

Still face down, Hick groaned. Tom checked the wound on the back of his head. His hair was matted and blood-soaked and he could tell it was a nasty gash. Tom gently rolled him over and as his did, Hick asked softly, "Did ya git 'em?"

"I hit a lung," said Tom, "He won't run far. Lie still now."

"Taught cha good, I did," uttered the hunter, "What happened? I cain't move my extremities."

"Hodge clan; knackered you good."

"Possum shits. They'll get theirs."

"Looks like they just got a measure," said Tom,

and he gently sat Hick up against a tree. Together they watched Dart try to help Loren. Keech however, only stood back, catching glimpses from a safe distance. He was never one for watching kin die.

Loren cried, "No, Dart! Don't move me ..."

Dart was helpless. So with tears running down his pock marked face, he held Loren as close as he might and blubbered, "Why'd ya stand, Loren? Why?"

"My fault. Dern short leg ..."

"I'm sorry I kilt you, brother. You know I'm sorry, don't you? You must know I didn't mean to cause this. Don't you? ..."

Tremors started to roll through Loren and he whimpered, "I cain't feel my legs."

This was in part because the entire weight of the boy's deaden body was suspended by the strong limb. It was also because the limb had passed directly through his spinal column. Remarkably though, this was the only time Dart had every heard Loren speak without a stammer, but Dart was too distraught to notice. He'd recall this fact years later while witnessing one of the twins push out another fetus; causing today's tragedy to resurface in his mind; in turn, giving him reason to again, act stupidly.

"I know I'm goin' to hell," Dart sniveled, "It's a fer-sure now."

Loren, turning paler by the second, was barely

audible, but still managed to whisper, "You was goin' there anyhow; fer sucklin' Bo's pooch behind the Church."

"How'd you know? ... Who telled on me?" but those were Loren's last words. The remaining air in the boy's lungs expelled in a low, guttural belch and his upper torso quivered as the bloody matter from his bowels worked its way off the limb and began splattering on Dart's bare feet.

Keech stood with his arms crossed, trying to hold back every emotion that wanted to surface, "He was slowing us down," he said in denial of his love of anyone or anything.

"Damn-it to you Keech!" screamed Dart, taking his attention away from Loren's corpse for a moment, "That was Loren! He always slowed us down!"

But Keech only advanced towards Tom and Hick, "Yer gonna pay, Fancyman; you too, Lafeet.

Hick, now able to feel his upper body some began to squirm for a fight, "Don't say that name you pig fucker! ..."

But Keech abided, "Fer Loren, fer stealin' Sarah, fer it all. It's yer burden now," and he drew his knife, but Tom pulled his pistol first and Keech froze; the barrel, only inches from the boy's desiccated face. And when Tom cocked the hammer, Keech wisely took a step back.

"Mr. Hodge," sustained Tom, "I'm going to say this to you one time --"

"I ain't got no ears fer you, Fancyman!" shouted Keech and he put his hands over his own ears.

So Tom thought to lower his voice in hopes the softer tone would be of some curiosity and perhaps more inviting, "Everyone knows John Farley died of natural causes." Dart heard Tom's words just fine and appeared surprised, so he stepped away from Loren's slumped over mass and listened more intently; because not hanging for murder definitely superseded any grief he might be feeling at the moment. And when Dart moved, Tom adjusted his pistol to cover them both and said, "The Red men came to trade with Farley and found him expired." Tom enunciated his words with no fear whatsoever in his voice or eyes, but deep down, the last thing he wanted to do was to shoot either of these young men, regardless of how disposed their nature; especially at this close range. He was fully aware of the damage his pistol could do, so he continued, "They found him just like you did, on the ground, clutching his chest, but unlike you, they went away. Unfortunately there's no excuse or law for the acts you've committed, except conceivably skinning a healthy mule, which could be judged as horse thievery; a hanging offence."

"That's just fancy talk!" protested Keech,

recoiling from the unbelievable information he'd just heard in his good ear, "How do I know those words ain't trickery and we won't be swingin' from 'Judge Elm!'"

"Because Mr. Hodge, you are still breathing American air. Can you smell it?"

Dart adjusted his nose like a rabbit and sniffed the space, "I can smell it," he said. Dart was also making half-sense of the situation; something of a rarity, but it became apparent when he grabbed Keech's suspender and pulled him from his reverie, "C'mon Keech," but Keech only stared at Tom and Hick, indirectly transfixed in denial; and as far away from his emotional state as he could get.

With his gun-hand, Tom waved the boys away, "Off with you now," he said, "Go make arrangements for your brother." And with that he kept the weapon trained on them as they slowly disbursed.

Tom placed his other hand on Hick who was squirming for a fight and said, "Hold still now. There'll be plenty of time for that another day."

Although Hick could barely move, if able, he would bar no holds in killing both brothers immediately. Guns or knives, it would not matter. He was completely conscious of the fact that he was not only aptly skilled, but psychologically capable of the act in either fashion and primed to commit it; and would not hesitate in its thoroughness. Nor would he look back or say a word after its culmination. He'd had his fill of the Hodges.

CHAPTER fifteen
a HAPPY DAY

SIX MONTHS LATER, a festive affair was underway at Morris's farm. Morris it appeared was a man that had it all: three farms, corn, cattle, tobacco and hogs; including his store in town and plenty of slave labor to work the land and perform every task 'n chore that came to his mind. He even had a designated area in the back of his oversized barn where the horses and wagons were stabled 'n parked by his Negro hands during such events – so to keep the front of the premises clear from anything that might be unsightly. Sadly however, for as sound as Morris was on the business side of a deal; he always appeared to be, in one way or another, a man with a *hand full of gimmy*.

Forty or so adults were in attendance with thrice that many children spread throughout the celebratory area. On the porch, Kentucky fiddles played in concert while Negro and white women alike set the tables that the men had carried out from the barn. All this while another indentured man of color attended three beautifully dressed pigs crackling on spits that had been suspended over beds of hot coals.

When a child shouted, "Here they come!" folks

excitedly started to assemble around a tall arbor covered with flowers; an arbor with a white picket gate swinging in the middle. Morris liked the idea of separation between his fellow citizens; even if his closest neighbor, Tom, lived more than two miles away. And because of this, connecting a fence line to the gate was unnecessary, as well as an unneeded expense, yet he still liked the arbor, and the idea of it.

Almost everyone watched as Pastor Skimerhorn, who was sitting beside his wife Rebecca in their wagon, along with some other carts and carriages began rolling up; everyone except about fifteen men and boys, (free blacks and whites alike) who were in a field behind the barn playing *baseball:* a rather new game that had caught on quickly with the American way of life; played with a stick, a ball covered in horse hide and some old feather pillows as points to run to after a player hits the ball thrown to him by another. Farther down the road, an additional group approached on horseback. Two of the men had custom carved hickory sticks tied to their rifle scabbards. They too were ready to join the game.

When Tom and Sarah arrived, a Negro stable hand stepped up and held Terry's harness. This allowed Tom to climb down from the old buckboard so he could help Sarah to the ground. When the two walked under the flowered arbor, guests started throwing rice 'n flowers and shouting congratulatory annotations of best wishes to the beaming bride & groom. Another Black stable hand stepped forward to control Terry, who was now becoming skittish over the number of voices and activity thus allowing Hick, the last to get out, a controlled egress. It was clear by now that alcohol had taken a toll on his once youthful appearance. His right arm hung with atrophy; and though he was able to walk without a cane or a crutch, a limp was plainly observed as he favored his left side while following the others under the whitewashed semicircle. When he passed under it, he took hold of his dead arm and tucked it into his jacket pocket. He then pulled out a concave flask from his other pocket, pinched the cork between his teeth and took a drink. This was followed by replacing the cork and spitting out some particles: a sequence he'd become quite good at.

With the PARTY in FULL SWING, Tom and Sarah sat at the middle table heartily devouring their meals. When Sarah noticed Hick leaning against a tree befogged with drink, she nudged Tom who replied somewhat annoyed, "What can I do? He curses me anytime I come close or say a word."

"Probably nuthin'", Sarah replied, "but he is yer good 'n best friend - last I noticed."

Reluctantly, Tom scooted his chair back and remarked, "I'm surprised he failed to pontificate a declamation of bedevilment in the church."

AT THE HOME of John Tweddle in Albany, Pinkerton Agent's Timothy Webster and Kate Warne were met at the front door by a Black butler. He showed them into a waiting area where Annaleez Tweddle would soon meet with them. Because of the success that surrounded the family's ale houses and investments, this established home; like that of Fraser Dunlop's was adorned with the finest money could buy.

FULL of LOATHE and SELF PITY, Hick leaned his bad arm into the rotten hole of an oak tree that stood on the other side of the arbor; a hole that a ten-inch round limb once extended from. With his back to the party, he faced the orange sunset and upended his flask.

Tom stepped up. Attempting to lighten matters he remark, "How lucky can one man get; I heard both Edmonia Patterson, and Katherine Frayser have eyes for you. What could be more desirable than two bible packing women who like to cook what you kill?" Hick's eyes however remained westerly when he replied, "Their kisses are sweet, but they ain't worth the pain. Besides, since when's Thomas Tucker resorted to gossip?"

Tom had seen this repeat-performance over the past six months more times than he cared to remember, therefore he simply replied, "I don't know how, or what to say anymore, Hick. I'm sorry this happened to you."

Hick looked Tom in the eye, the first time in a while, and drunkenly articulated, "All the way to Nashville to hear some sawbones tell me a word I cain't even pronounce. He even said he'd cut it off – fer free. I told'em if he asked agin I'll kill'em with my good one." Hick then returned his sights to the distant river and quoted a partial passage from Walt

Whitman's Spontaneous Me: "'*The limpid liquid within the young man, The vexed corrosion so pensive and so painful, The torment-the irritable tide that will not be at rest, The like of the same I feel - the like of the same in others.*'" Hick swallowed hard and tried to continue, but this time his words fell in between gasps of sorrow, "It's dead, Tom, and it ain't comin' back." He pulled up his sleeve to confirm it. When he did he spilled some whisky, "Look. See fer yerself. See how small it's gittin'?" He put his head against Tom's shoulder and began to sob even harder, "I cain't even write my name. I still have a terrible-hard time 'f dressin' myself and I can barely wipe my ass clean. Daddy says I should run fer office?"

Tom composed a valid effort to refrain from laughing at Hick's political accuracy while at the same time trying to stand him upright, "Maybe you should," said Tom, "but you must to do something, man - look at you."

"How?" asked Hick, completely teary-eyed, "That inblood took away everythin' important to me.

"No, he didn't take it all. You still have one good arm and you can walk 'n talk. And you still have your head to think with, if you'd only stop poisoning it." Right then Tom thought this was the wrong thing to say, and he was right.

Hick recoiled like a snake and turned on Tom,

"You're a fine one to talk with your charmed and perfect life! You don't know what it's like livin' like this!"

Fear ravaged Tom's face when Hick began to poke at his old shoulder wound, "What-da-ya take me fer, simple? I know what a ball-shot wound looks like, and it sure don't look like no wagon wheel mishap, if there is such nonsense!"

Tom looked around, but only a couple of folks took minor note.

"What's wrong," averred Hick, "runnin' from somethin!"

"Hick, please stop," and Tom took hold of the dipso's shoulders, but Hick wasn't having any and shook him loose. Weaving away he shouted, "You owe me Tom Tucker! <u>You</u> <u>owe</u> <u>me</u>! ..."

A few of the guests momentary looked Tom's direction but then returned their attention to the festivities. They'd already become used to Hick's new way of behaving. They also knew that Tom was about the only person who could get close to him since that day in Marion. So the guests rumored amongst themselves that even Tom was having a hard time of taking Hick's drunken back-sass.

Amidst a MYRIAD of airborne flowers 'n rice, Tom and Sarah walked under the whitewashed arbor that was now baron of anything remotely resembling plant life. When they climbed up into their wagon that had just been brought around, they noticed the back had been filled with the blossoms and vines that previously covered the arbor only a few hours before, and they smiled.

Final congratulatory words came from the remaining guests that now encircled them. Ida Morris called out, "Forty weeks from today, I'm a countin," and everyone laughed, including Tom and Sarah who ended it with their own sideways glance.

UNDER A CLEAR NIGHT SKY with a crescent moon waxing from anew, Tom drove the old buckboard up to the cabin. With Sarah's tipsy head resting on his shoulder, he stopped the wagon and when he did, she roused and looked around, "O look, Tom, how nice."

On the porch, along with more flowers were

handcrafted gifts wrapped in everything from cheese cloth 'n newsprint, to butcher paper and burlap. Tom shouldered his wobbly, new wife up the single step and onto the porch where he picked her up and kicked at the bottom of the door. Marred from opening it this way a thousand times, the door wouldn't open. Tom was tipsy too, so Sarah lowered her arm and lifted the latch, "Silly man." Tom carried her over the threshold and through the dark cabin where he dropped her on the bed with a thud. Sarah's short legs dangled as she laid back and looked up at the rough-cut rafters in a desultory sort of way. Tom on the other hand used the little bit of moon light entering through the open door to locate a small box on the table. It was something the couple had been wanting; ordered for them by Morris through his mercantile. So when Tom removed a phosphorus dipped stick from the box and dragged the tip over the pot belly stove: behold, he lit a kerosene lantern and the two candles on the table and kicked the door closed. He then watched the match burn toward his finger tips and thought how fast times were changing, and how these new inventions that ordinary people were coming up with made life less difficult. But he was quickly brought from his abstraction when his brain registered that his thumb and index finger were in contact with the flame.

With the cabin lit, the wealth of additional

offerings could now be seen: muffins, preserves, dried meats and sundries; another patchwork quilt, an afghan and more flowers; along with pies and sweets; all piled on the table and chairs. But instead of looking them over, Tom plopped himself on the bed beside Sarah and said, "Getting married is still harder than hunting bear."

"What do you mean?" she asked suspiciously, rising to her elbow, but before she could go on she saw all the gifts, along with a bear skin rug, "My goodness, you shot us a bear! Why Tom Tucker, aren't you full 'f surprises..."

A surprise to be certain, because lying before the fire place was the gargantuan hide of the bear that Tom and Hick took; its mouth and eyes closed, as if sleeping. At the end of each outstretched appendage, claws that extended to over five inches in length. The overall size was so immense; it literally took up more than half the living area.

Unfortunately, due to the predicament Tom and Hick were in after Hick's injury, they were unable to bring back more than the hide itself. Returning with hundreds of pounds of bear meat was purely out of the question. But luckily, not that far from where Tom had single handedly dressed out the monster, they came across a small group of Natives that were clearly in need. These people were grateful for the meat to feed their families with, and in exchange, gave the men two blankets along with a bow and a few arrows. Bear meat was good and an animal such as this was especially hard to kill, in particular if one didn't have a firearm, which they did not possess, so giving them the blankets along with the other items in trade was equitable to both parties considering the circumstances.

"So, Husband? ..." asked Sarah, "Has Hick been wanderin' about all this time with his arm danglin' just to fool me too?"

"No Sarah!" stated Tom firmly, and in a way needed if he was to keep her from asking more questions. He now realized his *hunting bear* remark; although well timed was a stupid thing to say and a sure means of getting her to think about his past. He also knew it was time for him to discontinue his use of alcohol; for he tended to be looser about his language when he took a drink or two; and a man in his position couldn't afford to do that, unless he wanted to become entangled in a web of lies that could ultimately lead him to the gallows.

"I'm sorry," said Sarah, "Fruit spirits tend to make me say hurtful things. It's a beautiful bear. Thank you, truly..." And with that she scooted off the bed, grabbed a chair and chattered it up to where Tom's legs dangled. Tom interlaced his fingers behind his head and relaxed back as Sarah lifted her new husband's foot to her lap and began unlacing his shoe, "If Mama were alive, she remarked coyly while struggling with the laces, "I'm not sure she'd've agreed to let-chew marry me." She finally managed to pull the shoe off and drop it on the floor loudly before lifting Tom's other leg to her lap.

"Why's that?" asked Tom, looking up at the same rough-cut rafters.

"Cuz she might 'f bin thinkin' you was out to rob 'er cradle."

"Not the case," said Tom, "I've been seeing it another way for quite some time. But tell me, did you not inform her about your ways with men?"

Some," she said, and she pulled Tom's other shoe off and dropped it equally as loud as the first, "but Mama didn't completely understand the younger ways; with me wearin' men's work clothes and makin' money like I did 'n all. Even to help out wasn't somethin' she cared fer much; and my tomboy conduct, well, that was behavior she didn't care fer *at all*. But I liked the outdoors, so it was hard fer us to git along in that way. She wanted me to marry up and be a lady." Her words caused her to reflect and become teary. "Mama didn't collect it all until she was about to pass. Then for about a hour or so, she got real lucid on everythin'. We had the sweetest talk; just us two girls.

It was like we talked on everythin' there was in the world for that short time. She told me where she felt I'd gone wrong as a girl; and the mistakes she'd made bringin' up us kids. I got to say where I felt she'd been wrong, and the bad things I'd done. I even told her 'bout the boys I fooled with, which I never felt bad about, except it was hard gatherin' the courage to say it. But after the first one, the rest come easy - and she didn't get mad - like I thought she was gonna. Like when I told 'er bout the time I snuck over; I mean went over, to Timmy Willbow's place. His folks had some means, so Timmy got to have his own room.

"My goodness," commented Tom, "How old were you?"

"I just got my roses, so, old enough to have a baby. Shush; you listenin'? ..."

"I am," he said, enjoying the story thus far, so he put a clamp on it.

"Good. Anyway, I found Timmy real fetchin'. So after the rest of the family went to bed, I clambered in through his window. I though he was-a-foolin' with his eyes closed 'n all, tryin' to make me think he was sleepin'. So I crawled under the covers. He was sooo warm, and he smelled sooo good, and I started softly rubbin' on him, like I do you, and he got real stiff, like you do, sept yer way bigger."

"Thank you, dear."

Then I pulled the skin back and put my mouth over his knob and started lovin' on it, like I do with you, sept I didn't know much then. His man-smell, or boy smell I reckon, got the best of me and I got to lovin' too fast and his nuts emptied in my mouth sooner than I wanted. I though he was-a-foolin' the whole time with his eyes bein' closed and snorin' 'n all. Later I found out he *was* sleepin' and had no recollection of the event. I knew cuz he paid me no mind in school. I felt embarrassed, but I reckon it was a good portent cuz later, after his family moved away, I found out he was a gossip and heeda told everyone. He also liked it with boys better, so that's another reason, but I do recall that smell, 'n that taste. Mmmm... It sure was somethin', and I've hankered for it ever since."

Sarah recalled all this while staring a hole through the cabin wall. She then looked down at Tom thinking she'd put him to sleep with her boring boy stories, but Tom was wide eyed and looking quite perky actually. "Go on," he said.

"I'm so happy me 'n mama had that chance to say our minds. I don't think I cudda lived with myself knowin' she passed without me getting' to say, 'I love you mama'. But also I reckon I'm sad cuz she didn't get to see me marry. She'd've been proud, Tom - real proud. Anyway, right before we was done talkin', she asked me in a voice I never before heard; soft, angle like, if we was *right*, and I couldn't help but weep. I said, 'Yes, mama, we're *right*. After that, it didn't take long fer her to get on with dyin'. So you see husband, it was the way you say it was, but only cuz *I* wanted it to be."

"But Sarah," argued Tom with a little bit of concern, "you told me you were a virgin."

"My cunny was always virgin territory, 'til I met chew, but my mouth 'n hands weren't, along with some other parts."

Sarah unbuttoned Tom's trousers and wiggled them off; no under-leggings needed. It was May and the weather was warming up. Sarah flipped her gown up, turned around and straddled Tom for a backwards saddle ride. No under bustles needed either, least by Sarah on her wedding day – or any day for that matter.

Akin to the manner in which she just spoke of her first boy adventure, Sarah would likely refrain from admitting to anyone but Tom what it was like when she first laid eyes on him. Truth be told, she stopped wearing under garments all together and was always ready for an occasion; a circumstance she would generally manipulate the preparation of due to the promise she made to herself atop the lumber wagon on the day she almost ran over Tom and Hick: that she would take this man and have him in every way she had ever dreamt, and at every opportunity that she could make manifest. For when she and Tom sat beside each other on the ten-mile ride into the valley, she felt her wetness escape at a volume she'd never experienced before; soon followed by a sensation that made the top of her head feel like it had popped above the clouds. Collectively this caused a wet spot so big, she had to keep her trouser-wearing legs pinched together so tight that when she stopped to drop the two off, she could only pray the enormity of the flow wouldn't be noticed. Thank goodness nearly every person had a difficult time with the humidity that summer, and that nearly every person's trousers, along with their wagon seats were almost always wet. But Sarah also knew that if a result like this could happen from a look and a feeling, she also knew she'd do whatever it took to have the rest of this man: every aspect; every emotion; every quality; every imperfection; everything, and at every likelihood.

On her knees, Sarah positioned her torso as flat as she could get it and then brought Tom's ankles as close to her face as she could; exposing her opening so to intoxicate him through his nostrils. Tom pulled Sarah's dress over his head and breathed in the strong evocative scent of his new wife's backside; a scent that overcame him every time, anywhere; a redolent coil that wound its way up her clothes no matter what she wore, past her bosom where it clung to her neck and interlaced itself between the strands her long red hair. A tang so prevailing that it had caused Tom to throw caution to the wind on many occasions, giving him solid basis to take and have Sarah in some dangerous and conspicuous places; and eye-catching enough to have caused quite a commotion if the two had been discovered.

One of the closest situations was at the Dycusburg Cemetery on the day Big John Farley was put in the ground. Right after Tom and Hick shot the melons; Tom took Sarah by the hand and said, "C'mon, shall we see what we hit?" When they arrived at the destroyed targets, they saw the men's attention was elsewhere, so the two ducked out of sight. After more time had elapsed than ought to be, two of the men wanted to see the damage done to the melons as well. Thank goodness however, that Hick was with them as they drunkenly walked the trail. These men may have been too intoxicated to care about where the musket balls hit, but not enough to have refrained from causing a lively frickus if one or both of them had seen what Tom and Sarah were up to. Because when Hick's eagle eye spotted *flagrande delicto*, or in other words, Sarah hugging a tree some yards in the distance and Tom lapping her fleshy hind-side with the veracity of the bear that filleted that trout, he turned the men back in the nick-of-time, but not before he'd made eye contact with the couple, forever sealing his fate as family.

THE CURVE in the small of Sarah's back was strong and evident as she straightened herself up. When she looked back, she witnessed Tom in another world, so she reached around to untie her own dress, but Tom opened his eyes and began to unlace the tight weave for her. Once undone he said, "Turn around."

Sarah then whispered, "I like it when you tell me what to do… in bed."

"Sarah, please," said Tom, rather embarrassed.

Tom, unlike Sarah you see, was never too vocal during their intimate times. So Sarah effortlessly spun her small frame around allowing Tom to reach up and caress her russet nipples through the material. He knew how to shut her up, or so he thought.

"Tom… ?"

"Mmm ..."

"What-da-ya-do in yer shed?" But Tom gave

one of them a loving nip, "O God!" she moaned.

"Stop asking questions," he said, "You know it makes me soft."

"God forbid you should get soft fer ten seconds. But tell me, what do you do in there?" she asked again.

"I tinker, and I think," he said. And with that he rolled her gown over her head and stuffed it behind his head as a pillow.

Sarah leaned in and looked deep into Tom's eyes; and in the most seductive shade uttered, "Then why don't you think on givin' us a baby."

Straddling her new spouse, Sarah unbuttoned Tom's shirt and ran her fingers over his chest. Tom wanted to pull his shirt back over his shoulder scar, but Sarah pinned his arms down. As she ground her soaked pelvis into him, she exposed *the mark* along with a number of other disfigurements. Unchecked, she buried her nose into his armpit. When she came up for air, she was completely foggy headed. It was then she began to sweetly inspect the old wounds, "You've seen my chest ferever," she said, touching and kissing the healed over areas, "and can you believe it, this is the first time I recall seein' yers this close, and this clear, with yer shirt all the way off."

Tom relaxed back. It's all he could do. He knew absolutely that no matter what, he could not show his discomfort during Sarah's cherished curiosity; inebriated or otherwise. He'd just have to get used to it.

"They're beautiful," she sighed, "Each one tells a wonderful story."

A THOUSAND MILES AWAY inside the home of John Tweddle, Agents Webster and Warne sat across from the man in his office. John Tweddle had clearly aged; not only in years, but he'd also been delimited by the strain of his son's circumstances. With his head in his hands, the ever watchful Annaleez remained at her father's side. She could feel his distress well above the persistence of these pesky detectives and could not wait for them to depart.

Agent Warne also sensed John Tweddle's pain, and as best she could, without expressing too much compassion in front of her partner, conveyed, "We apologize our questions were so difficult, sir." She then picked up a file folder along with a sketched likeness of Joseph from atop John Tweddle's giant oak desk and concluded, "Thank you sir; for your cooperation, and for your son's likeness. I know this entire ordeal pains you aggrievedly."

John Tweddle lifted his eyes and said, "There must be somebody who? ..." But Webster interrupted and with far less compassion said, "He shot your stepson, sir; I witnessed it."

"Yes, Mr. Webster," replied John Tweddle, completely overwhelmed, "You mentioned this - twice already I believe."

Warne stood up, "It's time we took our leave.

And at the throws of what appeared to be checkmate, the old man, out of courtesy, attempted to stand, but instead coughed and wobbled back into his chair. Annaleez quickly moved to him, "Father, you should be in bed, you're not well." She quickly motioned to an African servant man standing silent at the door, "Marcus, help me please," and the man immediately came to her. Together they shouldered her father toward the pocket doors. When they reached the threshold, John Tweddle stopped. He looked back at the agents and expressed softly, "If you find my son, please tell him I've never forsaken him-" But again Webster cut him short and stated without remorse, "It's a matter of when, Mr. Tweddle; when we find your son."

Under the LIGHT of a single candle, Sarah kissed another one of her husband's scars and asked sincerely, "Why do you hide them so?"

"I'm vain," answered Tom in a voice that coincided with being spent.

"You're not," she countered. "You're terribly handsome, but there ain't a foppish bone in yer body, sept this one I reckon," and she wiggled her haunches, bringing up a silly laugh.

To be precise, for as close as the couple had been prior to marriage, Tom rarely, and only by accident, removed his shirt in front of another person; including Sarah; always keeping the questionable shoulder wound away from bright light and direct eye contact.

"What about this perty little defect?" she asked, noticing a scar at Tom's belt line that was angular in nature and not as healed over as the others; still purple and somewhat itchy, "Have you been hidin' this one too?"

O, that one," he replied, feeling relieved.

Relieved because this scar you see had some actual truth around its acquisition. Tom quickly thought back to that day in Marion when he needed to draw his pistol in order to protect Hick and himself from Keech's advance. He'd pulled the weapon so fast that it caused his flesh to tear when the hammer of the weapon passed across his soft belly tissue. Even though this part of the story was true, he purposely failed to include the details of Hick's injury caused by the Hodge brothers by fabricating the (pistol pulling) portion of the story to include a devious man that had been tracking them in order to steal the bear hide.

Sarah on the other hand could never refuse the rush of a battle chronicle and mashed her haunches into Tom, "How heroic," she sighed, "holding off marauders while hunting bear for your woman... Mmm ..." Yet in order for her to keep her flow moving, she lightly petted him for another scar, but it was time the inquisition be thwarted and Tom aggressively rolled her to her knees and came around from behind.

"You are a big, fine suitor, husband Tucker."

"And tell me, wife, just how many suitors *have* you actually had?"

"Enough to know the difference between fine, and big..."

CHAPTER sixteen
1861

It was Dark outside and the early morning rain had been thunderously pounding the cabin's modern tin roof for hours; another one of the couple's wedding gifts, generously set-on and nailed in place one Saturday morning just a few months after they'd married.

A fire barely smoldered in the hearth and the patchwork quilt; also a wedding gift, now covered the wiggly couple lying on the pungent, yet warm grizzly hide.

Tom, who was lying on his back and half asleep with his nose in the bear's ear was being ridden hard by Sarah; her appetite for her husband's physical inheritances unarguably insatiable. The cabin was brightly cold and her breath could easily be seen chugging forth from under the quilt; stopping exactly where the cold air of the cabin met the warm air of the fireplace. She finished up and Tom rolled over. And though he still didn't care for the feel of animal hide against his own, he bucked up and accepted it when it was too cold to do anything but fall asleep in front of the fire.

Sarah awkwardly made it to her knees and finally to her feet. Bare naked, it was evident she was ready to give birth. She waddled to the door, but before unlatching it, she lifted off a long wool coat hooked to the back of it. Cloaking herself, William, a five-year old in a nightshirt ran up and yelled, "Mama don't go," and he grabbed hold of her leg.

His mother's need to alleviate nature's call was strong, so she turned the boy around and said, "Go climb back in with daddy, son - it's warm under *Mr. Bear.*" The comfort of his mother's words coupled with the gentle turning action agreed with the boy - and he let go. Sarah opened the door and the second she did, the sky illuminated with a flash and thunder clapped.

Making her way outside; the wind howled and the rain came at her sideways. A trickle of blood ran past her ankle and into the mud as she found it more difficult than usual advancing toward the barely discernable outline of the family's backhouse. Once inside the wooden box, she sat down, latched the door and breathed a sigh of relief. Staring forward, she sarcastically thought to herself what a far cry this gusty hole was from pissin' in tall corn. But she was relieved of her thought when a blast of wind-driven rain found its way through the heart shaped hole she'd carved in the siding and stung her in the face. She pulled off the last damp sheet of newsprint nailed to the door, but before wiping, she checked herself and smelled the discharge. The baby was on its way.

When Sarah unlatched the door and stepped inside the cabin sopping wet, Little William was asleep on *Mr. Bear* and Tom had just finished stoking the potbelly stove located in the cooking area, "Loosin' my water," she affirmed windily, "Won't be long." But before Tom could utter a word, Sarah averred, "We're outta bumf - and go fetch Doc McGinnis!..."

AFTER FIRMLY nailing another stack of newsprint to the inside wall of the family's outhouse, Tom backed out the door into horizontal sheets of rain. He also wondered if doing this before he went to get the doctor was a good idea because time was short, but as he walked away, he didn't give it another thought.

Walking towards the new barn, it was evident the farm had improved over the last few years. Hog pens now stood along the eastern fence line and two wagons sat under the covered structure that Tom and a group of neighbors finished last fall.

He snugged-up the girth-strap on a chestnut gelding, and despite the animal's attempt to expand the air in its lungs, Tom still managed to cinch it tight. He brought the stirrup back over the top, stuffed his boot into the foothold and mounted up. Lightly clad so he wouldn't sweat too much for fear of catching a chill, he galloped out of the barn and into the storm wearing little more than a shirt and a pair of trousers.

Tom laid a path across the back of his land for Doc McGinnis who lived on the other side of the river. Through puddles and over gushing ravines, Tom's well-bred mount turned easily and ran fast. Together they jumped a fence and then another. As he started to cross a harvested field, Tom lowered the reins and turned the animal flat out. This sweetheart could run. When he reached the ferry landing, without thinking, he led the animal straight on board. The ferryman, Connor Thorpe; an uncomplicated mid-thirties fellow possessing little motivation to learn more than what it took to safely operate the ferry, attempted to convince Tom that the wind was picking up and to cross could likely become perilous, but Tom wasn't having any of what the simple man had to offer. So against Thorpe's better judgment, he and Tom untied the lashings and began the process of crossing the river on what was now becoming an unstable platform.

Once to the OTHER SIDE, Tom led the animal off the barge and mounted up, but before continuing he turned and shouted back at Thorpe, "Wait for me!" Thorpe looked at the sky and felt the rain pummel his already soggy face; yet before he could absolute another word of discernment, Tom shouted again, "Wait for me, man!" Thorp avoided Tom's eyes. He simply lashed the vessel to the same rigging he had for the past five years and sat down on box.

Tom kicked the animal and galloped through Dycusburg 'n away. He jumped one more ravine, another fence and then crossed the last open field as fast as he could without allowing the animal to stumble, thus forsaking his efforts to retrieve the doctor and cause Sarah to give birth alone.

On a FLAT BARGE two hours south of Pittsburgh, Agents Webster and Warne huddled together under a single blanket on a slick and rainy boat deck. Cold and damp, Warne didn't look well. She continued to shiver even as Webster tried to keep her warm next to a wood stove that was almost completely out from the weather. When Warne argued the importance of capturing Tweddle, Webster replied, "Aye, Kate. I'm in complete agreement, I want him in custody as bad as you do, but we must return or seek shelter if you don't improve."

In the beginning stages of pneumonia, Warne coughed and replied, "I assure you, Tim, I'll recover. I will. And we'll capture Tweddle."

TOM slogged onto the front porch of the McGinnis house and banged on the door. Mrs. McGinnis, the doctor's five-foot-eleven inch, mid-forties Scandinavian wife answered, and in a Netherlander idiom asked, "Why Tom, what is it? Is it?--"

"Sarah's losing her water, madam. Is the doctor in?"

"No. He's gone off to tend to Morris's prize bull."

"Morris's bull?…"

"Ya."

"Tom looked back from whence he came and argued, "but Morris lives on the other side.

"And you didn't pass?" asked the woman.

"I didn't ride the roads."

"O dear," she said, "I don't know then."

Tom mounted up and rode for the ferry. On his way there he became irritated that Connor Thorpe failed to say that Doc McGinnis had just taken the ferry across from Dycusburg and would not likely be at his home. But Tom immediately settled when he realized that he'd boarded the ferry and strong-mindedly demanded the easy-going man take him across in spite of conditions. He'd also made the choice not to say a word to the operator while crossing; preferring to keep his private thoughts to himself. Therefore how was Thorpe to know he needed to fetch the doctor for Sarah… For that matter, Tom had never said a personal word or otherwise to Connor Thorp – ever. And this he felt needed to change.

When Thorpe saw Tom in the distance, he exhaled a sigh of relief. He was about to unlash the vessel so he too could get home, but he also knew he'd be harboring an insightful feeling of guilt if he were to have left Tom behind. Therefore along with his sigh, a profound sum of anxiety departed his body; and an ever-so-slight grin appeared at the left corner of his mouth.

SAFELY ACROSS, Tom thanked Thorpe, whom in turn simply nodded. He then mounted up and galloped the remaining miles to the Morris farm, which ironically was not that far from his own.

He dismounted and led his drenched 'n winded animal into the barn, "Morris!" he shouted, looking high and low, "Where's Doctor McGinnis? Morris! Where are you, man? ..."

From the back of the barn, Morris called out, "Tom, the nightmare's finally over." Tom made his way over to the man who looked winded himself where he continued, "Glad you stopped by. This bull a mine was sure givin' me a hard time –"

"I am sorry about your animal," spurted Tom, "but where's the doctor?"

"Everything right, Tom?"

"Bloody hell man, he was just here!"

"Gone an hour. What's wrong? Can I help?"

"Not unless you know how to deliver a baby."

"A human baby? Sarah? ..."

Tom waited for his answer.

"Sorry Tom, can't help ya."

The RAIN had temporarily subsided and everything for miles around was freshly soaked. The moon was descending on the western horizon and the sun was making its way into the eastern sky; its rays filtering through cobalt cumulus clouds and illuminating the distant fields in a mélange of colors and shade.

Tom rode up to his cabin and saw an empty wagon with a single mule team. Sopping wet and exhusted; he couldn't discern who it belonged to.

Concerned, he unlatched the door and trudged in. Rebecca Skimerhorn, who scarcely noticed him, had been gathering blood-soaked bedding. William, who'd been watching the fire on Mr. Bear, immediately jumped up when he saw his dad. Sarah, wrapped in her patchwork quilt, contently rocked while nursing baby Annie; the name she and Tom had chosen if they'd had a girl.

William plowed into Tom's leg, "Daddy!" Tom however, just stood in the puddle gathering around his shoes. The energy he'd just expended over the past three hours could have moved a small mountain, but apparently for not. Because what he was actually witnessing; which included his own feelings of serenity, was accomplished without any help on his part. This minor epiphany stimulated him to take note that he was powerless over matters such as these. This also caused him to softly utter in jest, "Please tell me there's something heavy I can move?"

A tired Mrs. Skimerhorn and a glowing Sarah said it all with their kind, yet knowing smiles. Therefore Tom knelt beside his wife of six years and checked in on newest member of the Tucker clan.

CHAPTER seventeen
SPRING CRAZY

Alleged INSANE; forty year old James Washington Shelby was being led up Smithland's Courthouse steps in leg irons and manacles by a competent looking thirty-something constable with a Spencer rifle strapped across his back and a Colt Dragoon holstered to his side.

From a side door, Hick exited onto the same landing his brother was being led up to. Dressed in trousers 'n suspenders along with a dark jacket over a white shirt; Hick's hair was just past his ears now; probably a good fifteen inches shorter than where it used to fall and nowhere near long enough to tie in a tail. In essence it looked like the barber had placed a bowl atop his head and cut everything below it. He also appeared frail and much older than a man in his mid-thirties who could only watch as the constable manhandled his unwilling, madman of a brother up each and every step.

Upon seeing James like this, Hick immediately recalled the numerous occasions Constable Alley had harassed his brother over small infringements; minutia really; and it meant just one thing: something dreadful had happened.

The event was later described in the local papers to the effect that: *Shelby and two of his slaves were repairing a fence on Shelby's northern most farm; that which is closest to the area of Lickskillet when Constable Alley rode up and surprised them. As Alley and Shelby argued over a small debt owed by Shelby, Alley's uncut mount began spinning uncontrollably. This caused the bigger of Shelby's slaves to approach the animal in an attempt to calm it down, but Alley pulled his nightstick and swung at the man, catching the top of his ear with the stick and peeling the flesh downward, thus causing undue harm. This action on Alley's part caused both slaves to become frightened and to run off. According to Shelby, Alley then pulled a Navy Colt and aimed it at Shelby's head with intent, but due to Alley's inability to control his animal; he could not accurately train the weapon on Shelby. In defense, Shelby took a number of steps back, produced the hand ax he had been using to repair his fencing with and beckoned Alley to shoot him. Shelby then stated that Alley fired his Colt directly at Shelby's head and missed, thus giving Shelby due cause to fear for his life and reason to: "act in defense of the only means by which God himself had provided me with to transport my soul while on Heaven's green earth." This was when Shelby threw the hand ax at Alley, but instead of hitting Alley, the ax hit Alley's horse with the hammer end. When Shelby was asked if there were any witnesses that he knew of, Shelby stated, "The only others that might have witness to the event* were my slaves, but they had run off, yet may have been watching from a distance." Shelby went on to say, "They are good slaves and they had been known to watch out for my interests when I was away." Shelby continued the account by saying, "Alley dismounted from his animal, aimed at me again and fired." This time Shelby was wounded in the upper torso. This caused Shelby to run for his ax. As he picked up the crude means of defense, Alley fired for the third time, hitting Shelby again, this time in his left shoulder, but because of unknown reasons, Alley's Colt discharged weakly, causing Shelby only severe bruising from the ball-shot. "Thank you Lord," Shelby stated, "that I had the forethought to put on my heavy shirt." Then in full defense of self, Shelby said that he threw the ax at Constable Alley, striking him in the collar bone area and severing what appeared to be an artery. This in turn caused Alley to run for his life. Shelby said that he gave chase and caught Alley as he fell to the ground bleeding. This is when Shelby produced the famous Dirk knife and stated, "It was handed down to me by my daddy's Uncle Isaac Shelby, Kentucky's first Governor. I keep it sharp too - with oil and a whetstone." Shelby finished by saying, "I then proceeded to stab the remaining life out of Alley with it."

On the COURTHOUSE STEPS, Hick and his older brother made eye contact. "Brother!" shouted Shelby, fetching Hick from his dream-state, but this also caused the constable to immediately size up the former hunter; and just as quickly pass him over as harmless; only to observe the pitiful shell of his once youthful nature. Shelby called again, "Check on the family?

Hick halfheartedly raised his good hand, "I will, James."

"He shot me twice!" shouted Shelby, "They're sayin' I stabbed 'em thirty times! LIARS! I counted as I stabbed! I counted! I know it was more! I was good at ciphering'! Remember, you told me I was! I'll take an oath to it! Told 'em not to come! Stole his life! Told 'em I would!"

By this time the constable had dragged Shelby to the landing and was attempting to get him through the doorway, but Shelby was pressing back against the lawman all while keeping precious eye contact with his brother, but this only forced the officer to work him more aggressively through the opening.

'Twas a **BUSY DAY** for law enforcement in Smithland. Climbing the steps behind Shelby was a seasoned deputy marshal in his forties. What was most perceptible about this lawman was the wet handkerchief he had covering his face; akin to something a highwayman might wear to conceal his identity. It was secured across his nose and mouth and protecting him as best it could from the stench of Dart Hodge. The deputy kept Dart positioned squarely in front of him, and though Dart's ankles were secured in leg irons and his good hand safely lashed behind his back to a bundle of his shredded britches, the deputy still had to push the adverse man up the steps. At perhaps twenty-seven; the youngest of the Hodge brothers looked more wretched and low down than ever a man could. His skin condition had become so appalling, his entire body and mind was all but absolutely afflicted. Huge patches in the shape of continents covered his chest, back and legs; bleeding through his shirt and trousers and *crustilizing* to a point that anyone close was repulsed by the odor of fresh blood oozing beyond layers of thick scabs. The itching, so intense; it caused the continual disruption of his thinking process. Not that his prior practice of thought had prevented him from behaving stupidly, because it hadn't, however a lifetime of continual suffering had created an entirely different matter.

With his stub of a right hand, Dart was at the perfect height to easily lift the deputy's hat from his head - and he did just that. He then sailed it into the street like a cow chip; causing him to laugh so hard that his one surviving tooth was actually visible at the back of his drawn and hollow mouth. And just as fast, the deputy stomped Dart's leg irons and pushed his face into the steps. Consequently he held him down with his other boot while he pulled a rawhide lanyard from his hip pocket and proceeded to lash the wandering stub to the only part of Dart's misfitted body that was available: his neck. This was the deputy's only insurance the hand wouldn't wander again. This also caused Dart some breathing discomfort, but the deputy had no feelings in this area.

A nicely dressed elderly man who'd been holding the hand of his granddaughter, kindly, yet with caution, handed the deputy's hat back to him, and in doing so, the deputy acknowledged the old man with a nod, slapped the dust off of it and awkwardly returned it to his head. He then reached down and promptly lifted Dart up by his britches and shirt; dry heaving in the process. Upon reaching the landing, he shoved Dart through the door; held open for him by another courtly citizen who quickly turned his head and retreated upon the passing inborn's smell.

As Hick watched Dart being escorted inside, he

recalled that awful day in Marion; yet for some unknown reason, harked back a passage from Walt Whitman's *Leaves of Grass;* a book he'd since given up the reading of: *'The murderer that is to be hung the next day - how does he sleep?'* ... Returning from his daze, Hick noted a crow that had just landed on the eve above him where it promptly crapped. He didn't know why his eyes followed the excrement to the ground where it splattered like all the other bird crap before it, but for some reason he wondered why they did. He also recalled the man, the third and youngest of the troublesome brothers, and he easily accepted that in the same way a bird effortlessly passes shit, he was glad to be rid of Dart Hodge.

In the COUNTY CLERK'S OFFICE, file cabinets, rolled up drawings, documents and clutter surrounded Hick's lonely corner area. He returned a pint size whisky bottle to the bottom drawer of his desk and before sitting down slid it closed. It hadn't been easy, and it still wasn't, but he'd finally learned to write, as well as dress himself and even wipe his ass clean with his left hand alone.

Both lawmen entered one behind the other and came to rest against the counter; each one tired in his own right from upholding the law. Hick removed himself from his desk and limped to the counter. The constable assigned to Shelby put his jailer's receipt down and said, "Yer brother, eh?"

Hick seldom felt the need to answer a rhetorical question, but this time he did, "Yes sir." While Hick's eyes carefully read the document, he asked the constable, "You take Alley's place?"

The constable waited for Hick to complete his reading, but in the meantime looked at the reluctant clerk precisely where their eyes would meet, and when Hick looked up from the paper, the lawman asked, "You right with that?"

"Fine by me," said Hick.

The deputy responsible for jailing Dart leaned in and remarked in a thick, Northern Louisiana accent, "Don't seem nary worth a two dolla levy agin a crazy man."

From the inside hallway, Tom was about to enter the clerk's office to say hello to Hick, but when he rounded the corner, he saw the lawmen, and just as fast, stopped and backed up out of sight.

The deputy marshal set his paperwork on the counter for Hick and then remarked to the constable, "A nickel says yo mad man walks."

Hick listened closely for the justification.

"He might at that," replied the constable, "Alley was outta line. He ought not've gone. Perhaps Shelby's mad, but he ain't stupid; and I got four bits says "Judge Elm" jerks your man's rotten head clean off."

With a smirk, Hick signed that paper without even reading it and filed it as the first case to be heard on the next day's docket.

Tom, whose business could wait, quietly walked past the door and exited the building. He double timed it down the steps and across to State Street and up to the general store where his wagon was tied.

"Fool's bet," chuckled the deputy, "Thievin' horse fucker, he is... Caught 'em lovin' on a nag, while jerkin' on the stud he thieved."

"Well, I'll be...," said the constable, taking a sideways step from the disgusting odor now rolling off the deputy, "You been a huntin'?" he asked, "What's that cher smellin' of?"

"One of the nastiest specimens of human I ever come across," replied the deputy, "I do hope he hangs, cuz I'd sooner quit the job 'n turn to clearin' out skunk nests than have the same task put upon me agin'."

"Cain't says I'd blame ya," replied the constable, "Grateful it weren't me the task was put upon."

"Whole holler of 'em outta Dycusburg," said the deputy, "but I ain't crossin' outta Livin'ston agin fo' mo' a that - makes no reason."

The deputy then turned to Hick and asked allegorically, "You're that hunter fella, Lafeet, ain't cha? Loose the use 'f that arm, ya did?" and he winked at the younger constable for some lawman like agreement. But the constable was a town official and though he might be obliged to exchange a word or two, he wasn't going to take it any farther. For certain he'd just taken Alley's place, but he wasn't new to the area and being acquainted with some of the Shelby's like he was, he knew of Hick and his prior reputation and he respected it.

"Mister," said Hick with fire in his eyes and his good fist clenched, "Don't chew call me by that name! If I had my arm back, I'd chunk you up side yer head like a--"

"Well you don't!" said the lawman and he took hold of Hick's good arm, "So get back to yer clerkin'," and he aggressively pushed it back at him, turned and walked out.

As soon the deputy stepped out the door, Tom's wagon was turning left onto Mill Street.

In a HECTIC shoreline settlement, boats and barges came and went while free blacks and slaves for the most part, trudged between the water and the beach tossing ropes and lumping cargo.

In the thick of the settlement itself; in the cracks 'n crannies of back alleys and stair-wells, to the corners 'n confines of rented room and saloons, to right out in the open street, travelers and merchants of seemingly every nationality carried on as they traded their wares.

Agents Webster and Warne, now dressed more rustic, yet still prissy for their environment, got nowhere as they circulated Joseph's likeness. This was a fresh and subjective land where the likes of big city law; seeking to capture and punish those who had done wrong in the eyes of absent law maker's was met with skeptical dissatisfaction. It also led the Chicago city dwellers to question their tactics. Warne, who was naturally slender, had lost more weight and still didn't look well. With a nagging body temperature higher than normal, she was finding it hard to keep food down. Webster's exasperation with the search however had finally become evident when his leg sank in a mud pocket clear up to his knee. Upon retrieving the leg, he realized his shoe was still at the bottom of the trap.

CHAPTER eighteen
PAST DIVISIONS

June, 1865. Fifty guests give or take, had accepted an invitation to attend Morris's annual summer time gathering. Couples happily swung their partners to an upbeat tempo provided by musicians on the front porch playing: guitar, washboard, spoons, fiddle and a saw; all tapping out the lively new melody of *Stephen Foster's, Camp Town Races.*

Ten or so young men; boys really, had just come in from a long game of baseball in the same field some of them played in back when Morris began throwing his summer time shindigs – the same year Tom and Sarah wed. These boys were hot and sweaty and proudly wearing the remnants of their military uniforms: grey and blue alike. But the war was over and this game was like a cool salve on a bad burn.

While some of the boys courted their gals; stealing kisses and sometimes a little more from behind the barn, others stood around and mingled. These boys; friends and neighbors since childhood, could be heard telling stories of gallant heroism, as well as those that contained a lesser courage.

Kentucky, like Delaware, Missouri and

Maryland, was a state torn between the two colors. Colors that looked equally appalling when soaked in the blood of husbands and sons regardless of the material's composition and color; men and boys, who in the end, never returned home to play another game of baseball.

Yet Kentucky was also a state filled with tremendously grateful families; grateful their soldiers, most of them anyway, were home now. Furthermore, they were thankful the differences between these two colors were finally on a path to healing. For some within this group of residents, the oppression of African slavery was something they had no direct experience with in their native countries. The fact also remained that Illinois, Indiana and Ohio; three states geographically north of Kentucky, had been *Free States* since the 1820s. So when the war came to their new home; in their eyes, being forced to patriotically choose one way or another was; as one might well imagine, an excruciating decision in more ways than purely political. There were also the well educated and politically savvy. These individuals knew the underlying northern politics that directly correlated with the rape and plunder of the south's beauty and commerce, was due in part to the obvious fact that the majority of foreign exchange came from the heavily taxed exports earned by southern states, and those in power; the ones that had already helped ruin the richness and beauty previously given to them by God, needed more land to call their own so they could spoil that as well; not to mention they now possessed the overwhelming bias, power and know-how needed to move west in order to eradicate the plains Indians.

While the smaller children frolicked in between dancing couples, preteens, too big to fool around in that fashion, spied on the romance from atop the hayloft of Morris's colossal new barn; the barn he'd ordered his slaves to hurriedly build from the lumber they'd cut 'n milled before the impending ratification of the new anti-slave laws were signed into effect, thus allowing them to leave.

Behind the barn, Isaac Martin, the twelve year old scruffy kid that Morris whiffed his boot at in Dycusburg was now twenty-seven and a soldier in the Union Army. He was sitting on a hay bale kissing on Mary Shelby who was barely eighteen when James Washington Shelby stepped up from behind. When Shelby caught the two off guard, they quickly stood up, "Daddy," said the girl, "I thought you were in Nashville, seekin' treatment?"

"The Aboriginals are still in th' hollers, Mary. They'll not allow me to pass," he stated ostensibly, no better that he was five years prior when he was sentenced to an asylum for the heinous killing of

Augustus Alley.

"Uh, Daddy," Mary continued with possible misgivings, "You remember Isaac Martin? ..."

Shelby extended his hand with sincere directness and enthusiastically said, "Mr. Martin, sir. It is a joy indeed to finally meet you face to face. Your family is well-known and you are deserving of an honorable discharge."

Isaac fearlessly looked Shelby dead in his eye and shook the man's hand; a man, for all intents and purposes, now appeared to be as sane as the woman he wanted to marry.

"Thank you sir," replied the boy with outward courage and inward nervousness, "It's an honor to finally be given the opportunity to meet Mary's father. I've heard much about your family's war exploits, and I especially have an interest in hearing a story or two that comes with your famous Dirk Knife."

That's when Mary gave Isaac a gentle nudge concerning his comment.

"I hope I have not offended you with my remark, sir?"

"No, goodness no," said Shelby in a kindly tone, "I take no offense whatsoever. The knife is famous, or should I say, infamous. No doubt on either side. It just recently, for that matter, saved my life. Mary may have spoken of it. And I have much gratitude in my ability, if need be, to filch a man's time with it. Some day soon boy, we'll sit down over a jug and chew on just how many folk it's kilt."

Isaac's face now reflected that the mentioning of the weapon was probably not a good idea.

HICK occupied a seat on Morris's front porch with the musicians. He looked more unkempt and scruffy than the aging Pastor Skimerhorn who was dozing in the chair next to him. Hick hadn't bathed in almost two weeks and at thirty-eight, looked twenty years older.

Tom on the other hand looked fit 'n first-rate at forty-seven. He was sitting at a long table with Sarah much the way he had during his wedding party, but now he was enjoying the surroundings with his entire family: William, who was ten; Annie who was almost five; along with Little Sarah who'd turned two. Sarah, at thirty-three, had finally grown some meat on her bones. Stronger than she'd ever been, she looked quite content as she breast fed Baby Mariah. "Annie honey," asked Sarah, "please go 'n get mama another piece of meat."

When Annie got up and went to task, Little Sarah snuggled in next to William who had his eye set on a stranger who'd just ridden in on horseback. The rider stopped at the barn where the former soldiers were mingling.

Morris leaned across the table for Tom's attention, but before acquiring it, looked around like he was about to reveal a secret, "Psst... hey Tom? See there? Yonder's Frank James of the Quantrill's. That's William Quantrill.

Tom looked over to see the young confederate soldiers gathering in praise around the rugged looking man who'd chosen to remain in the saddle. His thirsty mount nonetheless, stretched its head through a corral fence for drink from the trough. Murdering former blue boys in Kentucky was something James did not intend on doing right now, however those in blue weren't going to take any chances, so they moseyed off to tend to mock affairs while at the same time keeping a safe distance. As James visually scouted the farm; sizing up the youth and the adults alike, he swiftly decided it best he greet the boys and move along. Getting injured or killed by the likes of a woman with Sarah's disposition; a farmer's wife who could take him from a position he'd not seen or thought of, was

something he didn't require just now. And though
Sarah was nursing and less squirrelly than she once
was, she could still hit a mid-mark near as clean as
Hick could in his virile hunting days; and this was
something the qualified mercenary keenly recognized
from his purchase. Despite the fact he was only
twenty-two in years, his experience advised him that at
this very moment, Tom and Sarah were both looking at
him with those exact thoughts crossing their minds:
that if he were to as much as think about dismounting
or reaching for one of his weapons, he might start a
skirmish he couldn't finish. Morris again leaned
across for Tom's attention and said, "Showed them
nigger lovin' northerners a thing or two. That Lincoln
ruined more 'n half my business, freein' 'em up like he
did. Showed him, they sorely did. Got what *he* had
comin' after what he did to Atlanta. Too bad the
Pinkertons 're after 'em now. Too bad, it sorely is..."

Morris's comment sent Tom back in time to
Buffalo when the German businessman told him of the
Pinkerton's motto: *"We Never Sleep"*. But Tom was
more concerned with the present, therefore Morris's
comment also caused Tom to fix his eyes on the
infamous man burner the boys seemed to be falling
down over. Frank James continued to carefully look
over all the souls that might, or could do him harm if
he were to dismount. And though he was hungry, he

decided to gently rein his animal away from the boys and start out the same way he came in.

Tom then turned his attention to William who had craned his neck around the table so he too could watch as the soldiers paid homage to the departing gorilla rebel.

"Daddy?" asked the boy.

"Yes sir?" answered his father, eating his potato salad, yet still keeping one eye on James's exodus.

"I wish I could have gone to fight like the other boys."

Tom re-checked his young son's profile and his heart sank. William was barely ten and only a child, and though he could not lawfully enlist if the war were still on, Tom knew there were plenty of boys just as young that took up arms, fought and perished over the excitement of the idea. Tom then looked at Morris and while staring the sympathizing merchant dead in the eye, remarked with unreserved contempt, "Thank God's grace for not allowing it son."

Morris however was a steadfast and vocal anti abolitionist who'd heard it all before and could care less. Lately though, it was his neighbors who were clearly fed up of his hate. This was because all Morris had done since the impending laws were announced was carp about his faltering businesses due to either his 'niggers running off', or 'feeing their freedom oats before the actual ratification'.

On the other hand, there were plenty of folk that kept their, now free blacks on because they were an integral part of the workings as well as being akin to family for many of them. These folks were also implementing the *token commissary system*, or company store, that most of the other large farms and plantations were now using to provide the basic necessities to their help. There were also plenty of blacks with nowhere to go. You see, Morris never treated his slave brood with any dignity, so except the old and the weak, nearly all left prematurely, and permanently. Many of the men with riding and animal husbandry talents took up a nomadic existence and could be found heading west to drive cattle or fight Indians. Others found reason to take up with families that; although were unable to pay, treated them kindly for their labor in exchange for a roof and board.

So in actuality, most folks attended Morris's gatherings because it gave them grounds to socialize. And though the staunch southerner continued to use his get-togethers to advertise his businesses, he also provided everything for the party right down to the hard candy and liquor. And therefore anyone with half-a-wit would call their own attendance to such an event; human nature. Even so, because Morris had been so openly vocal and downright cruel over the

years; overtly condemning the families and the boys
that joined the union cause, a significant number of
locals called a secret meeting. End result: if Morris
didn't refrain from his verbal assaults against those
who'd helped him attain such an exceedingly good
way of living; and allow them to once again live
peacefully, nary would a soul attend his parties, and
his businesses would be boycotted. The message was
conveyed to him by a *reluctant* Pastor Skimerhorn
shortly after Abraham Lincoln was murdered.
Reluctant, because by now he too despised what the
northern aggressors had done to his beloved Southern
States. But he was also abhorrent as fellow priests of
Episcopalian denominations, where it was customary
to pray for the leader of a country, were ordered by
northern authorities, in no uncertain terms, that if they
did not order their congregations to pray for the
assassinated president in the southern areas that had
been conquered, the priests would be taken away, and
the churches turned over to northern denominations.
Skimerhorn had every right in the world to ignore both
orders: federal and the one from the community, but
being the pacifist he was, he timed his delivery to
Morris perfectly and with just the right amount of
weight to get the point across; emphasizing future loss
of income and opportunity – the only facet that had
enough shine to get the merchant's attention. He paid

little attention to the federal order however;
mentioning to his flock that it might be appropriate to
pray for the fallen president because he too was a man,
but barely a head bowed by those in attendance and he
therefore never mentioned it again.

the Growing **TUCKER CLAN** had once again forced
the expansion of their cabin to include another room
close to the same size as the main living space.

With the children asleep throughout, Tom and
Sarah laid in bed with Baby Mariah between them.
Drowsily Tom remarked, "Parties wear me out."

"Well, I'm double tuckered," countered Sarah,
"and grateful for it."

Tom smiled sideways at her pun. He knew his
grammatical influence had helped his wife's voice and
diction improve greatly over the years. Her wit
conversely, had remained unabated and razor sharp.

"Grateful I am," she continued, "that this
terrible war's finally at an end. And that party, well,

that party made it so; least wise in my mind it did. But I still feel terrible about our beloved president losing his life over it. Truly... but yer the lucky one," she said changing chords, "All you have to do is get up before the sun does, milk the cows, feed the hogs, till the west field, pick ten bushels 'f corn and shoe the mule. Did I leave anything out? O, and take care of mama; and she moved the baby over and snuggled in for some close up time with the ol' man.

"But Tom felt the need to interject and said, "You failed to include one important detail, my dear,"

"And that is? ..." asked Sarah.

"The fact that we have created workers who are maturing and will carry out the vast majority of the labor you feel I am so lucky to have the honor of performing."

"Well, aren't you one fer conjurin' up a fancy solution fer gittin' outta yer chores."

"That's me all right," answered Tom in a dozy, cock-hard fashion, "Fucking your cunny, thus producing worker bees that will grow up and help is a lot easier than doing it all myself."

"Come here," said Sarah softly, "lay yer head down right here. Too much has already been said for one day."

Regardless of any supplementary information Tom may have been lacking about relationships, he knew when it was time to change the subject around Sarah. So he laid his head down on her tummy and sighed, "Wife? ..."

"Mmm ..."

"Did you ever dream of a bigger existence?"

"You mean, like a life in the city?"

"Uh huh."

"I reckon I did, when I was a girl," she said, "but then daddy took ill, leavin' us shorthanded, so that perty much ended my dreamin', till you come along," and she batted her eyelashes at the ceiling. "After meetin' you, I couldn't stop dreamin' of all the places you'd take me - and have me."

This was an aspect of their relationship that Tom was more than aware of, so he attempted to clarify, "What I meant to ask was, what do you dream of now?"

"No need to dream; for a purpose anyway."

"Not at all? ..."

"Not fer a different outcome if that's what yer referrin' to. I'm as happy as one woman can be: healthy family; a good man who provides, and friends from the top of Livingston County to the bottom; a few in Crittenden and some in the others too."

Sarah propped herself up and looked down at Tom, "Is there somethin' yer wantin' to say?" But Tom couldn't seem to get it out. "Husband," she said, "we been married pert-near eleven years now, and by my cipherin', unless you're fixin' on takin' up with another, or leaving us, I figger we'll be married a sight longer, so--"

Tom pulled Sarah down from her little soapbox and brought her in close. She was always easier to handle from a proximity of inches. Sarah snuggled in and continued, "I know I'm good fer at least three more younglin's, and if need be, I'll wait eleven more years fer you to tell me what you do in that dark ol' shed." For Tom, this continued to be the epitome of Sarah's strong and patient side. He looked at her and for a brief moment recalled how Amanda held him the night before he departed Albany for Buffalo. He then leaned over the edge of the bed and in the same way he had for the past eleven plus years, blew out the paraffin oil lamp.

"Good night, husband…"

CHAPTER nineteen
AUTUMN, 1875

On THE PORCH of the Hodge cabin, the cross-eyed twin, now in her forties, sat on a bench holding the hand of a thirteen year old girl. Like years before, they were dressed in nothing more than soiled flour sacks with holes for their heads and arms, but because it's been abnormally cold, Norman had graciously allowed them to share a small blanket that covered their shoulders. And though their ashen faces reflected no actual expression per say, they did project an appearance that came from years of an existence with a Satin seed; a look that revealed a peripheral, yet at the same time, deep and hidden horror.

It was only last year that her twin, who'd conceived and passed more than nineteen fetuses ranging from stillborn to healthy, died. Not during childbirth as one might have expected, but in a freakish accident. One morning in the chicken coop while she was gathering eggs for Norman's breakfast, a board let loose and struck her in the forehead. The board itself was not all that heavy or powerful in its descent; yet it did have a rusty six-inch pole spike protruding from it. After falling to the ground, she was dead inside an hour. This infuriated Norman. Not because he'd lost kin, but because when the woman collapsed, the eggs she'd gathered for his breakfast had broken.

📖

Inside a dilapidated CORRAL situated under some trees and to the side of the Hodge cabin, Keech, also in his mid-forties along with Norman was attempting to breed a beautiful black stallion with a swayback nag.

Angered that the animals wouldn't join, Hodge jagged, "Why'd ya go'n take the biggest dern stud there was? Fuck yer stupid! More stupid than that son-a-her ma's," gestering to the twin on the porch, "fer gittin' his self hanged; fer the same goddamn thing - bein' stupid!"

"I'm sorry, daddy, there was only one animal that didn't run off."

The old man sent the boy a killing look, and Keech lowered his head. "Wadda ya want me to do?" he asked.

"Take it back! Before it's missed and we…, I

mean you, get hanged. Now git! ..."

But at that moment, Norman's character oddly changed, taking on to a seemingly trance like state. At the same time he began to blindly stare at the sun, he grabbed hold of his balls. Squeezing them, he stood up and started for the cabin as if an unnatural force had taken him over. In a steady yet deliberate fashion, he smoothly rolled his suspenders over his shoulders and easily unhitched his britches. He then shouted at the girls, "Git inside! Both 'f ya!" And before he reached the porch, he was completely naked; trousers in the mud with a full-on pikestaff before him. Without as much as a thought, the twin and the young girl stood up and obeyed; entering the dark precincts to once again hold a meeting with the impious.

In CHICAGO, the functions of *The Pinkerton National Detective Agency* were stronger than ever. In an upscale and boastfully ornate office with a view of a city that was rebuilding itself from the ashes of a disastrous fire that devoured three square miles only a few years prior, a maturing Allan Pinkerton rose from behind his desk and walked over to a large wall map depicting the U.S. territories including all of her rail ways, mountains and rivers. On an adjacent wall was a memorial to his agents lost in the line of duty. It included mementoes and photographs. Among them: Seth Yondell, Timothy Webster and Kate Warne.

Agents Liam Stone and Albin Bennett, two no-nonsense, capable men in their thirties stood with Pinkerton at the map. Their derby hats rested on chairs in front of his desk.

Pinkerton touched his finger to all the rail lines and townships leading westerly from Buffalo and stated sharply, "Webster and Warne only made it as far as Evansville before I called 'em back. I know this case is old lads, but we never sleep, eh?"

Bennett studied the map and replied in a clean British tone, "But Mr. Pinkerton, how do you know Tweddle is--"

"Tweddle likes city life!" snapped the boss with certainty, chopping off Bennett's words with his thick burr. He tapped the map even harder and continued,

"He's close to the biggest burgs with rail access. I know it! I feel it mair by the day!"

With this, Pinkerton walked back to his desk and picked up a file folder. Shaking it he said, "I want this one closed lads; before the New Year! Too many people disturbed, far too long!"

It was a **SWELTERING DAY** and Tom had been furrowing the lower field with a mule and plow for the last four hours. He stopped and took a drink from the military canteen Isaac Martin gave to William upon his return home from the service. He lowered it, wiped his brow and looked towards the river. The family's cabin however, rested on the bluff abeam Tom's shoulder.

Everyone on the Tucker Farm contributed: nineteen year old William threw buckets of slop to the hogs; thirteen year old Annie was having a hard time pinning damp sheets on a breezy clothes line, but she was managing; Little Sarah at eleven was thrashing a rug strung between two uprights with a wicker carper beater and nine year old Mariah was showing five year old Mary how to pump water; all this while four-year old John played with a puppy on the porch.

While keeping an eye on John and the puppy, Sarah leaned against the hog pen to spend some idle time with William. The boy stepped from the pen with mud 'n slop past his ankles. After closing the gate he asked his mother, "You really think the four-hundred pounder'll bring six dollars?"

"It will. Maybe more as long as it don't taste like catfish," she chuckled.

"You mean like Ol' Ecklas Coleman's do?"

"They taste like what you feed 'em, son," and she looked back at Tom in the field who was still plowing and she waved, but he didn't see her as his figure moved behind the cabin. "I recall daddy tellin' me a story years ago of a feller in England that raised chickens just so he could feed 'em to his swine. Now that's somethin' I'd be interested in tastin'; chicken-hog. Think there's a market for it? This one got William to scratching his head. The boy knew a hog would eat just about anything, so he started thinking on all the different critters he could feed one so it would taste special: possum, squirrel, pheasant, rabbit, dove, pigeon, etc, etc...

"Ecklas," his mother continued, "should stick to

fishin', and leave hoggin' to those who grow crops.

The children had moved onto other chores and Tom had finished furrowing the field. He was on the mule's back and riding towards the cabin with only a rope halter on the animal.

Sarah appeared to be content rocking on the porch with John and the puppy. She kept the boy and the pup wrangled close with her callused, bare feet while at the same time cooling herself from the humidity of fall by fanning her face with a folded flour sack that doubled as a diaper. "Seen the stud?" she asked Tom who'd just rolled off the back of the mule exhausted.

"He's out there," he answered, soaked in sweat.

"He didn't come when Mariah put oats out for him. He always comes fer her."

Making his way towards the cabin door, Tom passed a half dozen sock stretchers standing in various places with the family's garments pulled over them. Seconds later he emerged with a spy glass. He stretched it out and walked up to the fence by the garden to have a look himself. Through the instrument he saw a stubbly field with some cows and a few horses, but no black stud. He panned the device towards the far corner where the giant pecan tree stood; the tree he and Sarah had so much fun under. It was also a shady spot where the animals liked to stay cool, but no stallion. Then he did a double take, "Well, I'll be..."

"What? ..." asked Sarah.

Through the glass, Tom watched Keech Hodge lead the glistening animal into the pasture through an opening in the fence where he'd taken down a couple of boards. Once loose, the stallion snorted 'n bucked and then galloped off in an animated floating stride.

Tom collapsed the device with a crack and handed it to Sarah in passing. When he hastily rolled back onto the sweat-drenched mule, his concerned wife shouted, "What'd you see?!"

"It's that damn Keech Hodge!" he called over his shoulder and he began riding off.

"You best be careful, Tom Tucker!" shouted Sarah, "That clan's full a trickery!"

Beyond the farthest FENCE LINE and well out of sight from the cabin, Keech quietly walked the middle of the road. Distancing himself from the Tucker farm, he swatted at pebbles with a willow switch. But when he heard an approaching rider, he turned and saw Tom on the mule, "Bloody horse thief!" he shouted, "I should have mistaken you for a bear when I had the chance!"

Keech dropped the switch and grabbed up a piece of limb wood from the side of the road and ran for Tom. Tom reined-back hard, but it was too late. Keech smashed the solid limb against the mule's shins and the animal pitched him over the top where he skidded along the roadway, finally coming to a stop in a drainage ditch along the side. Bruised and dazed, he tried to right himself, but before he could, Keech grabbed another stick and walloped him unconscious with it. Tom slid into the shallow trench, face up with his legs on the roadway – as if sitting in a chair.

ALWAYS ONE to investigate matters, Sarah, as she approached in her buckboard, witnessed Keech bash Tom and uttered, "O Lordy... and then snapped the reins, "Git up!"

Keech started unlacing Tom's shoes and pulled one off, "Always wearin' nice shoes eh, Fancyman," but when Keech saw Sarah's wagon, he quickly ducked in the bushes.

Sarah applied the brake and reined the animal back. The wheels locked up and the wagon came to a chattering standstill. She collected up her 12 gauge and jumped down, "Husband!" she called on her way to the ditch. She positioned herself next to Tom who was altogether unconscious. She set the scatter gun on the road and began nursing him.

Keech watched from the bushes. Needless to say, Sarah's anger caused the effort Tom had put into the improvement of her language to fly right out the window, "You'd better turn yer tail up 'n run Keech Hodge! Dern yer clan! If I as much as eye you from a corner, I'll gut you like a flounderin' catfish! ...--"

But before she could finish, Keech picked up the shotgun and used the butt end to shove her away from her husband. Her small frame was no match for the bully, but Sarah wasn't afraid of Keech and never had been. She slapped at his legs and then found a small stick and stabbed at his bare feet in hopes of puncturing one, but Keech just stepped back.

For the first time really, the middle Hodge boy reached inside his soul where he managed to unearth a shred of decency, "Hello Sarah, he kindly said, "It's been a spell."

"Keech Hodge!" she shouted while continuing to check on Tom, "God gave yer clan nutin'! Hear me, <u>nu</u> <u>thin</u>! That's why y'all steal 'n injer!"

But her words passed right over him and he asked, "Remember when you kissed me?"

"No!" But she actually did.

"I do," he said, his eyes looking clear through the woman.

"Well, you can just carve that thought right out of y'all's brainless head!"

"I cain't. I tried; hard too, cuz it hurt when it'd turn up - unexpected like. But then, after, it seemed to be the only good thought I was left with. It was a thought I could rest on a spell, and not feel all twisted inside."

"You're ill Keech," said Sarah, trying for a skosh of humanity, "and there's no treatment for what y'all ain't got!"

"It don't matter," he replied, his tenderness short-lived, "cuz I'm gonna finish yer bunch, kids too. I've set my mind to it."

Sarah choked some, but still managed to scoff,

"Better git to it then, 'cuz last I ciphered, y'all was runnin' low on kin." And said with as much sarcasm as she could muster. "They're gonna hang you up like they hanged yer useless puke of a brother. Even chicken crap's worth more than yer bunch!"

📖

DOWN the road a piece, Hick was unmindfully kicking a stone as he walked to the ferry crossing so he could get to Smithland. On his way to work at the court house; his arm was tucked deep into his jacket pocket and his limp was ostensibly no better than it was over twenty years ago. When he rounded the bend, he saw Keech standing over Sarah with her 12-gauge under his arm. As soon as Keech raised the butt of the gun to strike Tom dead, Sarah and Hick simultaneously shouted, "NO!..." Sarah leaned forward to protect Tom and instead of the gun-butt hitting Tom square, it struck Sarah's head with a glancing blow. She immediately folded. Her face scuffed the roadway and her unconscious body slumped onto Tom's.

Hick lit out as fast as he could, but he was slower by far, and before he could get to Tom 'n Sarah, Keech managed to jerk Sarah up from the ditch and flop her into the back of the buckboard along with Tom's one shoe. He then hopped onto the seat, slid the handle of the shotgun under his ass and picked up the reins. Just as Hick got close enough to perhaps do something, the squalid inbred snapped the rawhide. Extending his leg, Keech knocked Hick to the ground shouting, "Cripple!" and he roared on by.

At the CINCINNATT TRAIN STATION, Agent Stone was having a difficult time showing Joseph's likeness to a railroad worker who was bent over while inspecting the tracks. In his thick Scots intonation Stone asked, "Well, man, have you seen him?" After a quick glance at the likeness, the man replied, "No sir," and returned to his job. But this was insufficient conviction for the investigator, so Stone raised his voice, "Are ye sure!?" he shouted, pressing the likeness closer to the man's face, "Look harder!"

On the other side of ten or more sets of tracks, in an area far less congested from where the train cars and workers prepared to depart, Agent Bennett had been surveying the area between the station and the Ohio River. When a boat whistle blew, he honed in on the vessel sounding it. By the time Agent Stone had stepped up to his partner, Stone's entire body was enveloped in agitation; half of him frustrated and the other half just hot and sweaty, but before he could utter a word of discontent, Bennett annotated with confidence, "Pinkerton's wrong."

"He's never wrong," exclaimed Stone.

"He is this time. Tweddle didn't travel by rail. Besides that likeness is worthless this far north. It's been too many years. It's why the others couldn't track him."

Perplexed, Stone asked, "How do ye know all this?"

With analytical precision Bennett stated, "Tweddle feels guilty. He'll have wanted to punish himself."

"Make sense, man," said Stone and he took off his derby and ran his hand through his remaining hair...

Still looking at the river, Bennett posed, "Ask yourself this, Liam; how would you feel if you killed your brother?"

I don't have a brother," the agent replied, wiping sweat from his face and brow.

So to make his point, Bennett turned to him and said, "He traveled by river. Judgment dictates he wouldn't want to risk a second train escape. He was also aided. He wasn't a woodsman, or a hunter."

Feeling the need to conceal his thinning hair, Stone arranged his head cover and looked to where Bennett's gaze was set. Adjusting the lid exactly how he liked it, he argued, "The file reads that his father made clear mention on more than one occasion that he gets deathly ill on the water, and will do almost anything to avoid it. The old man has no reason to fabricate an alibi. He wants us to find his son as bad as the law wants to see him hang. The shoreline townships are a sure giveaway. Besides, why would he subject himself to torture?" At that very moment; when Stone had finished asking his question, both men knowingly, turned and looked at each other, yet remained silent. Stone contemplated for another moment, and then, without any conscious input, began nodding ever so slightly. The heavy-handed Scot was beginning to understand.

ON THE ROAD to Smithland, the mule stood lame while Hick cared for Tom who was still laying caddywhompus in the drainage ditch; completely unaware of his surroundings.

"Tom?..." pleaded Hick, "C'mon, you gotta wake up. C'mon now..."

Tom groaned; and with his own might, made a weak attempt to adjust his position, and then with Hick's help, finally righted himself. "He whacked ya good," said Hick, "Would've kilt-cha, but we shouted."

"You're like a brother, Hick," uttered Tom, "Thank you..."

"No time for sentiments. We need to git after 'em."

"Who?"

"Keech, that's who!"

"Let him go. There's time for that another day."

"But he stole Sarah!"

Concerned, Tom tried to turn his head in the direction of the farm, but that brought on pain.

"C'mon," said Hick, "we need to trail that melon fucker."

OUTSIDE the Tucker home, six children congregated around Hick who quietly held the reins of both the stallion and a bay. The children looked worried, and by rights should be.

Tom, who was clearly not himself, faltered as he exited the cabin. He was laden with his Indian trade rifle; Hick's old Sharps '51; a Colt .45 revolver and his old flintlock pistol. These black power *hand-sticks* that were now being turned into surplus for the faster discharging revolvers, had always been, ironically, Tom's pistol of choice since losing his first one on the train from Buffalo all those years ago.

"Remember this?" he asked Hick, showing him his old sporting rifle that had been inside the cabin since that day in Marion.

"I rightly do," replied Hick, and he nodded accordingly with a thought of using it once again; perhaps to shoot some dinner should they find the need to camp. Once Tom tied the scabbard containing Hick's rifle to the bay, Hick used his left arm to hold the saddle horn and he mounted up. His bad leg it turned out was close enough to the extra weight and momentum needed to put his body into the saddle without too much offset. Not as difficult as he'd been thinking all these years; just a bit more right-leg heave and he was up and in. It felt good he thought when he sank into the seat; hearing the leather squeak when he waggled his ass and settled in.

Tom said, "I always knew a day would come when you'd likely get to discharge it again." And even though Hick thought he might shoot some food again with his *old friend*, he also knew that it was Tom's wife that had been taken; and for as much as he yearned to put one through Keech Hodge, it was Tom's duty to do it and therefore resided; knowing that he was only part of the posse in support of his friend.

Tom then turned his attention to his family and said, "William, the farm's in your charge until I return."

"But Daddy," the boy worriedly protested, "what if Keech shows?"

The girls shuddered at the mere sound of Keech's name, let alone the thought of him coming onto their land or within sight of the cabin.

William became even more fearful when Tom placed the Colt revolver in his hand. "But daddy," he exclaimed, "I never shot - *a man*."

When William said this, Tom could feel his sincerity and became even more grateful his first son never went to war, "I've always prayed you'd never need to son." But when Tom mounted up, William worriedly asked, "What if it fails?..."

"*This* weapon will not fail to fire. If Keech shows, cock it like I showed you, aim for the heart and squeeze the trigger. Discharge it two times. Shoot the head if required. After he dies, you'll cry. Keep the girls safe." Tom drove his heels, now fitted with another pair of shoes, into the stallion's flanks and the two friends rode away as fast as their animals would carry them.

HOT 'n CLAMY was the nature of this cave situated on the face of a limestone hillside; a place the brothers had visited many times. Along with the normal smell of dampness; it reeked of spoiling greens and saturated smoke. In the blackness towards the back of the cavern, water oozed down the walls creating tiny flows that made their way to the front of the sun-lit opening. There they terminated into puddles to finally spill over and trickle down the mossy face. Inside, the walls were adorned with deep Native engravings; hieroglyphics of sorts. Once beautiful representations of a sacred life, since desecrated by the brothers: their meanings changed to symbolize the overwhelming damage their clan had done to themselves and others over the years. For the last few minutes, Keech had been sitting on a log poking at a newly built fire with a stick. He knew as sunset approached, a chill would soon follow.

With her hands lashed before her and her ankles hobbled so she could only walk short steps, Sarah had settled into a dry spot against the wall. Her head ached from the black 'n blue egg that had formed on her forehead from the butt of her shotgun, but this didn't stop her from speaking her mind, "So Keech," she sputtered in a foggy, yet informative tone, "You steal me away from my husband and six children so you 'n me can settle down and have a family of our own, eh? I reckon you've done yerself some sober cipherin' on how yer gonna provide fer us while we live here in this fine little cave dwellin' you've decorated."

"Shut yer hole! No one'll find us in here, not even that cripple."

Sarah scoffed and under her breath said, "You found it – and the Injuns found it." Keech pondered the rebuttal. "And you don't know my husband."

But Keech sat up and responded even stiffer, "I know I hit em real hard. Maybe kilt 'em in that drain. And if he didn't pass," he argued, drawing his hunting

knife, "I'll make sure of it - you too, and yer brood.
Then I'll eat yer mule. That's what I know!"

ON a lightly traveled path surrounded by moderate
woodlands, Tom and Hick rode up on Sarah's
buckboard. Hick surveyed the surroundings with a
keen eye: ground, bushes, twigs, trees, sky, and more
notably, wind direction and its speed.

In token form, but no less serious, Tom also
looked for tracks, but he was unsteady and nauseous.
He needed to rest. He bent over ready to vomit and
with his hands on his knees asked, "You can track
anything, right, Hick?"

"Like huntin' possum I reckon, sept possum's a
might smarter than the likes of Keech Hodge."

It's not the answer Tom had hoped for, but it
was one that allowed him to feel that his friend still
knew what he was doing.

"They're close, Tom," said Hick, "By my
reckonin', they're in that formation yonder," and he

pointed, but Tom was busy coughing up.

At the same time Keech poked at the fire, he coveted Sarah's lightly sleeping body through the flames. Languorously through the thick malaise of a tortured soul he craved her wholesome beauty; inside and out. He always had. "I was always there," he softly supposed, "keepin' eyes on you, but you never saw me."

Sarah roused, but Keech was in a trance, "You always picked the boys that didn't care none fer you, like Timmy Willbow. But I was there, watchin'. I always kept eyes out fer you. But Timmy liked gitting' with us boys, and this got me all mixed inside. Why Sarah..?"

Realizing she was still bound, Sarah tried a more subtle approach, "Please let me loose, Keech? That way no one'll be injured."

FOUR-HUNDRED yards away, Hick had been leaning against a thin hickory trying to open Tom's spyglass all the way. He had the big end pinched between his knees, but because his leg was weak, he couldn't seem to get the small end to extend. Tom stepped up half bent over and extended his hand, and Hick begrudgingly passed him the device. Tom stretched it out and handed it back. Because of Hick's prior independence, accepting help from others has been difficult, but this time he found it within himself to acknowledge his friend with a grateful nod.

Hick set the glass on a limb and looked through the eye piece. He slowly searched the wooded areas and then aimed it into the hills. He panned the instrument as far to the right as the tree would allow and then to the left almost as far when he stopped after seeing some rising smoke. He tilted the glass down and saw more of it oozing from the top of the cave mouth. He then saw Sarah standing on the sandy hillside in front of the opening with a long rope attached to her hands. He watched as she stepped out and beyond the opening. Using the hillside to support her back, she lifted her dress as best she could, squatted and peed.

Hick turned to Tom who was loosening the girth strap on the stallion while still trying to recover from his bout, "Tom?" whispered Hick, holding the glass up. Tom forwent the task and made his way to where Hick was pointing, "Yonder's Sarah…" With vengeance, Tom put the glass to his eye. Through it, he saw Sarah stand up and with the aid of the hillside, work her dress back down. He then watched Keech pull her back inside. Without thinking, Tom handed the glass to Hick and angrily started for the cave.

Hick whispered as loud as he could before it was no longer a whisper, "Wait Tom!" Tom kept walking then turned. "Take a rifle..." and Hick pointed to Tom's *Henry*.

Tom pulled the black powder pistol from his belt and showed it to Hick.

"The time's not right," Hick pleaded.

"The time's right now," argued Tom, "Keech Hodge has my wife!" and he started for the cave.

"Dang you Tom Tucker," whispered Hick, scuffing dirt with his shoe, "Why'd you bring me if you was fixin' on gittin' yerself kilt?"

"I didn't bring you," replied Tom, "You brought me," and he started walking.

Hick thought about the remark for a moment and came to realize that he did bring Tom, and therefore still actually had what it took to track. And this too made him feel better about himself.

SARAH returned to her place against the wall and again pondered a way to convey a simple importance to Keech so he might understand the consequences of his actions, "Please, Keech?" Sarah appealed.

"I cain't," he said, staring at the tiny flame that was now making more smoke than heat.

"Why?" asked the woman with honest query.

"It's too late," he said.

"Turn me loose, please?…"

"It don't matter no-how," Keech remitted in a timbre about as sad as any voice could muster. As blood trickled from his wounded ear and saliva drained from the corner of his disfigured 'n unfeeling mouth, he lifted his eyes from the fire and looked directly at the woman, "I cain't," he reiterated; his face, the one that Sarah was *now* seeing through the heat waves, appeared smoother than it actually was; angelic like. "They're gonna lynch me; fer my life," his eyes lowering again to the tiny flame, "Fer what I ain't, and never could amount to. After the Woman-Talbot's devil-cat cut me, I begged daddy to let me die; more times than I recollect, but he wouldn't. He just kilt us, slow-like, by lettin' us live. We all begged 'em, 'Kill us daddy, please kill us,' but he wouldn't. He just kept makin' the girls have more babies. He wouldn't stop. He couldn't. When Doc Sanders was stitchin' up my face, I could hear 'em talkin'. Doc asked daddy why he did that to his girls. He told 'em cuz it was done to him, and that's the way it always was. It weren't my fault I was born. He told me once my ma was a whore who run off after she pushed me out. I hoped 'n hoped fer long spells she'd come back 'n take me with her, but daddy said she run off cuz I was so ugly. When I cried, he beat me and had his way with me. If any of us cried, he'd have his way with us. It weren't my fault he wouldn't kill me and bury me with the rest. He kilt plenny others. It weren't my fault I was born, Sarah. All I ever wanted was to be dead, but I was too scared to do it myself; afeard I'd mess it up and daddy would let me live. You were the only person that made livin' a little more bearable.

Outside THE CAVE, Tom signaled Sarah with his mourning dove call, "Coo ye coo…, coo coo…."

Inside, Sarah's ears perked when she heard it and applied to Keech, "I need to make more water."

"You just made water," he argued.

"I'm with child," she blurted, conjuring a bold face lie, "I need to make more water!"

Outside, Tom waited.   Hick however, sensing it was time to do something; anything, limped over to the stallion and pulled Tom's *J. Henry* from its scabbard. This weapon, if loaded and sighted properly, could hit a mark at the distance he was currently at. So he managed to raise the barrel of the almost canon like weapon onto a small, dead branch, but snap, the branch broke and the muzzle hit the dirt. In its current position, Hick feebly discovered the weapon had yet to be loaded. He left the barrel in the dirt, leaned the butt against the tree and limped over to Tom's saddlebags and began looking for the ammunition, but soon discovered it hadn't been packed, "Dang you, Tom Tucker!" he whispered, scuffing his feet again.

At the same time Tom crept closer, Sarah waited for Keech's response to her request. Tom's bird call sounded again...

"I'm *not* gonna make water right here if that's what yer waitin' to see," she spouted.

Keech wasn't exactly pondering on that visual, but it would be nice to watch he thought.

"Keech Hodge!"

"Alright!" he answered, finally submitting to the woman's bitching.

"Thank you," she replied sincerely. But Keech turned baffled; lost really from Sarah's unfeigned gratitude. These two words you see; chained together and spoken to him, on his behalf, and in that particular tone and inflection were quite possibly two sounds he had never absorbed until now. This caused both of his eyes to become weepy for a few moments. He then wiped a rolling tear from one of them. Looking at it, he became sincerely mystified by its appearance and the emotion connected to it.

TOM'S *J. HENRY* rifle was useless. So Hick balanced the weapon's weight in one hand while positioning the tip of the barrel into the scabbard. He then lifted the butt and allowed the gun's weight to take it all the way down into the covering. This is when he scuffed the ground again with more frustration. Walking over to the bay, he pulled out his Sharps '51 from its old home. And like a blind man in his own barn, he opened the side pouch on the scabbard and retrieved everything necessary to ready the weapon. He lowered the breech and loaded in a special linen cartridge containing extra powder; a cartridge he recalled creating shortly before the tragic bear hunting trip. This was followed by a smaller conical mini-ball that he always carried several of for long distance shots; shots that *always* made him money when he wagered. Upon raising and locking the breech, he inspected the percussion cap for corrosion or damage - and set it in place. He then pried back the weapon's brass hammer.

TOM CREPT CLOSER. Crouching low, he watched Sarah emerge from the mouth of the cave. When she spotted him, she strategically stepped to the side where she squatted and pretended to pee, but the steep incline between them obscured Keech and the shotgun under his arm.

Tom stepped into the open and pointed the black powder pistol at the rag of a man and shouted, "Keech Hodge! Release my wife!"

Keech raised the shotgun, but Tom squeezed the trigger first, yet the pistol failed to discharge. Sarah helplessly watched as Keech raised the lethal weapon on her now defenseless husband. Leveling the weapon, Keech shouted down at Tom, "WHERE'S YER LAFEET NOW, FANCYMAN! But suddenly Keech's body folded forward like a rag doll as if violently jerked by a rope from around his waist and blew backwards. Sarah too was knocked off her feet because the leash she'd been secured with was tied around Keech's foot. A second later, Tom heard the echo of a gunshot report. He looked around as it made its way from the wooded area to the hillside.

At the twelve-hundred foot mark; well beyond the Sharps' effective range with a standard load, Hick awkwardly leaned against the thin hickory he'd chosen as a firing platform. His rifle barrel resting on a limb; the rear tang sight raised to its maximum and his left index finger on the trigger. The weapon's breech and barrel oozed burnt powder and gasses and because there was no wind, a cloud of smoke lay before it so thick, the surrounding scape was barely discernable. "Gotcha this time, Keech Hodge," he said out loud, "I warned ya - stop callin' me by that name."

CHAPTER twenty
THE GOWER HOUSE

TWO-WEEKS LATER on a stormy night in Smithland, a thin, drawn man sat at a piano playing saloon melodies from an upright box. The notes were accompanied by an atmosphere of card playing and drinking inside the small, yet noisy front room of The Gower House. Although the house was a bit raucous due to the current nature of the socializing being conducted, rain could still be heard pounding the tin rooftops outside. Whores joined in the proclivities; leading men upstairs to engage in a poke; the carnal pleasure that only the exchange of currency or trade could provide those traveling or not. And whether the man was single or married, these sporting women; girls mostly, formulated no judgment upon those they entertained for the money or goods they received in-kind for their services. They provided the township with something no less important than the farrier who shod the horses; the blacksmith who fabricated the shoes or the difficulty the mayor had to go through spending the money generated by the tax collector.

Seated in the corner, Ned Buntline, at fifty-three, was playing poker with a few other men. Ned was winning. Also mixed with the smell of smoke, sweat and whisky, Agents Stone and Bennett closely mingled amongst the souls. Stone had been passing Joseph's likeness around relentlessly asking the same questions over and over in his cold and uncaring tone. And with each man asked, he carefully watched his eyes when he answered. Meanwhile Bennett not only kept an eye on Stone's back, he also watched the escape routes in case something he'd not thought of occurred. He was also aware however that The Gower House was a boarding establishment; and as a general rule, only birds of passage came to stay; and therefore believed constructing a lead on Tweddle's whereabouts from here would be slim as best.

OUTSIDE, a man staggered from the front door of The Gower House and into the pouring rain of the dark street. And if it wasn't for the candles and the paraffin lanterns seen from the windows, he wouldn't be seen at all. He was a transient, yet in his hand was Joseph's likeness, and in his shoulder jutted a knife. He stumbled a few more steps then collapsed to his knees.

Stone walked out the same door and stood for a moment under the eve looking at him. Then in measured footfalls, the agent stepped off the planking and into the downpour towards the man.

Fearing for his life, the man held up his hands; Joseph's likeness was in the bloody one, "Don't kill me, mister, please. Here, take it..." Stone snapped the paper back. "I'm drunk," slurred the man, "I was foolin', that's all -..."

Stone placed his foot to the man's shoulder and in one callous act, levered the blade from his bleeding flesh. The man cried out, but this only caused the hardened operative to shove Joseph's likeness back in his face and growl, "Do ye know him, or don't ye?" - the claim made only inches from the sniveling man's ear.

"No!" he whimpered, "No..."

Stone tucked the likeness into his jacket and walked back under the porch eve and out of the downpour to meet Bennett who was now standing by a few men, including Buntline. They'd come out in time to watch the wounded man stumble away. And for as much as this man was a drifter of sorts, some of the others had played cards with him before, however none of these men knew the agents who were now aware they'd pushed their questioning too far. So when the smartly dressed investigators started to overhear a hush of 'inquiring tones' as to the true nature of their business, they strategically ignored the men and walked away to a dryer portion of decking. As they did, Ned turned his back to the agents and opened his arms around the men like a cobra and gently turned the small crowd of intoxicants back inside, "C'mon now. The excitement's over. Let's go play some cards." And though Ned was a brawler to the end, he knew an interface between these representatives of the law and a card player or two would surely end in an injurious outcome. All the same, before walking in, he looked back at the agents who had stopped to quietly converse amongst themselves. Never shy on the talents of observation, Ned watched their body movements in order to garner even more information. After a moment, he followed the others inside to where it was warm and dry, and to collect his winnings.

"These are all wanderers," Bennett claimed.

"He's close," argued Stone, cleaning his blade with a white handkerchief before returning it to the sheath he had hooked to his suspender. Neatening himself, he did a double take on the outline of a person some steps away that was blending into the shadow of the overhang like a chameleon. Rainwater was literally sheeting off the roof above the silhouette's head and splashing into the muddy street, thus making it difficult to ascertain whether it was a man or a woman.

Stone was tired and wet, so he handed the likeness to Bennett and gestured for him to make the approach. Bennett was also tired, yet never one to shirk a task, stepped over to the figure and leaned in, "You - standing there?" he called.

The tattered looking individual, who Bennett now made out as a man, was too intoxicated to care about anything more than the tare he was currently on. He simply clung onto post while pissing in the street. Unfortunately he was getting more on his shoes than in the puddle he was aiming for. But because of the weather, it was nearly impossible to tell the difference between the rain drops and the stream of piss.

Thoroughly worn-out from asking strangers the same question; and at the same time irritated he didn't get a response on his first request, Bennett shouted, "You! Drunkard? Seen this Man?" and he put Joseph's likeness directly before the figure's slumped over torso. In turn, the man grabbed Bennett's arm with an endeavor to focus. He looked hard at the drawing. Slurring his words, Hick answered, "That's Tarm Tucker. I just saved his life – again...

CHAPTER twenty-one
Wagon APPROACHES

BARELY A SOUL stirred on this bracingly cold Sunday morning. The black stallion, which had matured and settled down some due to an ongoing list of requests for its studding services, was saddled and tied to a post outside the ten-by-ten shed. When Tom stepped from the small structure, he was caught off guard by Ned Buntline who'd just pulled to a stop in his buggy. Off guard due to the light covering of snow that had fallen an hour before, allowing him to approach in virtual silence. Plumes of exhalation departed the animal's nostrils while its driver continued to sit bundled; the man's shoulders draped in a Union Army blanket and his legs covered with two plaid woolen beddings.

Tom, who was dressed warm yet unencumbered, closed the door behind him. Ready to mount up, he declared, "Well, Ned Buntline... I failed to hear your advance. I must have lost some of my hearing. What brings you to the valley?"

"Well, you do, Tom," he replied calmly, "or should I say, Joseph Tweddle?"

Tom's stomach jumped into his chest and his

heart began pounding. He immediately scanned the area. He wasn't sure if he should run to the cabin for a weapon; mount up and attempt an escape, or do both.

"Where's the family?" asked Ned as Tom continued looking for others that may be near.

"It's Sunday... They went on ahead to church, like they always do..."

Buntline nodded and diplomatically admitted, "Not being a church going man, I do regret these matters escape me at times." He also saw no need to climb out from under his warm covers, yet his small movements didn't escape Tom's eyes; including the fact that Ned's hands were under his blankets.

"Listen Tom," he said in an unruffled tone, "I like you, always have; ever since I witnessed you save your man there in Albany."

"He died," Tom stated as a fact, stepping back from his hard address of the stallion. He'd also established that Buntline didn't come to cause trouble and therefore placed his hasty thoughts of mounting up and riding across the frozen countryside on hold until he could ascertain more about why the writer had traveled this far.

"Even so," said Buntline, "you acted mighty fast; tying that severed arm like you did. I was truly divided with my own behavior that day." Ned wanted to remove his hat in revere of the factory foreman, but feeling the cold, he refrained and only pulled down the brim with respect. Tom however, questioned the man's humanity; something Ned hadn't demonstrated a tremendous amount of during his intermittent visits to the area.

"I was rude to him," Ned acknowledged, "and all of a sudden it happened. I could not retract my words, and have since been regretful for their expression. But you built my buggy," he continued, trying to smile after his emotional recall of the terrible accident and the subsequent news of the foreman's death, "and I'll add, you did a fine job."

Tom needed to only glance at the buggy, "I didn't build that."

"This one, hell no you didn't. Devil built this contraption, but I owned the one you constructed for seventeen years – fine workmanship it was, and I'll attest to it. Eventually sold 'er for parts."

"Get to the point, Ned."

"Please forgive my procrastination, Tom. I'm a writer, but I'm also a reader," and Ned pulled a cigar from under his blanket, but doing this caused Tom to become wary. "I meet my challenges square on," he continued, offering a second cigar to Tom who declined, "and I study as much as I can about this rapidly expanding nation of ours." The now corpulent man struck a kitchen match against the firewall of the buggy and lit his leafy roll. "When you first came to town," he murmured, puffing away, "I knew I'd seen you in Albany. So I looked for a story."

Tom mocked, "The infamous Joseph Tweddle, now living in Kentucky under an alias. Exploiting others; is that not your livelihood, Buntline?"

"I admit it," he replied without shame, "So I looked in past publications for any indication of why a well brought up English engineer from New York would show his face a region well removed from any populous, and the reading I do say, was not as plentiful as I'd hoped."

Tom waited for more.

"I've turned plenty against me, Tom. My stories've put me in a perilous purchase more than a time or two; and like you, I enjoy spending time here. The area is truly glorious."

"So why didn't you speak your truth?"

"Written on a page or handed down," he answered in earnest, "stories are about timing, and at that point I was newly married." When he said this, his voice cracked from genuine grief. "I'd already taken too many unnecessary chances on my beautiful, *heart of sweetness* leaving me, or even worse, leaving me for another."

"I heard the news about her passing," said Tom and he removed his hat, "My sincerest condolences."

372

"I'm still distraught," replied Ned without pretense and he pulled a handkerchief and wiped his eyes. "Heartache's not a feeling I harbor well; perhaps why I remarry quickly. But I will say, that one, I loved with all my heart."

"I truly regret your loss," said Tom, replacing his hat. "It caused me to seriously reflect on what it would be like to lose Sarah, and I felt sorrowful."

"Thank you, sir," responded Ned, "I'm touched by your authenticity; I justly am. I do believe the candid grief that others feel and share over another's loss is what allows those who've yet to lose a loved one, the ability to recognize how short life can actually be." Tom nodded in agreement and wanted to comment, but only watched the man regain his composure. Ned continued, "That's why I felt it best I leave you alone twenty-five years ago; to sort out your own demons."

"What made you suspect I was harboring demons?"

"Your eyes," he said, looking at Tom while puffing on his cigar - trying to get it lit again.

Tom petted the stallion's neck, "Are you here to capture me, Ned?"

Buntline chuckled, "Capture you? I'm far too old for that campaign. I'd need a sight more than a suit and buggy to bring a nefarious desperado like you up the courthouse steps to meet blind justice."

And though Buntline had admittedly given up his brawling days; with his knees bothersome and his joints susceptible to the cold; truth be told, he got into a scrap just last week with two sober card players at The Gower House and came out the victor. In other words, Ned could take Tom in a bar fight, but attempting to capture him would furnish an altogether different outcome, and Ned knew this. Besides, Buntline had customarily been motivated by writing a well crafted story for money, not both. And this situation presented neither, because by this point in his career, he'd already published a significant number of novels and money wasn't as important as it once was.

"O, I don't know about that," said Tom in resign, "I'm tired, Ned. I might even find it a relief."

Ned shook his head, "I wouldn't take that line too far, Tom. Just so's you know; some years back, I felt the end of a lynch mob's rope. After swingin' fer what felt like a life time, I was cut down. It was some good quality luck fer me, which I've always had, so don't go thinkin' that gettin' your neck extended is a relief. Fortunately I don't have much of a neck to lengthen; kinda thick," and he chuckled as he felt the chill around his collar.

On the FRONT PORCH of the Tucker cabin, Tom was sitting in his favorite straight chair while Ned was enjoying the porch swing that Tom had bought Sarah as an anniversary gift by way of a catalog a few years back. Ned was also sipping from the cider crock that Tom allowed Hick to keep on the porch for cold mornings such as these. Even *if* Hick didn't come around much these days, it was still a nice reminder of the times when he did.

"*Edward Zane Carroll Judson,*" Ned proudly announced in a soulful drawl backed up by a few ounces of mash that was now splashing around in his forceful belly.

"And *who* exactly is that?" asked Tom as if he'd just heard a foreign language.

"My given," replied Ned, handing the jug back to Tom, "I felt it might settle your state some if you knew."

Tom accepted the jug and nodded with understanding because it did actually make him feel better to hear once again that he wasn't the only, or the last person who'd changed their name for the sake of past deeds committed. He then gave himself permission to take a tiny nip of Hick's pumpkin mash whisky - the first since he'd promised himself on his wedding night to refrain from such actions; for a loose tongue came by way of a liquored up mind. Therefore he was lucky that Buntline's arm was in the perfect position to take the jug back after his small swig.

"Mmm, mm...," Ned decreed, wiping his chin, "I do enjoy a warm mist over me on an icy mornin'." He exhaled thick fog and concluded, "From what I've gleaned, Tom, the Agency's been searchin' a spell. And you remaining clear of The Gower House all these years appears a good forecast."

Tom squared his chair, looked across the pasture and plainly held, "It's been twenty-five years, Ned, and I can't say that I've ever heard of, nor read about any person, company, or country for that matter, seeking a single individual for so long."

"Well, you can thank manmade statutes for that," Ned supposed, "or the lack there of, cuz there ain't one fer murder."

"You're a gambling man, Ned; am I out of options?"

"You can shoot cain-cha?" he asked, sputtering some; his diction now starting to slip.

"Learned from the best," answered Tom while continuing to stare across the field.

"Yes sir, and my sincere condolences to you over the slow and steady decline of our friend, Hick Shelby. I feel partially responsible for the mishap leadin' to what disabled him: informin' y'all as to the whereabouts of those bears - should've never said a word. Been cursed as a know-it-all my entire life."

The story you see, the one that Tom and Hick agreed to on telling others about how Hick became injured, was an easy yarn to commit to memory: *'The grizzly took Hick by surprise and in taking a swipe at him, caused him to fall backwards where he bashed his head against a rock - and this is when Tom shot the animal.'* The story was fabricated so those who knew and cared about Hick wouldn't lay n' wait to murder the Hodge clan for their act; which one or more of them would have surely done.

"We killed the bear," said Tom, "and that's what matters. Hick would say this too, so try not to be concerned over it. We're both grateful for the clean lead that took us to the area."

"I know, I know," said Buntline, feeling bad over the unpleasant incident, "Well then, join my new act. I've been contractin' out Buffalo Bill. You've heard of William Cody?"

"Of course I know who Cody is."

"Either way, I'm gonna sell 'em on another tour. We can open in New York as soon as next month. You can play an army scout – just like me."

"I have a wife and six children, Ned. My sudden departure would rend the family. Besides, New York's where I'm wanted - remember?

"No difference if the Pinkerton's apprehend

you; either way, you'll be gone from the area."

"Point taken, but I'm not leaving my family; at least not voluntarily," said Tom, who was now thinking that even Buntline was now running low on ideas.

Ned took another pull from the jug and established, "What about that undomesticated Hodge fella? Seems for a pair of trousers, he'd make any ol' body, or two disappear."

"No more killing," asserted Tom, remembering Hick's unyielding message to him: "Stick to the yarn, no matter what". This was chiefly due to the unavoidable fact that most folks had a good degree of ordinary sense and were going to ask how he became injured and who the responsible partiers were. Therefore he wanted no other soul to know the humiliating truth: that he allowed a Hodge to get the drop on him.

Ned nodded and though he'd never been short on passionate schemes; he *was* known to amicably agree with regular sense when one of his fanatical ideas fell short of execution.

A SONG of PRAISE ascended from the pews of the First Baptist Church in Pinckneyville where eight Tuckers, amongst friends and neighbors sat singing their hearts out. Everyone but Tom was taken in by the feeling, so Mariah, being the song loving girl she was, tugged on Daddy's sleeve for him to get in the Spirit.

The singing ceased and an ailing Pastor Skimerhorn, over eighty-five and a widower now, got up from the front bench and found his way to the pulpit. And though the man had never been injured in battle, he began to speak with a sincere reverence; an unaffectedness that might come forth when one's been mortally wounded and lay dying. "My days're numbered dear ones," he said lowering his head. This small action caused the congregation to shutter. He then lifted his eyes and looked at Tom with the one eye he could barely see from and continued, "All our days're numbered. And I can only come to y'all now from a place of great humility." The congregation muttered with curiosity because in all their years of listening to the man's dogmatic preaching, they'd never heard words that held such feeling in their delivery. "Before, I was a hypocrite. I could not read, and I still can not read. I would memorize the scriptures as they were read to me, but my heart; my heart was empty.

The congregation clearly denied the admission of his misgivings. Still he humbly raised his hands for them to quiet down, "Up till now," he said, "I've had no real advice for any of y'all. But my heart is full now, and I ask you to sincerely live yer lives to their fullest. Forgive yer neighbor, and those who might be closer. Shut the door on past sins; yours and theirs. Let those old thoughts loll like a sleeping dog, and if the dog wakes up, tell it to go back to sleep and pay it no mind."

Sarah took note that Tom, for the first time really, was touched by the old man's words. For you see, one day when Tom was out for a pleasure ride, he came upon Rebecca and Alfred Cummings, her lover at the time. Alfred had Rebecca lain atop the fallen sycamore behind the Skimerhorn barn; his face under her dress and well inside her jam jar. Neither of them saw Tom; still Rebecca took ill soon thereafter, catching a chill that turned dire after she'd spent hours in the rain looking for a brooch given to her by the pastor; lost that day while loving Alfred. Her search was spurred on by the pastor's innocent mention that after he was finished cutting John Farley's head marker, he was going to turn the remains of the downed sycamore into firewood. This caused Rebecca to panic over the though that he might come across the brooch and accuse her of an affair. Silly really, because she simply could've alleged she'd lost it – nonetheless, what happened was ironic. The one sure way Rebecca knew to keep her men in line was to remain on a constant, accusative vigil of them perhaps having an affair; a female tactic she'd cultivated from an early age. This was a behavior that rooted itself early on when she'd learned that her twenty-nine year old mother, a paint 'n putty beauty, had been murdered by her Baptist preacher of a father after returning home from an afternoon of secret love making with her paramour.

Rebecca Skimerhorn died after a short bout with bronchial pneumonia; only three months after she'd aided in the birth of Tom and Sarah's first born son, William. Insultingly she owned the manipulative foresight to create a will bequeathing her entire estate to Alfred Cummings, the man she'd been having the forbidden affair with for the previous five years. For poor Rebecca, in her forty-nine years above ground, couldn't get the simple permutation of unrestrained, passionate sex in correct order with marriage and the appearance of looking refined in public - all perplexing issues for her. The pastor, who'd known of the affair for some time, said nothing of her transgressions, yet still changed *his* will back to that of 'husband and wife' if he were to pass first. But much to his chagrin, after receiving the news that Alfred Cummings was to arrive at their home to collect Rebecca's belongings;

some of which had substantial value because she'd been collecting revolutionary war trinkets since she was a girl, changed his resolve again, bequeathing the remaining portion of his estate upon his death to the church. But this was accomplished to no emotional or spiritual avail. You see, Pete Skimerhorn truly loved his one and only wife with all of his heart. Even after his anguish had subsided and the single position he could not change was the shame and embarrassment that gripped him when passed by those who knew how she had treated him – he still loved her.

PASTOR SKIMERHORN stood outside and greeted the last of his flock as they exited the front doors of his church. Shaking their hands with both of his, genuinely thanking them for their attendance, he could barely make out the blurry outline of Tom's figure as he loaded up his family into their wagon.

"Husband?" asked Sarah, "Tell me? …

Tom lifted John over the side and set him in the

back with the others, "It was just something Pete said."

Sarah leaned down from her seat and whispered, "I know that! What'd he stir up?"

"I'll see you at home," said Tom and he gave the horse a pat on its rump and it took its first step.

Displeased, Sarah snapped the rein over an animal that was already in motion. But it knew where to go and how to get back to the ferry for the ride back across the river.

Tom turned to see the pastor looking at him from the steps of the church. Everyone else was either silently tracking away over the light cover of snow or loaded up and would soon be gone.

Skimerhorn caned his way in Tom's direction and Tom walked toward the Pastor until the two met somewhere in between. Together they watched the Tucker wagon with five children frolicking in the back along with William next to his mother disappear beyond the tree line.

Skimerhorn took hold of Tom's arm and began walking, "Is there something you'd like to tell me, Tom," said the old man, "before we both depart?"

SARAH brought the wagon to a stop in front of the barn and the children leapt out. William lifted John over the side and the older girls took the younger ones by the hand, spreading out across the farm for their weekly free-time after church.

Sarah however, remained seated with a woolen blanket over her legs and her old patchwork quilt covering her shoulders. Motionless, she mulled over Tom's previous silence. The freezing autumn air unsurprisingly compressed the surroundings, thus restricting where a person might set their gaze. And therefore due to its close proximity, along with its natural whereabouts, Sarah's eyes easily landed on the door of the ten-by-ten shed and the open railroad lock hanging from it, "Well I'll be," she said, finally being hand delivered a compelling reason to investigate her husband's private space.

Keeping her shoulders covered, she climbed down and prudently made her way toward the shed. In doing so, she looked around to all the places the children usually played after church, and carefully listened - counting each of their voices. Upon reaching the door of the shed, she gently pressed the squeaky slab forward. As she pushed, she was caught off guard when she felt her sleeve hook on something, but it was only Little Annie, now fifteen and not so little anymore tugging on it, "Mama, what're you doin' in daddy's shed? He's gonna be real mad."

"Shush girl," her mother commanded in a tone that told the child: fifteen was still not old enough to hold any decision making power, "Now go about yer play time, and don't you say a word to anyone; hear me?" "Yes Mama," answered the teen respectfully.

Little Annie was raised to share her *own* life openly, yet refrain from allowing private family matters to roam freely, and the tone in her mother's voice dictated this was one of those times. So the girl did as she was told to do, however when she walked away, she looked back and asked herself aloud, "Why do men get to have a place of their own when the rest of us have to share?..."

Sarah stepped up and into the shed. She closed the door, but left it ajar enough for her to see by. As she looked around, she saw the walls had been randomly covered from top-to-bottom with drawings created in charcoal, ink, and pencil alike. She could only stare; drop jawed at the display of artistic and creative talent. She briefly noted a table at the far corner littered with drawing tools and partial sketches, but then paid it no further mind.

With a critical eye, she looked closely at the exquisitely crafted and idealized renderings of her friends and family that had been done over the years. She softly ran her fingers over the images that now brought on heartfelt memories. These were tender moments indeed: moments of her children and their friends growing up; her and Tom during their courting days; friends passing on, and rivals getting their due; including Sarah's kidnapping and the death of Keech Hodge.

However tacked to the opposite wall was a series of layered drawings that reenacted the shootings that took place on the train from Buffalo to Albany twenty-five years ago. She studied these with care and took note of the remarkable precision and the astounding particulars; especially those that contained expressions on the faces of the people involved, because these specific illustrations had far more attention placed on their detail and eventual outcome. In total, more than thirty pages could be seen that accounted from the time Joseph watched the agents escort the chained man aboard; to Robaré harassing the woman in her seat; to the first shots fired; to Joseph being wounded and ultimately fleeing for his life.

When she looked closely at the drawing that explained how Tom received his shoulder wound, she took a shuttered breath, and a rare, yet discernable tear rolled off her cheek and landed on an image lying on the floor. The tear caused some of the ink on the paper to run, but this was a drawing she had no interest in.

The moon above Kentucky's western sky was waning to a sliver. It was nearly dark and Tom was finished putting away the saddle and tack from his ride in from Church. He started for the cabin, but then remembered his previous haste while encountering Buntline that morning. When he turned for the shed, he saw the door was completely closed. And because he'd performed that act himself, he also saw the lock had been secured. Again his stomach jumped into his chest and his heart started pounding. He immediately contemplated the possibility that his entire family knew the truth about his past because he, more than anyone, knew what was pined to the walls of the shed.

Inside the expanded three-room cabin, William was tending to the fire while John was asleep on a well-worn Mr. Bear. In another room, Annie and Little Sarah were in bed reading to Mariah and Mary.

While Sarah cleared away the last of the dinner dishes, Tom sat at the head of the table only picking at his biscuits and beans. Sarah removed his plate and exchanged it for the drawing of Agent Webster shooting him in the shoulder, "Yer quite the artist," she established in her matter of fact drawl; her own air tempered and impenetrable. While Tom stared at the drawing, she sat down and asked, "Yer name ain't Tom, is it?" When Tom failed to respond, she declared, "O Lordy..."

Tom reached for her hand, but Sarah pulled it back and whispered harshly, "Don't you touch me!"

Immediately they both looked at the children. The girls were nearly asleep and only William paid minor note. But he'd seen his parents argue before, so he returned to his thoughts of becoming a doctor; a career he'd settled on at the age of 5 after witnessing Rebecca Skimerhorn help his mother give birth to his younger sister Annie.

"Don't you dare touch me!" she repeated, her eyes darting between Tom, the drawing and her 12 gauge shotgun by the door - loaded and ready.

"Sarah, please..." Tom implored.

"Don't you come *near* me, or I, I, don't know *what* I'll do..."

Tom retrieved his hand and politely replied, "Like I've said to you all those times and for all these years, wife, I am the man who loves you."

"Well I *don't* love you!" snapped the angry woman. "I don't even *know* you!"

Tom stood up, and as a father, checked on the children again; all were asleep: John with William by the fire and the girls in their beds. Then without a word, he unlatched the door and walked outside, yet for no apparent reason, left it wide open. When Tom stepped into the night air, the slivered moon had become covered by a thin layer of clouds, but still visible, back-lighting the sky enough for him to see by. Sarah moved to the door and watched her husband of more than twenty years walk towards the shed. A light snow flurry swirled up from behind him and dusted his head and shoulders.

"You get yerself some air," she said closing the door, "cuz yer gonna need it."

Two inches of SNOW now covered the single step in front of the shed's open door. By lantern light, Tom calmly looked over the drawings of his life with a new and different perspective.

With the drawing in hand, Sarah walked from the cabin toward the shed; snow flakes landing on her red hair that now had some strands of grey in it. She stopped at the door of the small structure and looked inside at her husband's profile to witness the once brazen and dashing force of Tom Tucker visibly shaken and weeping. She stepped up behind him and set down the drawing. She placed the side of her face to his back and hugged her arms around his waist.

"Remarkable..." said Tom in a tangible tone, "That for all this time, no one took it upon themselves to look inside. All these years you trusted me implicitly and without question, and I lied to you. I've lied to everyone."

"This ain't something I can choose fer you, husband," said Sarah, "but either way, I'll stand by you."

"I don't know what to do," he said, disgrace and heartache at the root of every word. "There are some men who've been tracking me; apparently for years. If I'm captured, I am afraid I'll never see you or the children again."

"We'll manage," Sarah said in a voice that was also beginning to crack.

Tom wanted to say more, but Sarah held her tears back and continued, "You know me; I can shoot 'n fish better than most, and skin 'n cook anything *with* legs or without. And I won't die on you while yer away, I promise."

"Joseph Tweddle," said Tom, barely able to contain his emotions.

"Huh?" blubbered Sarah, wiping her eyes and her nose on the back of his shirt, "Who's he? ..."

"My given name is *Joseph Daniel Tweddle*. We were Presbyterian."

This time when Tom spoke that name, he listened to how it actually sounded when the words left his mouth, and they resonated - different and unfamiliar.

Sarah stepped around Tom and with compassionate focus, looked up and gave him her full attention, but neither one said a word. She then put her head on his chest and uttered, "That's not what I care about. Besides we're Baptist."

📖

Inside THE CABIN, Tom's drawings were now spread over everything - and there were many more than Sarah had first seen in the shed. She was shuffling them around; looking for an order, her own sequence of sorts.

"I'm failing to understand," said Tom while helping to arrange them, "What are you looking for?"

"Shush," spurted the woman, "I'm gettin' a feelin'. Tell me now, is this how it happened?"

Tom carelessly looked at the order of the pages.

391

He had mentally replayed the events so many times, and inspected the drawings for so many years; it was as if he knew the sequence by heart and at the same time was blind to it. "Yes," he said, and then, "No. That one needs to be here, and those need to go there, like that - I think. God, it's been so long. All I've tried to do is close my eyes and forget it happened."

Sarah looked intently at the arrangement and asked, "Are you seein' what I'm seein'?"

Tom craned his head one way and then the other in hopes the display would make better sense and said, "Should I be?"

"I shore hope so, Tom Tucker or Joseph, or whatever yer name really is."

Because on the table and the floor; across the counter 'n into the living area; laid out in sequential order were sixty-three detailed illustrations that Tom had drawn shortly after building the shed. Images that depicted the exact way the shootings on the train took place from *his* standing points. Everything he saw that morning relating to the event. Tom didn't draw these because he felt he might need them at some future point in defense of his actions; he drew them because he was an artist, and he knew he needed to rid his mind of what continued to surface in order for him to move forward as such. You see, before the shed was built, he had no place to draw or keep the finished works. In fact he didn't actually know why he kept them to begin with because his real artistic passion was drawing his family and his friends while living his life in Kentucky. He also felt that if he would have informed Sarah of his talent, or attempted to display some of the pieces; it would have only served to bring up more questions about his past. So he kept it all locked away. There were also a number of other sketches Tom had completed after he'd met Hick. These contained the beauty they experienced traveling the rivers south to Kentucky, and since Sarah initially took everything from the shed she felt pertinent, she eventually put these to the side in order to get to the heart of the incident.

"Because she contended, "what I'm seein' ain't murder."

"My god woman, I shot him in front of an agent of the law! I think I'd know. He was my stepbrother; my father's favored."

"I don't care if you kilt 'em on the courthouse steps," said the detective in her, "Stepbrother or not, I'm seein' self-defense."

Frustrated, Tom ran his hands through his thick, yet graying hair and said, "Who do you think a jury will believe; a fugitive on the run for twenty five years, or the men that work for a company like Pinkerton? ..."

With that, Sarah looked Tom in the eye and clearly stated, "I need to know somethin'."

"Anything," said Tom with resign, "Anything at all – please, ask."

"When we married, you said somethin' on our wedding night I've been carryin' since. You told me, 'Gettin' married was *still* harder than huntin' bear'. I need to know; was there another, before me, that you justly loved?…"

Tom took his own shuttered breath. He slowly stood up and gazed out the kitchen window into the blackness. He then went to the door, unlatched it and quietly walked outside.

📖

TOM stepped into the cramped quarters of the shed and stood motionless before his drawing table. He knew this was the end. He knew he had to tell the truth; the whole truth from this point forward if he was to have any remaining self regard. He pulled the middle drawer completely out and set it on top of the table. Reaching all the way to the back, he retrieved the oval locket containing Amanda's portrait-painting along with his gold wedding band. He refrained from opening the locket, yet at the same time realized that even though he knows nothing of her disposition, nor any other family members for that matter, this part of his life was over.

THE CABIN DOOR unlatched and Tom stepped back inside. He softly set down a few more drawings on the table before Sarah; drawings of the life he and Amanda shared in New York. He also set down the locket and his gold wedding band.

Sarah looked up at Tom with more tears in her eyes than in twenty-five years of marriage combined. Because at this particular moment, her sadness didn't have anything to do with the trouble her husband was in; it had to do with the fact, that even though his life in New York was admittedly different and had nothing to do with her, it was a life she too wanted to know about; a life she could have shared in, but alas; would it have helped, or even mattered?

Sarah looked at the drawings, but what she was interested in was the locket and the ring. She picked them up and clutched them hard. She felt their power and began to openly cry; an extended out pouring of love, and at the same time, grief; something she hadn't done since her father died over thirty years ago. Slowly she opened the locket and looked at the painting of Amanda and declared in a covered breath, "O Tom; she's enormously beautiful."

HOGS and CHICKENS freely roamed in and out of the Hodge cabin; a filth laden structure now best suited for lodging the wealth of varmints 'n vermin that have pissed and shat on everything in sight. This is where the decrepit Norman Hodge sat cross-legged on his manky black mattress. With sleepy eyes, he stood up and stumbled to his favorite break in the floor to shit through. Other cracks in the floor also served as entries into the maggot infested cesspool under the structure; something that became necessary when there was no one left to repair the outhouse that finally collapsed. But it was also necessary because Norman had become too feeble to make it outside to the hole that still existed even though there was no structure.

Outside, snow had been making its way through the breaks in the roof of the chicken coop; also fallen to pieces. Inside the structure, the cross-eyed twin was gathering a few brown eggs in her tattered flour sack. By her will alone, she'd kept the holes in the coop covered so the critters wouldn't eat the chickens. Her teenage daughter stood close as she too shivered from the cold.

From inside the cabin the old man shouted, "Have 'em cooked when I git up!" Then he laughed, "Or I'll beat cha, both y'alls..." and he fell back into his own muck.

ON SMITHLAND'S PIER, people were in constant motion in an attempt to keep the falling snow from dampening their spirits. It was an exciting day when the steamship, *J.C. Drouillard* stopped on its mail run to Nashville; her steel hull rocking to and fro as she pulled at her ropes causing the dock timbers to creek out a song filled with low and muffled tones.

Tom had been chatting with a middle-age couple who were waiting for a package of medicine to arrive for their ailing daughter. Not completely dressed for the cold, they'd been standing around shivering for some time because the ship had been delayed due to weather. Simultaneously as a crewman began to wheel the mail cart down the gangplank, Tom saw Hick fishing by the bow of the ship where the water lapped the shore, but because it was so cold, it was where thin ice met the frozen mud; Hick's cane pole stuck in a hold he'd dug out with an axe just before the freeze came.

Tom called and waved, "Hick? Hick, man!…"

Hick looked up and meekly waved, but then reached into his winter coat and pulled out a bottle.

Tom turned to excuse himself from the couple, but they'd already made their way to where the mail was being handed out, desperately hoping to receive the parcel they'd waited so long for.

With his family's MAIL IN HAND, Tom had made it to the edge of the water where he greeted Hick, "Hello, my friend," he said with pleasure. "It's been some time."

Playing with his line and pole, Hick replied in short, "Tom..."

"We'd like to have you over for dinner – sometime soon...?" Sarah's preparing one of your favorites; red beans 'n rice with squirrel brains."

From Tom's vantage point, Agents Stone and Bennett, who were seated in a boat manned by two oarsmen, had well cleared the bow of the ship and were now pulling ashore a number of yards in front of where the two friends were standing. The agents got out, straightened themselves and began their approach. Tom saw the men, but because he didn't know them, and also because there were so many other boats in the water, along with men working around the shore, he thought nothing of their movements.

Stone and Bennett spotted Tom and Hick; yet Hick, still having retained his keen eye sight, also saw the agents from the corner of his.

"Well, what do you know," Bennett remarked in stride, "an on time drunkard."

Once again, Stone rechecked Joseph's likeness. And though it was smudged from the incident outside The Gower House, Stone was able to confirm, "It's him."

"I'm sorry, Tom," said Hick, lowering his head.

"Sorry? That's not like you, man. Sorry for what? You can surely make it to dinner? It's been months since you've come over. I'll even cross over and pick you up."

As the agents closed in, Hick became nervous; his words hurried and erratic, "They said I was yer, accomplice. They said, I'd, I'd hang fer helpin' you.

Again, that feeling arrived in the pit of Tom's stomach and he immediately became anxious, "What are you saying, man?" he asked, craning his head for Hick's attention, "Hick, look at me!" Hick signaled with his eyes towards the agents and Tom followed his track, but it was too late. The agents stepped in.

"Thank you Mr. Shelby," Bennett artfully acknowledged, lumbering his heavy hand on Hick's easily collapsible shoulder, "Your services are no longer required."

Motionless, Hick recalled every terrible thing he'd ever said or done to Tom; this one resting at the apex. Hick extended his hand and nodded for Tom's mail. In disbelief Tom slowly handed the post to Hick. Tom could only watch as his friend turned around and staggered away; his head so low that if weren't attached to his neck, it would've surely scraped the ground.

"Me O my," said Bennett with praise, "Joseph Tweddle, at last. *At last*..."

"I don't know who you're referring to sir. My name is Thomas B. Tucker."

"That's a lie!" blurted Stone, making sure his voice was heard, "We know who ye're. We've followed your trail since Buffalo! This one should make record!" which he said even louder as he looked around for an audience, but there wasn't one. Anyone within earshot was simply interested in being done with what they'd come to do – all the while keeping warm in the process. Besides an arrogant Scot wasn't something new to the area, so why should anyone take an interest.

(Wil*liam* Jaeger Stone), the only son of an Irish barmaid and a German salesman who'd chosen to remain in Glasgow, noticed no person was taking an interest in his loud and obnoxious words. He did however; see Tom looking at him in a curious way. He could also tell that Tom was far from a southern ne'er-do-well; even after twenty-five years, and therefore chose to refrain from more strident talk.

YARDS AWAY by now, Hick stopped when he remembered that he'd left his pole, so he turned and looked back. It was wiggling with a fish-on, but he also saw the agents hadn't finished with Tom, so he turned around and kept walking. Upon reaching the top of the pier, he looked down at the men. By this time Tom had taken off his coat and opened up his shirt so the agents could look for themselves at his shoulder; a key piece of information and the only mark to actually identify him by this many years after the incident. Hick knew this was Tom's biggest secret, so he took a drink from his bottle and nervously watched.

"Will you go peaceable?" asked Bennett. When Tom heard the question, his stature fell at ease and a look of relief unveiled itself over his entire body. He nodded, almost with gratitude, and the agents picked up on this.

Tom then asked, "Would you mind waiting to place me in irons? I'd rather not have my friends see me chained."

In any other situation, neither agent would have honored such a ridiculous request; however the glow on Stone's face after realizing he'd actually captured a man wanted for twenty-five years was enough to relax *his* stature as well. Therefore he easily nodded, granting the request. Stone also knew that if Tom were to run, he and Bennett were good enough marksman to easily shoot him down, and this Tom also knew.

Tom began redressing himself as the agents escorted him to the rowboat. A few people glanced at the men, but because Smithland had seen so many characters come and go over the years, (carrying on with so many colorful behaviors), seeing a man pull his shirt over and put his coat back on was nothing out of the ordinary – even if it was freezing cold out.

The agents helped Tom aboard and the oarsmen pushed off. The craft maneuvered away from the icy shore and towards the moving current. Once into the flow, Bennett wasted no time putting Tom in chains while Stone kept a sharp eye for any trickery that Tom might attempt to execute, but there wasn't any.

It was time for the *J.C. Drouillard* to depart. So her whistles blew and her bells clanged...

CONVERSERLY a *clang* of a different nature came from the inside of the Hodge cabin. The clang was heard again - and then once more, but on the final sounding the resonance was less sharp, dull rather.

The cross eyed twin walked out the door and dropped a cast iron skillet; burnt eggs and all into the virgin snow. When the newly formed flakes landed on the blackened metal, they absorbed the fresh blood around a whip of hair that had just been abrasively removed from the head of Norman Hodge upon the skillet's final carry.

The twin then picked up an improvised bag she'd built from tying together a pair of filthy trousers found in a corner of the barn amongst a pile of rags; found near the burrowed out corner where Norman made the boys sleep.

With a few narrow belongings stuffed inside, she stepped off the porch and reached for the hand of the young girl that stood just outside. In silent vigil, the snow had been piling up on the girl's head and shoulders. The two looked at the cabin, but the snow wasn't falling near hard enough to extinguish the roaring flames now erupting from it. The structure's grimy nature made for a swift ignition. Pigs, chickens and anything with consciousness bolted out the openings. In seconds enclosure was engulfed. Without emotion or words, the woman and child walked away hand in hand where they vanished into the woods behind the collapsed outhouse: the last resting place where so many of Hodge's offspring met their end.

HOURS BEFORE where the large ship had caused a frenzied excitement, Hick leaned against the pier piling of the now vacant dock. Covered in snow, he was alone and trembling. With his good arm wrapped around the piling, he slid to his knees and began sobbing uncontrollably, "Lordy, what have I gone 'n done this time? I've given up the only friend that ever treated me like a man, and with the respect I asked for... I'm good for nuthin' and no one." Crawling to the edge of the dock he blubbered, "God forgive me," whereby he barely lifted himself up and stood unsteadily with his toes over the edge.

Contemplating his bitter fate, the drunken man noticed something in the water. Looking closer, he thought at first it might be a large fish, a gar perhaps, but it wasn't. It was the ghostly image of Keech Hodge looking at him through what appeared to be a layer of ice, as if alive and attempting to escape the tomb that encased him.

"It cain't be he mumbled. Keech is dead. I shot 'em; punctured his heart and made sure it stopped. We stripped him nekid and buried 'em in the hills. Burnt his clothes too. Even if wolves dug 'em up, it cain't be. It just caint!"

Hick continued to stare in disbelief at the apparition. He then pulled the bottle from his pocket and examined his caramel-colored friend and lover of more than thirty-five years, "I HATE YOU!" he screamed. "I HATE YOU!… Taking hold of the bottle's neck, he awkwardly threw it down as hard as he could against the wooden planks. When the fragile, hand-blown glass shattered, the dark bourbon inside quickly melted the snow around it. Hick looked at the water again and Keech was gone.

GIANT snow flakes quietly departed from the heavens above. The ones that made it to earth had been piling up on a man curled in a ball on the pier at Smithland. Moses Lafayette (Hick) Shelby was a crushed and broken man.

CHAPTER twenty-two
EXTRADITION

SPEEDING to NEW YORK in a passenger car drawn by a newly built locomotive, Tom, whose hands and legs were cuffed and shackled, was being guarded closely by Agents Stone and Bennett. While he soundly slept, his head bumped against the window of the car as it rocked from side to side. In some ways not much had changed: ticketed passengers looked at him much in the same way they looked at the shackled prisoner all those years ago, but unlike then, Tom was happy to be rid of the uncertainties that had haunted him for so long. Accordingly, while the train stopped at every town for passengers, freight and fuel, he ate lightly, relieved himself; with the assistance of an agent, and returned to his seat where he blissfully went back to sleep. He hadn't rested this well in years he thought.

INSIDE the offices of an Albany law firm, Tom sat in a bolstered chair across from a well dressed, full-bodied attorney in his sixties wearing an obvious toupee. There were also two other smartly dressed lawyers in their thirties with neatly trimmed facial flarings who stood to either side of the stout man ready to respond to his smallest request.

Instead of being defended by an unremarkable counselor; who would have surely lost the case, thus forcing Tom to be remanded into the custody of the warden at Sing-Sing Penitentiary where he'd be awaiting execution for the murder of Robaré Pulling; he was speaking with someone who was actually hired to help him.

"...and the carriage factory?...," asked Tom, not really caring one way or the other of its disposition, but at this point, his curiosity had been piqued. It was also clear that his manacles and leg irons had been removed.

"Sold," the portly man responded in a formal Queen's tone, "shortly after your disappearance. Your father Evidently had high expectations for it, and for you, but he was only one man and a wheelwright, not an engineer. And since malt brewing and banking was his primary source of revenue, he chose to remain with what he knew best considering his most trusted was no longer about."

Hearing the man's response was not unexpected. Tom was familiar with his father enough to know he would have never gambled everything he was worth on one venture.

"What of Annaleez?" asked Tom.

"Your sister Ann Eliza has a residence in San Francisco. I've drafted a letter informing her of your whereabouts. It was her efforts that uncovered the woman's intensions."

"Woman?" asked Tom with an increased interest, "What woman?…

The old man glanced at both young attorneys and replied in a manner denoting that everyone in the office had been aware of this information for some time, "Why your stepbrother's accomplice of course."

Tom thought back to that horrifying day on the train when only a few rows up, the nicely dressed man, who turned out to be Robaré, was Evidently working a ruse with this woman all along.

"Yes," said the attorney, "You can well imagine the puzzle the agencies had to piece together: a body smashed against the rocks; expensive cargo scattered along the tracks; your stepbrother dead and, well, you get the picture."

"Yes sir," murmured Tom, staring out a side window, "I'm well aware of the pictures."

"She's passed now," the man continued, "Some

blight I'd expect. But her objective was to distract you long enough for your stepbrother to destroy the cargo, thus making you look incompetent in your father's eyes." These last few words brought Tom from his solemn. It also helped him recall what Robaré shouted to the captive man in chains after his plans had been interrupted, that he'd *"ruined everything!"* Now Robaré's actions made sense.

The lawyer turned his attention to a folder where some drawings became visible and said, "Twas an unexpected yet fortunate turn of events that ensued. In any case, we'll keep these until we're certain nothing more will arise. Quite remarkable they are."

The expression on Tom's face revealed an acute misunderstanding of how his secret drawings came into this man's possession.

"Your depictions," said the attorney, "are rather noteworthy. You have a little talent it appears."

"But how, …   … did you get those?" asked Tom, however Tom didn't ask his question loud enough or soon enough.

The man closed the folder, looked at him squarely and stated, "Twas a shame you just missed your father's service, sir. The entire city came out. He was a loved man. People are still speaking of his generosity and I imagine will for some time to come."

"I loved him," said Tom softly, "and thought of

him always."

"Yes sir," replied the attorney, "and ironically it twas best your return was not sooner. The alleged contempt you had for your stepbrother is what kept the formal investigation open until '62, when the only remaining eyewitness; Agent Webster I believe it twas, hanged as a union spy - and that ended that. It twas Pinkerton that kept it open on his end, but only until recently. Your sister it seemed, through tireless correspondence, dispelled all notions that you'd conspired with the alleged murderer being returned here for trial; in turn dispelling any truth that you had something to do with the death of Pinkerton's young agent aboard the train; self-defense you know."

The rotund man carefully turned a page in the file and clearly enunciated, "Under the provisions of your late father's will, the estate *only* provides for one Joseph Tweddle and his heirs." The man then leaned the bun of his short body across his desk where his stubby fingers opened an engraved silver box. He removed a cigar and rolled back into his chair, "Therefore you will be required to reassume the name Joseph Daniel Tweddle and remarry any wife you have taken in the meantime, under that name, if you so choose."

Both young lawyers struck a match at nearly the same time, but the old man turned to his left and it was that lawyer who lit his mentor's cigar; in return receiving a gentle pat on the back of his thigh as a reward. Puffing away, he asked, "Will you be able to comply with your late father's request?"

The attorney didn't really care which answer came forth, but he did see that Tom needed some time to think. Therefore he stated, "Upon this firm's receipt of such record, the first disbursement of the three million dollars, including the aforementioned trust and land deeds, including your share of the proceeds from the sale of the carriage company, will be drafted to an account of your choice."

The old man closed the file. Puffing hard, he filled the surrounding space with thick, aromatic smoke. He noticed the new heir was in shock, so he nodded to the younger men to come around and helped him to his feet.

WHEN THE DOOR opened to the reception area, Agents Stone and Bennett immediately rose from their chairs. Before them was the man they'd just delivered in chains; standing with a junior counselor to each side of him. The young men stood down and allowed Tom his own balance. When they were satisfied he wouldn't topple, they returned to the large office and without a word closed the door behind them.

Bennett removed his hat, "Mr. Tweddle, our sincere apologies to you, sir. We were only just informed of your specific circumstances. Our instructions changed upon reaching the terminal when we were ordered to bring you here."

"Quite all right Albin," said Tom, "You both did a fine job of trailing me. There's only one other man that could've accomplished that."

"And whom might that be, sir," asked Bennett.

"Ironically it was the man that helped you find me."

"Aye, your friend?" Stone confirmed, "Lafayette Shelby."

"Folks just call him Hick," said Tom, "And that's *all* they call him by."

"Aye sir, Mr. Tweddle. Is there somewhere we can drive you during your stay in Albany?"

SULLY; Fraser Dunlop's former butler, now in his late-eighties, stood in the foyer of the Dunlop mansion looking out at a clean shaven, smartly dressed man in a new tailored suit for the times, "Well, I God," Sully said smiling big, "Masser Tweedle, sir."

"You remember me?.." asked Tom, who gently took hold the old man's hand and shook it ever-so-gently with both of his; heedful not to squeeze the fragile, bird like bones; all the while knowing in his heart this man had been nothing but kind to him and Amanda.

"O, yasser, Masser Tweedle, I sholey do recall," his eyes brining and his wrinkled face coming to light. His puckered mouth and cheeks drawn in from barely a tooth in his head, yet his smile was so filled with life from the sight of Tom, "Yes sir, I sholey do!" he said and he began to openly weep. "I still have the renderin' you marked up fo me. The one Masser Dunlop gimmy at Christmas. Yasser I sholey do love that renderin' you marked up. Yes sir…"

Tom allowed the man a moment and then attempted to suppose, "Is, Mr. Dunlop - in…?"

"Sad to say sir, Masser Dunlop passed on pert near twenty year ago."

"A loss to us all," said Tom removing his hat.

Sully bowed his head, "Yasser, we all became real remorseful at the news. He was sailin' to fetch mo 'f his lovely liquor. A disease on ship I reckon."

Tom also bowed his head in penitence, "I am sorry," he said. "And what of Innes?"

"Also sad, sir. Innes passed from knife wounds received while defendin' the masser's name."

"O my…," said Tom, taken aback, "I know he was a tough lot."

"Yasser," confirmed Sully, "Three. He ended three of 'em befo they took him. But the new folks kept me on," he said with a smile. "Real nice'a dem to do dat; specially wit me gittin' on in years. Real nice'a dem." In silence, Tom gazed at Sully, but the former slave could easily tell he was being looked clear through.

"Masser Tweedle, sir?"

"Mmm? …" mumbled Tom, coming from his thoughts.

"We heard the bad rumors, sir. Everyone became so heart broke when you failed to turn up. Their lives I mean; just fell to pieces."

Solemnly Joseph nodded, "An unexpected turn of events, my friend. More sorrowful than I can ever possibly recount."

"Yasser Masser Tweedle, I reckon they was. I shoely reckon so."

416

A CARRIAGE turned off the dirt road and rolled beyond a set of iron gates onto a cobblestone drive. Slowly it circled behind Joseph Tweddle's former Albany residence. From inside the carriage, Tom looked at the house 'n gardens as if he had entered a dream.

The coach patiently waited as Tom walked up to the back door and softly knocked. When it opened, he was received by a heavyset maid in her forties with an Irish inflection, "Can I help you sir?"

Tom removed his hat and said, "My name's Tom… I mean Joseph Tweddle. This used to be my--"

"O heavens…," said the woman with excitement, "Aye sir, this was ye home. The news is everywhere that ye turned up. People're still grieving ye father's passing. I'm so sorry for ye loss, he was a great man. O my, well, please come in." Opening the door she continued, "The owners are away, but I'm sure they'd be fine with it; ye being a celebrity 'n all.

Tom took a small step back, "No, but thank you," he said, "I've come unannounced." But still he craned his head around the woman for a look inside.

"O my," she said, "ye want to know what happened…?"

On the brink of tears, Tom could only nod. He was grateful that he'd come here for some answers instead of asking his father's arrogant lawyer. For if he'd learned one thing living in the south all these years; it was if one wanted the truth, one needed to ask those closest to it. And it wasn't that Sully wouldn't have been an appropriate source for the information; he surely would have, but Tom didn't want to upset the fragile man more than he already had from his unexpected visit.

"For pity sake," she said remembering, "I was just a lass when I heard aboot Miss Amanda passin' - the way she did; ya know, durin' child birth 'n all. The baby turnin' like it did, and so late in comin'."

The woman's delivery forced Tom's emotions to get the better of him and he began to openly weep.

Continuing in her blunt manner, "Some say the gossip's what killed're. People talkin'. Tellin' lies ya know - that ye'd run off with another. But I know ye didn't. I knew in my heart Miss Amanda had true feelings for ye and would never choose a man that would leave'er. I believe her heart broke when ye failed to return; but what do I know, I'm just a servant."

Joseph leaned against the door jam and proclaimed, "She was the love of my life. I thought of her every day."

"And ye were hers, sir; and ye were hers..." The maid contemplated for a moment and then asked, "Would ye want to know?" But Joseph only looked at her in question.

"The baby's sex, I mean?" Only Joseph's eyes revealed the answer.

"Twas a little boy. Joseph Daniel, named after ye, sir."

Simultaneously the woman stepped forward and Joseph fell into her sobbing, "There-there now," she said, patting him softly, "I'm sure there was good cause."

In the end, this Irish woman with more than fifty years of meager service behind her recalled this humble demonstration of emotion from a man she'd only heard of in folklore as remarkable. This event would also help catapult her toward those she would eventually help transition from this world into the next as a caregiver to the dying.

SIX DAYS later, a locomotive pulling seventeen cars, heaved to an almost deafening stop at Kentucky's busy Paducah depot; a far cry from the up and coming township it was twenty-five years ago. With people everywhere, Tom stepped from the first of three *Pullman Palace Cars* onto a long boardwalk. He set down the brown paper-wrapped package he'd been carrying and straightened himself. He brushed the lint from his shoulders and adjusted his hat and tie just right. When he glanced up, he saw Sarah at the end of the boardwalk dressed in her usual farm garb. Behind her, Hick was at the reins of a four-seat buggy reading a book. Tom and Sarah began walking towards each other. Sarah kept her eyes locked on Tom until they met. The contrast between a clean shaven, impeccably dressed English aristocrat and a Kentucky farm wife caused a few bystanders, as well as some newly ticketed passengers that were now seating themselves inside the plush passenger cars to look on.

Tom kissed Sarah on the cheek and inhaled a deep breath of her neck scent, "Hello wife."

Sarah looked him over, "Fancy garments," she said in her matter of fact tone.

"An unforeseen turn of events," said Tom.

"Evidently," she remarked.

"Thank you for sending the drawings."

"Thank Ned Buntline; personal currier on horseback I reckon. You home to stay?"

Tom slipped the package he'd been carrying under his other arm and then locked Sarah's arm inside of his in a committed fashion. Walking towards the wagon, Sarah nuzzled her nose in close to catch a hint of Tom's scent, or that of another woman's. Upon reaching the wagon, Tom helped her into the back, but before he sat down, he placed his hand on Hick's shoulder and in a brotherly way asked, "How are you old man?"

Hick closed his well-read copy of *Leaves of Grass*, and without a word, reached across and placed his good hand on Tom's. Tom then slipped the parcel he been carrying into Hick's lap. "Open it," he said and he glanced back at Sarah who was seating herself.

Hick felt completely undeserving of anything much less a gift from the man he'd nearly sent to the gallows and he began to weep, but still managed to pull the string on the package and work his hand under the brown, waxed paper.

"Only the best for my friend," said Tom, observing the joy on Hick's face as he removed a garment along with a framed illustration from the wrapping. Hick held up a pair pants and inspected the quality. With tears streaming down his face, he looked back at Tom and said, "I read about these, Tom, "These are made by Levi Strauss. They say they're the best work pants ever made." He then looked closely at the drawing and could not help but to openly heartedly cry. It was a highly detailed pen 'n ink illustration of him and Tom riding the *Nunna Dual Tsuny* Trail in 1854; only hours before everything changed for both of them. It depicted Hick reading *Leaves of Grass* and Tom scratching his head in dismay. To date it was the most distinguished and honorable rendering of anything Tom had created.

Then as best they might, the aged frontiersmen quietly wiped their tears and resumed their seated positions. Hick called, "Git-up," and the wagon rolled across the bumpy tracks where it merged into the busy Paducah thoroughfare.

- End -

- EPITAPH -

TOM TUCKER returned to his perfect life in the Cumberland Valley; and to the township that would later be named *Hillsville* and then finally *Tiline*, (pronounced *Tileen*) after the beautiful little girl, *Tiline Doom*. Tom remarried Sarah Jones and soon thereafter registered at the St. Felix Hotel in Smithland under the names, Joseph D. and Sarah Tweddle; after which they collected their full inheritance.

Joseph's honorable countenance coupled with his fresh prosperity benefited Livingston County well beyond the day he died in August of 1893. He rests in the Tweddle Family Cemetery in Tiline, Kentucky. He was seventy-five years old.

SARAH TUCKER - TWEDDLE, like the smart woman she was went along with the name change and remarried Tom for the sake of record, but never stopped referring to him as Tom or husband. Because of her poor and rural upbringing, the Tweddle's newfound affluence witnessed Sarah as having what few would argue as a spending dilemma; ordering items from catalogs in vast quantities and then sadly discarding most of what she'd bought. She lived twenty-three years beyond her beloved Tom, passing on September 1st, 1910. She was eighty-one.

MOSES LAFAYETTE "HICK" SHELBY eventually married Katherine Frayser. Sadly though, little of his life and whereabouts were recorded. He died at the age of sixty-seven in February of 1894, only six months after his best friend Tom. He rests in a small family cemetery on the road between Salem and Pinckneyville; just across the Cumberland River and not far from Tom and Sarah's farm on Tweddle Road in Tiline.

JOHN TWEDDLE; Joseph's father was involved in many business ventures throughout his life. He was a wheelwright, a brewer, a banker and above all, a magnanimous and generous man to all whom knew him. He erected Tweddle Hall in Albany and when he died in March of 1875, the city publicly wept.

JAMES WASHINGTON SHELBY was in deed committed to a Tennessee asylum for the horrific killing of Constable Augustus Alley; however serving not one day for his crime, he died in April of 1905 at the age of eighty-one.

NED BUNTLINE, coined, *"King of the Dime Store Novelists"* went on to write and produce William F. "Buffalo Bill" Cody's, "Scouts of the Plains" which played to packed houses for years. After writing some 400 novels and marrying at least six times, Ned died in July of 1886 in New York. He was between sixty-three and sixty-five years old – leave it to Ned.

ENOCH T. POTTS, Isaac Martin's childhood friend went on to take advantage of a military pension promised by the U.S. Government for Union War Veterans. Being one of a microscopic handful of men to receive the pension, Enoch collected it to his dying day.

ALLAN PINKERTON, founder of *The North-Western Police Agency*, which later became *The Pinkerton National Detective Agency*, died at the age of sixty-five in July of 1884 when he slipped on an icy street in Chicago, biting his tongue so hard that it caused gangrene to which he eventually succumbed.

AGENT TIMOTHY WEBSTER, was one of Pinkerton's top agents until he was indeed hanged as Union spy in 1862. He was forty years old.

AGENT KATE WARNE was credited with being both America's first female detective, as well as obtaining key surveillance information that thwarted a plot to assassinate Abraham Lincoln. Kitty, as she was fondly referred to by Pinkerton, died on New Year's Day in 1868 of phenomena. She's buried next to him in the Pinkerton Family cemetery in Chicago. She was thirty-eight years old.

ISAAC MARTIN went on to wed **MARY SHELBY**. Their daughter, Blanch Martin, married John Walker Tweddle.

JOHN WALKER TWEDDLE, Tom's youngest child, remained in Livingston County and inherited the balance of Joseph and Sarah's estate until ironically in 1929, at the age of 57, the same age Tom inherited his wealth, he lost nearly all his prosperity to the great depression. Being the child to experience the least hardship and the most wealth, John Walker Tweddle died a depressed and broken man when he had no skill or trade to rely on after the loss of the family's money and home. Today, those same assets would be worth almost eighty million dollars.

IN THE END, the details surrounding the events that happened on the train from Buffalo to Albany that spring morning in 1850 remained a guarded family secret and vague at best. It was not until Joseph's youngest grandson, Martin Irvin Tweddle, on his death bed, shared these previously undisclosed events with his son Charlie Tweddle; the author's good friend and the inspiration for this book - Thank you Charlie and Barbara for such a wonderfully inspiring yarn.